Poison Pen

A DI Ambrose mystery

To Summer and Pauline Kirk

by P J Quinn

Stairwell Books

Published by Stairwell Books
70 Barbara Drive
Norwalk
CT 06851 USA

ISBN: 978-0-9833482-8-3

Printed and bound in the UK by Russell Press Ltd.

Layout design Alan Gillott

Also by P.J. Quinn

Foul Play – A DI Ambrose Mystery

About the authors

Pauline Kirk is the author of two novels: *Waters of Time,* Century Hutchinson 1988; Ulverscroft 1991, and *The Keepers*, Virago (Little, Brown), 1996 and 1997. Ten collections of her poetry have been published, including *Walking to Snailbeach: Selected and New poems*, and the most recent, *Dancing through wood and Time*, in which some of her poems are set to music by the York composer, Martin Scheuregger. She is a member of the Pennine Poets group, and editor of Fighting Cock Press. Her poems, short stories and articles have appeared in many anthologies and journals, and been broadcast on radio.

Jo Summers has written numerous articles for the legal press and national newspapers. Her books include *Islamic Wills, Trusts and Estates: Planning for this World and the Next* with Mufti Talha Ahmad Azami and Shahzad Siddiqui (Euromoney Books) and *The Offshore Trustees' UK Tax Handbook* (Euromoney Books). Future projects include a UK tax textbook for the University of Connecticut, USA.

With thanks to Paul Summers, Nicky Pallis, Frances Pearce, Mary Sheepshanks and Marian Smith; and to our editors Rose and Alan.

To Paul and Pete

Book One

28th July 1959

The heat was suffocating. He was breathing too quickly.

"Hey, you alright pal?" the American asked. "You look a little green around the gills."

The rattle of train wheels echoed round his head. He couldn't think.

"I feel dreadful," James Marshall said. The smell of stale sweat, food and smoke made him worse with every minute. He should have waited 'til he could travel first class, but he couldn't bear to stay in that tiny hotel room any longer. He *had* to get to Calcutta.

"You got Montezuma's revenge?" the young man asked, looking concerned. "Why don't you get off at the next station? There must be a doctor somewhere."

"No. I've got to get to Calcutta," James insisted. "There won't be any doctors here." He peered out on a horizon of brown fields and the occasional dusty village. A livid yellow sky dazzled his eyes. "Could you let me have a drink of water?" he asked. "I've drunk all mine."

"You don't want to be drinking water," the American replied. "Not in this country. Here, have a proper drink."

The scotch made James cough. At the end of the carriage a man was frying okra on a primus stove. The smell of ghee and paraffin made James feel sick. Urgently he stood up and stuffed his head out of the window. The air was almost as hot outside but the wind against his face revived him.

He'd been poisoned, he was sure of it. When he went to the Hall he was fine, on top of the world with Lizzi agreeing to marry him. On the second day he started to feel odd. And as each day passed, he felt worse. It couldn't have been something he'd eaten before he arrived. His check-up with his GP had been thorough. With him going back out to India for a year it had to be. He was sure the poisoning had started at Chalk Heath Hall. And it was still

1

poisoning him too. Every day since he docked, he'd felt worse and worse…

"You really should get off you know," the American's wife said. "It's probably the train. Everything's so *primitive* isn't it? Jack Kerouac never travelled in India, that's for sure," she sniffed with distaste.

With an effort, James turned back into the carriage. He must be going mad to think such things. Why should anyone poison him? How could they? They'd all eaten the same food, shared the same tureens. He must have a touch of the sun. It was sending him half mad.

But he *had* started feeling ill at the Hall, his mind insisted. It couldn't be the sun. Couldn't be India at all. He had an aerogramme in the front of his bag. He must get a message to Lizzi.

His hands shaking, James found the aerogramme and a pen. Resting against the wooden slats beside him, he tried to write. There was no time for pleasantries.

"Lizzi," he began, "if anything happens to me go to DI Ambrose at Chalk Heath police station. We met when he investigated poor Jessop's death. Tell him I was poisoned at Chalk Heath Hall, while I was at their retreat. Don't laugh. I'm not joking. I've never felt so ill in my life. I'm trying to get to my parents but I don't know if I'll make it. If you hear I have died, or never hear anything more from me, go to DI Ambrose. Ask him to find out what happened to me. I love you, Darling."

For a few moments James stared ahead of him, his eyes barely focusing on the crowded carriage. "If I'm imagining things we'll laugh about this together some time," he added. "Longing to see you again, Jamie." Then he addressed the letter as clearly as his shaking hand would allow: "Miss E Chalfont, The Old Rectory, South Wold, nr Chalk Heath, England."

The train was pulling into a small town, spluttering and grinding to a halt beside a dusty platform. Some of the passengers got off to relieve themselves beside the railway lines. Quickly James sealed the letter and felt in his pocket for some rupees. The usual hawkers were crowding around the train, hoping to sell refreshments. He spotted a couple of young girls offering fruit. You could often trust the girls more than the boys, James said to himself. He called across to one of them, slipping into the pigeon Bengali of his childhood. Telling himself to slow down, he started again, more carefully. "If I give you money, would you take this to the post office?" he asked the girl. "You take this, send it to England? Here's money."

She looked back at him uncertainly. "Please," James pleaded. "It's to my betrothed. To tell her I love her."

"Ah!" the girl replied, smiling. She was about twelve but already wise in the ways of men. "Love letter," she said. "How much you give me?" Her open fingers reached up to the carriage window.

The train would be leaving soon. Urgently James pressed the letter and a handful of rupees into the girl's hands. "Please don't forget," he pleaded. "She must know that I love her. We may never see each other again."

"Poor man!" The girl looked at the money he'd given her. It was more than she would earn in a week. "I will post your letter, mister," she promised. "You must love your lady a lot."

The train was pulling away from the platform, doors slamming and latecomers still hauling themselves on board. Some of them were climbing on to the roof for a free ride. Exhausted, James fell back into his seat.

"You don't think that kid'll keep a promise?" the American asked scornfully. "She'll spend your money and use your letter to light the cow dung."

If he'd been feeling well enough, James would have called the man a bigoted fool. Instead, he settled back against the hard wooden seat and tried to sleep.

As the train rattled across the plain, the hum of voices swelled. The smell of cooking and stale sweat grew stronger. The heat stifled every breath of air. Each seat and window frame rattled and groaned.

Gradually the sounds blurred in James' mind. It was going dark. He was confused. "It's not night yet," he tried to say, but nothing came out his dry mouth.

He didn't feel a thing as he slumped to the carriage floor.

Chapter One

13th September 1959

The blow stunned him. Reeling, DI Paul Ambrose sank to his knees, clutching his temple. He nearly cried out in pain.

He moved his hand: there was blood on it. Urgently he grabbed his handkerchief and looked round for some water. He saw a jug on a table near the window. Pressing the cloth to the wound, he got up. He felt sick, but deep breaths helped. Almost crouching, he moved towards the jug.

It wasn't easy. The ceiling slumped and the walls bent. Everything was at an odd angle. Ducking under a beam, he inched towards the tiny window.

As he'd hoped, there was water in the jug. Pouring himself a glass, Ambrose drank until he felt a little better, then he soaked his handkerchief. He pressed it to the wound until the throbbing eased. Sighing, he stood very still, looking out the window.

He could see the Hall's driveway stretching in front of him, quartered by the leaded glass. Carefully he turned back and looked around the room he'd been allocated. It was a crazy, misshapen attic with thick beams, just waiting for him to crack his head again. It wasn't a good start, he thought ruefully.

Working undercover was difficult, especially with so little to go on. Even his closest colleagues didn't think James Marshall had been murdered. Yet Ambrose's famous instinct wouldn't let him move on. So here he was, at Chalk Heath Hall, with its rambling staircases and overgrown gardens. The door to his room creaked like it was straight out of a Hammer House of Horror movie. And the first thing he did, Ambrose thought crossly, was nearly knock himself out.

At six foot four Ambrose had often found his height an advantage, particularly in a professional capacity. Now, he most definitely wished he were smaller. He'd watched with envy as other guests were shown into spacious rooms. It was just typical, he thought, that the tallest man had been given the room with the lowest ceiling.

It was cold, despite the autumn sun outside. Ambrose shivered. The radiator looked new. Presumably in the past the attic hadn't been heated. He wondered why the owners had bothered. There was no way a pump would reach this far.

Crossing back to the bed, Ambrose avoided the beam, but only just. He took out his writing pad and pencils and laid them on the oak desk. He'd better look as though he was keen to start work, in case someone checked his room.

Then he hung his dinner jacket and trousers in the wardrobe. It wasn't often he had to wear a dinner jacket for work. If nothing else, this case was giving him a week away from the Station. Ambrose felt he couldn't lose. If his hunch were right, he'd unmask a cold-blooded murderer. If he were wrong, he'd have a whole week to focus on writing. He decided not to unpack anything more yet. Perhaps one of the other guests would take pity on him and swap rooms.

Feeling better now he had a plan of action, Ambrose looked for a mirror. There wasn't one and his was at the bottom of his case. Running his fingers through his hair and straightening his tie would have to be enough. He wanted to look around before the welcoming party started.

Gingerly he made his way back down the stairs to the floor below. He walked along the landing, towards the main stairway with the mahogany banister. At the sound of footsteps he turned. A woman was coming towards him. As soon as she saw him she let out a gasp, then clasped her hand over her mouth. "You poor man!" she said. "What have you done?" Her voice was low and husky.

It took Ambrose a few seconds to realise she was addressing him.

"You have blood on your face," the woman persisted. "You must sit down." Unceremoniously, she took Ambrose's hand and made him sit in a deep armchair near the top of the stairs. Her manner suggested she was used to being obeyed.

"It's nothing," Ambrose assured her in acute embarrassment. "I hit my head on the beam in my room. That's all."

"Well, it's still bleeding. Not a lot, but it looks bad. You just sit here and I'll get my first aid kit. I'm Sheila Butterworth, by the way. Miss not Mrs. I shall expect you to be here when I come back. Won't be a tick."

Patting his handkerchief against his forehead, Ambrose saw fresh blood. Miss Butterworth was right. He couldn't go downstairs as he was. Besides, it was a useful chance to get to know one of the women on his suspect list. He tried to recall whether she was one of the artists or a writer. With her short, cropped hair and loose slacks, she looked sporty. The plimsolls suggested she'd been about to go for a run around the grounds.

Waiting, Ambrose listened to the sounds below him. Other guests had arrived. He could hear their chatter as they explored the ground floor. He could just see the black and white tiles in the lobby below, showing the scuffmarks of generations. The step of the front doorway had worn in the middle to almost half its original size. The heavy oak door, now propped open, couldn't possibly do its job any more. The gap between door and step would be big enough to let a small rodent through, never mind the breeze.

Miss Butterworth reappeared, carrying a first aid kit. "I never go anywhere without it," she explained. "You can tell I was a Girl Guide, can't you? Now do you want me to nurse you or should I leave you to it?" Seeing Ambrose's face, she laughed. "Well I can see you're the independent sort. Good job I've brought my compact mirror, so you can see what you're doing. Help yourself to whatever you need and then put it all back inside my room. First on the left. The door's not locked. I don't think there's even a lock on it. I'm just off for a quick run. See you at the Welcome."

Thanking her, Ambrose took the first aid kit. "You're very kind," he said.

"Not at all!" Sheila Butterworth smiled. "You gave me quite a start standing in front of me, at least ten foot tall, with blood on your face. Pity I'm not writing a gothic horror novel! You'd have fitted in nicely."

"Sorry," Ambrose apologised, smiling back. Now his head was clearing, he could see the funny side. Being mothered by one of his suspects hadn't been in his plan.

"See you," she repeated and ran down the stairs, through the door, into the sunlight beyond.

It took Ambrose a few minutes to patch himself up, hiding the plaster under his hair. It would be agony pulling it off later. Then he slipped the first aid kit and mirror inside Sheila Butterworth's room. As she'd said, the door had no lock, just like his room. Out here on the edge of town it was probably safe enough, but he wasn't happy with the front door being wide open too. It also complicated matters. An outsider might have been responsible for James Marshall's death, sneaking into the Hall unnoticed.

Taking a quick look round the room, Ambrose didn't have time for a full search. Beside, he wouldn't even know what to look for. The woman was clearly neat and tidy. Her bag was already unpacked and writing materials were on the desk. Closing the door quietly, Ambrose decided to investigate the ground floor.

It was still too early for the welcome party, so Ambrose went to the dining room to check where he'd be sitting for lunch. To his surprise, he found his hostess setting the table. He hadn't had chance to look at her closely when they'd met earlier. Now he was able to examine her without being noticed.

She was leaning forwards, putting out the cutlery, her pearl necklace colliding gently with the water jug. Her baby blue cardigan and matching jumper contrasted with her pale skin and green eyes. A tweed skirt, stockings and court shoes finished her attire. She wore her fair hair up in a loose bun held in place by an ivory clip. Lest anyone forgot she was an artist, she had skewered her bun with a long paintbrush. A few wispy curls at her neck added charm. She clearly took as much care over her table as she did over her appearance. Ornately scribed place names marked where each guest should sit.

Ambrose slipped back into the corridor, almost colliding with a stranger with piercing blue eyes and floppy brown hair. He looked to be in his early twenties. "Geraint Templeton!" the young man announced with a swish of his fringe. It didn't seem to help. A wayward lock settled resolutely back over his right eye.

Ambrose was immediately alert: another of his potential suspects. "Paul Ambrose," he replied.

Geraint looked at him quizzically then roared in amusement.

"Don't tell me, let me guess. Ruthie has put you in the corner room in the *attic*!" Geraint laughed. He moved past Ambrose towards the dining room, sticking his head around the door.

"Ruth darling. You haven't put this *giant* on the top floor, surely?" he guffawed.

Ambrose heard the clatter of suddenly dropped silver then hurried footsteps towards the door. Ruth Yates looked flustered.

"How could I *possibly* have known how tall our distinguished guest is?" she complained hotly.

Chapter Two

"Distinguished?" Geraint turned to stare up at Ambrose, as if the explanation would be written on his forehead.

"This is Detective Inspector Ambrose," Ruth's tone suggested she was talking to a young child.

"Good god Ruth!" Geraint exclaimed. "Even more reason not to stick the poor chap in the smallest room in the house. You'll ruin his career if you turn him into a hunchback."

Geraint tipped his head on one side as if assessing the embarrassed Ambrose.

"Why don't you give him the speaker's room, Ruthie?" the young man demanded. "I mean he's only staying one night, presumably. I really don't see why you have to keep a whole room for him. Surely he could bunk up with one of us chaps?"

"Absolutely not," Ruth Yates looked horrified. "We always take the best care of our speakers," she added, turning to Ambrose.

Geraint sighed theatrically. "Look, tell you what, why don't you swap rooms with *me*?" he smiled. "That's presuming Ruthie here has kept my usual room for me and not given it to anyone else." He turned back towards their hostess.

"Of course the Yellow Room is ready for you," she said tartly. "It always is. Although why I don't give your room to a *paying* guest I really can't imagine."

"Because you adore my company," Geraint replied. "And because I help you out with your tiresome art students. Plus, of course, I'm the best looking chap for miles and you know your lady guests love having me around."

Ambrose was torn. He desperately wanted to change rooms, yet he really didn't want to accept anything from this annoying young man. Fortunately Ruth settled matters.

"Well you might as well make yourself useful for once, Geraint!" she pursed her lips. "Go upstairs and collect DI Ambrose's suitcase, presuming he's not unpacked yet."

"Just my Dinner Jacket and writing things," Ambrose replied. "I can collect them later."

"Good. Then put his case in the Yellow Room," Ruth ordered Geraint. "That's on the first floor, at the end of the corridor, opposite the gentlemen's bathroom," she explained to Ambrose.

"Yellow Room?" Geraint snorted. "Milky grey would be closer, Ruth darling. That room hasn't seen a drop of paint in decades. If you're not careful, I'll paint it myself. Multi-coloured spots would look good don't you think? Or perhaps a nice tartan to match that ridiculous dress you insist on wearing in the evenings!"

Geraint started up the stairs before Ruth could reply. Ambrose turned to his hostess.

"Geraint is my most successful student," she smiled thinly and shrugged. "He's making a real name for himself. Of course, it helps that he doesn't have to earn a living like the rest of us." Jealousy dripped from her voice like melting ice. "Still he's quite right: you can't possibly sleep in the attic. You'd better follow him up now."

She moved back into the dining room as if relieved matters had been settled.

Ambrose considered Geraint as he walked with him to the so-called Yellow Room. He wondered if the up and coming artist really was irresistible to women. Sadly it probably was true. The studied insouciance had almost certainly taken years of practice. The open necked collar and elegantly scruffy jacket were designed to appeal. At the very least, the whole effect would make a certain type of woman want to mother Geraint.

Ambrose wasn't keen to spend too much time in Geraint's company, although he'd have to get to know him soon. As quickly as possible he swapped rooms and unpacked properly.

11

The ceiling here was certainly higher and more suited to a guest of his stature, but Geraint hadn't exaggerated about the faded paint. He could have added the threadbare carpet and sagging mattress. It was going to be an uncomfortable week, Ambrose realised. Mary would never believe him. Like most people who'd never been inside Chalk Heath Hall, his wife was convinced it was palatial. He wondered how Mary was getting on with their son Joe. Better perhaps, with Ambrose away. She always said he made things worse.

He'd been worried that taking the week off on his own was unfair on Mary, but she'd insisted. "You're always saying you can't get any writing done, and now's your chance, without feeling guilty. You just tell yourself you're working on a case and not wasting time." She understood him rather too well.

Walking back down to the lobby, Ambrose nearly collided with Ruth's husband who was hurrying towards the dining room, out of breath.

"Sorry old man," he gasped. "Lost track of time. My wife will be furious with me," he added. "I should be setting the table for luncheon!"

Frank Yates whisked past in a flurry of tweed jacket and flannel trousers. Ambrose just managed to spot the shirt, cravat and the leather patches on the elbows before Frank disappeared. Ambrose felt almost disappointed. He wasn't sure what he'd expected of his host, the once famous novelist. Perhaps he subconsciously thought that anyone who'd managed to get a book published, let alone two, would have a god-like appearance. Frank looked decidedly human. His dark hair was slicked back, slightly greying at the temples. His brown eyes looked smaller behind his pince-nez spectacles.

The chime of a silver gong echoed down the hallway. The welcome party was beginning. Clearly Frank was far too late to lay the table.

Chapter Three

Only three other guests were at the Welcome when Ambrose arrived. They were standing in the dining room, near a pair of French windows, which opened on to a terrace outside.

"I think I'll be over there," a young woman was saying, pointing towards a place on the far side of the dining table. "Mine's the vegetarian meal. Let me guess – potato soup again?" she grinned ruefully.

"I'm afraid so," Frank Yates said, smiling uncomfortably. "We'll try to do something a bit more imaginative tomorrow lunch. Do you like artichokes?"

"Love them, Frank" the girl replied, offering her hand to him in greeting. "You'll remember me, Edith Greenwood."

Frank smiled in surprise. "Of course. How nice to see you again," he replied. "So you remember we use first names during our weeks. I find it so much better for getting to know everyone. It worked when you were here last time, didn't it?"

Though he pretended to be reading the place names before joining the others, Ambrose considered the girl with interest. If she'd been here before, he must find out if she'd met James Marshall. Whilst not exactly pretty, Edith Greenwood was striking. About twenty one, she looked as though she could wield a hammer as easily as a pen or paintbrush. "Doesn't do badly on a vegetarian diet," Ambrose thought to himself.

With her long red hair tied back in a ponytail and her clear blue eyes, Edith would have been noticeable anywhere. In the dining room of a faded stately Hall she seemed utterly out of place. Every item of her clothing was black, apart from a small red blanket wrapped around her shoulders like a shawl, even though the autumn sun was streaming onto the terrace. Her sweater looked as though it hadn't been washed for weeks and the boots peeping beneath her heavy long skirt were definitely Army and Navy surplus. "Art student," Ambrose decided. "Has to be."

"Goodness! Can you get artichokes round here?" the man next to her asked. "What expensive tastes you have, my dear!" He laughed nasally, like a seal honking.

Edith glanced in his direction, clearly not sure whether to laugh or be annoyed. She settled for an amused reply. "We grow them, so I have to like them."

"Do you live on a farm, then?" the third guest asked. Her manner was uncertain, as if she felt she ought to make an effort to join in the conversation, but hated meeting strangers.

"How did you know?" Edith asked, laughing. "Is it the mud on my boots?"

"Oh, I didn't mean…" The older woman flushed in confusion. "I was just interested. I'm sorry. I should have introduced myself. Mrs Henry Williams. Oh, did I hear that we have to use first names? Betty Williams then." She was becoming more nervous with every word. "I – er… Are you a writer too?"

"Lord, no. Can't spell for toffee. No, I'm here to paint," Edith replied.

"Believe me, you don't need to be able to spell if you're a writer, do you Frank? It didn't stop you getting published, judging by the errors I spotted in your book!" another nasal laugh.

There was an awkward silence. Frank looked at his watch. A number of the houseguests still hadn't arrived. The guests wouldn't even have a small sherry to help them relax. Instead, Ruth began pouring each of them a glass of apple juice.

"As it said on the booking form," she explained, "this is a teetotal house. I was brought up strict Methodist, and the dangers of alcoholism were drummed into me as a child."

"Stalwart of Old Chalk Heath chapel," DS Winters had warned Ambrose earlier. "You'll have a dry week."

"But that's not the only reason," Ruth was continuing. "I've seen what drink can do, and I hate to think how many fine artists and writers have thrown away their talent that way. I wouldn't want to harm anyone, and who knows what serving alcohol here might lead to? The wine of inspiration will be sufficient," she added sweetly. "I'm sure we'll have a wonderful week together. Let's raise our glasses to that."

Dutifully, they each held up their apple juice.

"There are hors-d'oeuvres on the table just outside the French doors, on the terrace," Frank added. "To keep us going until lunch is served. We'll do the introductions after more people come down."

"How many of us are there?" Ambrose asked.

"Ten, plus our distinguished speaker, and Geraint. Oh, and of course, Frank and myself," Ruth replied. "We'll be joining you for all the activities. I always find I gain enormously from our gatherings. Other people's ideas are so stimulating. It makes me paint. It's just too easy finding excuses not to be creative."

"Yes, isn't it?" Betty agreed, rather too vehemently. Blushing, she moved back towards the dining table and began to check the nameplates. Ambrose tried to avoid watching her too obviously. He couldn't help wonder why the woman was there. She was totally unlike the other, more flamboyant guests. Everything about her said 'respectability': fawn twin-set, brown pleated skirt, flat brown shoes. With her pale brown hair clipped back, she reminded him of a little sparrow. She wasn't on Ambrose's list of suspects, having never been to the Hall before, but he would keep an eye on her anyway.

Two other guests appeared. One was Sheila Butterworth. Pleased to find a familiar face, she crossed to join Ambrose just as he stepped onto the terrace. "Hello again," she began. "Good to see you looking more human! I'm afraid I didn't catch your name but I gather you're a policeman."

Smiling, Ambrose shook his head. "I'd rather you didn't advertise that fact," he said softly. "I'm here as a writer, at least, I'm trying to be one. You write too, don't you?"

"Like you, I try," Sheila replied, helping herself to a small cheese cracker from the nearby table. "By day I'm chief librarian at

Jenners Park Central, surrounded by other people's masterpieces. At night I dream of writing one myself. Haven't managed it yet. One day though… We live in hope. After all, even Virginia Woolf had to start somewhere. But you still haven't told me who you are. Clever man!"

"Not deliberate," Ambrose assured her. "The name's Paul Ambrose."

The other newcomer, an older woman, was standing near them. "May I join you?" she asked in a melodious, elegant voice. "It's DI Ambrose, isn't it? We met at last year's Remembrance Day Parade. I was at the Cenotaph in the Council group, with my late husband. You were presenting the police wreath."

In surprise, Ambrose considered the speaker. "Upper crust," he thought to himself. "Definitely well-heeled. But charming with it." He didn't recall meeting her. "I'm afraid I have a poor memory for names," he apologised.

"Why should you remember me? I'm Margaret Astin. My husband was Colonel Astin. You might have known him?"

Ambrose did indeed recall the Colonel: one of the more sensible members of the Police Committee. A Diplomat in his past life, Colonel Astin had been good at banging Council heads together without their owners feeling pain. Intrigued, Ambrose studied Margaret as they shook hands. Though in her sixties, she was remarkably attractive, and contrasted with the other guests as vividly as the far younger Edith. There was something faintly exotic about Margaret's appearance. Her white hair was loosely but elegantly arranged, held in what looked like a real tortoiseshell comb. The scarf that fell nonchalantly across her shoulders was a beautiful deep green silk, surely from India. She had a way of listening, too, that made you feel important. Before he knew it, Ambrose was talking to her about the changes in Chalk Heath and the extra demands they made on policing.

"The population's increased by a thousand over the past two years," he explained. "It's not just the new estates being built, but

16

the older houses being split up. Most near the Heath have been divided now and I'm afraid some of the newcomers are, well…"

"Not what we're used to," Margaret suggested, completing his sentence. "My parents must be turning in their graves. But then, change happens, doesn't it? And I wouldn't want to go back to how things were when I was a girl. I had to fight to be allowed an education. Embroidery and French were supposed to be enough for me," she smiled. All the while, her brown eyes sparkled with light and intelligence.

Ambrose was beginning to enjoy himself. If Margaret remained a widow, he reflected, it would surely be out of choice. He found her low voice attractive, almost seductive.

The man with the seal's laugh interrupted their conversation. "Hello. I'm John Harper," he announced, "but call me Jack."

"The travelling salesman," Ambrose thought immediately: this was another on his suspect list.

Jack seemed to swell as he spoke. "I'm a writer," he continued, "working on a comic novel at present. And you?"

He'd addressed his question generally, and Shelia began to reply, but Jack didn't listen for long. As soon as Sheila mentioned spirituality and stream of consciousness he took two steps back. Within minutes he'd returned to the table. The crackers were clearly more interesting than any writing other than his own.

Geraint joined them on the terrace. "Budge over," he said irreverently to Jack. "I'm starving and you're hogging the food, not to mention the only decent bit of sunlight. It's perishing upstairs."

"Oh come on," Frank remonstrated. "It's far better since we had the new central heating put in. You must admit that."

"All relative, dear boy!" Geraint replied cheerfully. "You don't actually freeze now, just go a delicate shade of blue." He held his hands up for the company, or rather the women, to see. "Quite an attractive colour, wouldn't you say?"

"He thinks a good deal of himself, doesn't he?" Margaret remarked quietly to Ambrose. "Ruth and Frank must find him... rather tiresome. "

Two new guests arrived. The first was a quiet, insignificant man in his 40's who spoke so indistinctly that Ambrose heard the name as 'Geralson'. It took Ambrose hours to discover the man's name was actually Gerald Thompson and on the list of possible suspects. When trying to memorise the list earlier, Ambrose had chosen objects as an aide-mémoire for each suspect. 'Fancy fountain pen' hardly seemed appropriate for Gerald Thompson, unless it had run out of ink.

His total opposite, Jonathan Prentice, breezed in with a pleasant smile all round. "Pleased to meet you," he announced. "Sorry I'm so late. Had to drive up from darkest Surrey and got stuck in traffic." Highly confident and rather handsome, if a little grey, he announced that he'd been in Dorking on business. "I run a literary agency," Jonathan explained. "Set it up just after the War, when my dear wife died. We specialise in non-fiction, Natural History, autobiographies, that sort of thing. It struck me as an under-developed genre. Some of the best writers are on our list now. We're still growing too."

"Excellent," Frank replied. It seemed to be his all-purpose reply. "We're delighted to have you with us. When you visited last month, you said you might stay with us regularly?"

"I'm sure I will," Jonathan said affably. "I shall need a week's peace and quiet every so often. I'm writing myself now: a biography of Stalin, working title, *Uncle Joe*."

"What a brilliant title!" Sheila enthused. "Ironic and yet familiar. As enigmatic as the man himself!"

Jonathan beamed towards her. He clearly liked having a fan club.

There was a pause. Ambrose counted the people around him. Two guests were late. Fortunately, lunch didn't seem to be ready yet either. "We're a bit short-staffed today," Frank apologised as Ruth slipped out to the kitchen. "The chef's on holiday."

"Timbuctoo?" Geraint suggested.

Ambrose was beginning to wonder if every member of staff was 'on holiday'. He certainly hadn't seen any servants since he'd arrived. He appreciated that Frank and Ruth wouldn't want to advertise if they'd lost their staff. Or perhaps they just couldn't afford any.

Frank continued heartily, "I may as well announce it now. We'll be sharing the cooking from tomorrow onwards. It's an excellent way of getting to know your fellow artists and writers. We find that talking in a kitchen often brings out the shyer members." He glanced in Betty's direction. "Don't worry!" he added reassuringly. "Ruth and I will be around to help."

There was a mutter of consternation, especially among the men.

"Come on chaps," Frank chided them cheerfully. "Cooking's not that difficult! After all, women do it every day." This produced a loud protest from the women and much laughter. The house party was beginning to relax.

"There'll be a rota for you to sign up," Frank continued, "and menus will be left out for every meal. The special gala dinner at the end will be cooked for you, but you'll be doing all the others."

Ambrose smiled to himself. He had to congratulate Ruth on such an innovative solution to her lack of kitchen staff.

"Well, I hope you lot cook better than the last group who stayed here," Geraint commented. "I was ill for weeks afterwards."

"Nonsense," Frank snapped. "You're always ill."

"Only when I'm here, dear boy," Geraint replied.

"You shouldn't be such a delicate flower," Frank said and they all laughed.

Acting as Master of Ceremonies, Frank was working hard to keep everyone patiently waiting for the last arrivals. Judging by the constant glances at his watch, they were running very late. Conversation faltered a bit, and the group began to split up into twos and threes. Ambrose found himself trapped by Jack Harper and being lectured on the perils of being a commercial traveller. "I've a huge fund of good stories," Jack assured him. "They'll make a hilarious book. You've no idea some of the things that happen when you're on the road. There was one time last year when I was up in Manchester…"

The man droned on, relating a series of increasingly questionable tales. At first Ambrose listened, trying to gain an idea of the man's character, but soon he found himself losing interest. He'd never found risqué jokes funny and this man's humour was becoming decidedly blue. Hoping he was nodding in the right places, Ambrose examined the other guests.

Since he was a child, Ambrose had found watching other people more enjoyable than joining in. The habit had earned him the reputation of being 'the strong silent type', but it was no pose. His keen observation had stood him in good stead and was probably why he became a detective in the first place. Now he had good cause to watch the people in the room around him. There were enough egos banging around to fill an auditorium. If James Marshall had been poisoned, such creative tensions could have taken a murderous turn. Or perhaps the deceased was as boring as Jack Harper? By now, Ambrose could cheerfully have dropped something lethal in the salesman's apple juice.

Ashamed at his own thought, Ambrose turned to Jack. "Aren't the autumn colours beautiful?" he asked. Even so banal a topic would be a welcome change.

He was spared Jack's reply. There was a small disturbance in the hallway outside the dining room. At once Margaret, who was nearest the door, was holding it open while a woman came in on crutches, stumbling a little on the uneven floor. Two or three people rushed to her assistance, glad to have something to do. "Thank you so much," the woman said, several times. "I'm so sorry to be a trouble."

"No trouble at all," half a dozen voices assured her. A chair was pulled out and she was helped to it. "You must be Phyllis Hey,"

Frank said. "I'm sorry to see you've hurt your leg. Nothing serious I hope?"

"No, just a nuisance," she assured him. "An old war wound. I won't bore you with the details." Her manner suggested she soon would, however, whether they liked it or not.

"Phyllis is an illustrator," Frank explained, ignoring her look of surprise. Clearly she hadn't been aware they were all on first name terms. "She does colour pictures for children's books. Had a lot of work published you know."

"But I've come here to learn how to paint landscapes," Phyllis insisted, smiling. "And where better than in such a lovely old house, with such lovely views." She nodded towards the garden beyond the French windows.

"Yes, I'm itching to be out there myself," Edith agreed.

It was the first open suggestion that the guests were losing patience and their host went uneasily to the door. "I can't think what's happened to Christina Wright," he said several times, as he looked down the corridor. "She arrived about an hour ago and insisted on going straight to her room. I carried her case up."

"I must admit I'm getting rather hungry," Betty said mildly.

"Ah!" Frank called suddenly, his voice sharp with relief. "We were just getting worried about you. I hope you didn't lose your way? This old house can be confusing."

The last member of the house party had arrived. Ambrose had expected someone colourful and extravagant, used to making dramatically late entrances. Instead Christina Wright was plainly dressed, almost dowdy, in a baggy shirt-dress that would have hidden a multitude of sins. A mouse-coloured cardigan matched her hair. Frank had already told them that the missing member was a teacher at Chalk Heath Grammar, but Ambrose couldn't imagine Christina keeping order, even in a group of sixth form literature students. There must be more to her than met their eyes that lunchtime, Ambrose decided. "I'm so sorry," she said, slightly breathless.

21

"Good job the lunch wasn't ready," Geraint whispered loudly. "Or it would have been cold by now."

"Did you feel unwell?" Sheila asked in concern.

"I was reading, and lost all sense of time."

"Reading?" Edith repeated incredulously.

"Yes, that's what a good book can do for you," a voice agreed tactfully from the door. Their hostess, with a large tureen of soup, was at last entering the room.

Chapter Four

Ambrose breathed in deeply, smelling the autumn air. Frank's instructions were simple: "Find somewhere quiet, on your own, for an hour or two, and let yourselves go. You can write or paint or just think. It doesn't matter. This is your week and it begins now!"

Ambrose decided to walk up to the village. He'd noticed a telephone box and post office as he drove past. With Mary having the car now, it would be useful to know how long it would take to walk there from the Hall. He'd promised to ring her at least once, to check how she was coping on her own with Joe. Not that Joe would be likely to listen to fatherly advice, especially over the phone, Ambrose admitted.

He walked briskly up the drive and out through the Hall gates. He was pleased to find the phone box was only a few minutes' walk, near the end of a row of cottages. The post office was next door combined with a small general store. On the other side of the main street was a small village green, once surrounded by railings, now mere stumps of metal sawn off for the war effort. Crossing a small side road, Ambrose found the Chalk Heath Arms, firmly shut until opening time. Ambrose glanced at his watch. He had time to go a bit further. He passed the pub and a terrace of modern houses. Almost immediately he was out of the village, heading towards Chalk Heath. On the other side of the street an ugly church squatted like a stone toad, but there was nothing else of interest.

As he walked back down the drive, Ambrose considered the Hall in front of him. With its elegant frontage, it was typically eighteenth century. The windows were carefully balanced, the aspect pleasing. It was a lovely building, though going into decline. Ambrose could see gaps in the pointing and there was an ominous sag in the roof between two chimneys. "I'll bet those slates let the rain in," he thought sympathetically. It was hardly surprising Frank and Ruth Yates needed an income. Entertaining cultured house parties must be better than taking in lodgers.

Turning left, Ambrose entered a courtyard between the Hall and a derelict building, probably the old stables he thought. Going through an arch at the far end of the courtyard, Ambrose found Ruth's market garden, with neatly planted raised beds and fruit trees. Canes stood like tepee frames, bean stalks rotting back at the end of the season. Sprouts swelled on thick green stalks, and a few cauliflowers and cabbages still waited to be cut.

He wondered how Ruth could run a market garden, entertain monthly house parties and keep a rambling old country house clean. That would be more than enough for most people. How she could also paint lovely, finely drawn nature studies was well nigh incredible. That explained why she looked so tired, Ambrose thought in sympathy.

Leaving the market garden through another arch, he began to explore the grounds behind the Hall. Lunch had been surprisingly delicious, but strained. He was extremely glad to be out in the open, away from the tense atmosphere of the dining room. Even now, details of conversations and behaviour occupied his thoughts.

As soon as they gathered, there had been a sharp edge to Ruth and Geraint's banter. "Darling, do stop monopolising the ladies," she said to him before they'd even sat down. "If you're not careful, you'll use all your charm today and have none left for the rest of the week!"

Geraint smiled, only to come back at Ruth a moment later by picking up a glass near him. "How clever of you to mix and match," he remarked. "It's all the rage." One of the glasses didn't quite match the others, presumably replacing a broken one.

To Ambrose's trained ear Ruth's animosity was hard to miss: the little snide remarks, the deliberate condescension as she 'helpfully' and publicly told Geraint which spoon to use. Geraint retaliated easily enough, "sorry, I thought that was a spare, so you could show the whole set," but his mouth tightened.

Ambrose was grateful that Margaret had moments before quietly explained the cutlery to him and Edith. Neither of them would have had a clue otherwise. He'd been to formal dinners before, with the 'top brass', but the intricacies of Ruth's silverware were beyond him. Did they run classes at posh girls' schools, on how to confuse your guests with the cutlery?

"How did you cope last time you stayed here?" Ambrose whispered to Edith.

"I should be ashamed of myself," she admitted quietly. "It's not as if this is my first meal here, but I'm still not sure which knife to use for the butter. I spent several days last time pretending I wasn't well, so I didn't have to come down to dinner. Bless her, Ruth carried my meals up on a tray. At least no one could see I sucked the peas off my knife!"

"When were you here before?" Ambrose asked nonchalantly.

"The month before last. Ruth's a brilliant tutor, and I begged to be allowed to come again. I can learn so much from her."

Ambrose knew there was only one house party each month. So Edith had been missed off DS Winters' list. Five, not four, of the present group had been at the same house party as James Marshall. Edith must be watched carefully too, pleasant as she seemed.

He had to admire her determination. Other than himself, she was probably the only one there from a truly working class background. Coming on such house parties must be part of her training, paid for by a local charity or scholarship he suspected. The meals were an ordeal, but she was taking full advantage of the chances she was being given.

It wasn't just the cutlery that was a challenge, Ambrose reflected. Listening to the conversation at lunch was like eavesdropping on children in a playground: "Look at me!" "No, me!" "I can be wittier than you!"

He'd even found himself joining in, telling everyone about the short stories he'd had published in the local paper. They were probably all nervous, he reflected, thrown into an unusual situation. Christina had implied as much, suddenly blurting out, "You all make me feel so insignificant. I'm only a novice, and a week like this is quite different to real life, isn't it?"

It was a penetrating remark and made Ambrose look again at the woman. Apart from Betty, she was the least predictable member of the group, apparently a nobody, yet as Margaret had whispered, "Who knows what passion lurks beneath that baggy cardigan?"

Yes, an odd lot, Ambrose thought wryly, and he would never have imagined himself spending a week with such people. He wasn't sure whether James Marshall had done him a favour or a disservice, leading him here.

Clasping his pencil and notebook, Ambrose wandered down the lawn towards the wooded area, glancing around him. He was surprised by a twinge of jealousy. He'd never been of an envious nature before, and could quite happily do without the large house. His own little home was far more comfortable, and better heated, than Chalk Heath Hall. The long driveway and extensive lawns, now somewhat overgrown, left him cold. But having your own woodland, that was something else.

He wondered why Ruth was so keen to put Geraint down. On the face of it, she had everything: breeding, class, a wonderful if ramshackle stately home. Ruth was renowned as an artist in her own right, quite apart from Frank's fame as the local novelist. Geraint surely couldn't be a threat to her, could he?

Ambrose was so preoccupied that he nearly fell over Geraint's easel.

"Woah, there!" Geraint called out cheerfully from behind him. "You need to look where you're going old boy!"

Making his apologies, Ambrose stopped and looked at Geraint's painting.

"How long have you been working on this?" he asked, surprised.

"Until you interrupted me, about half an hour or so," Geraint replied, licking the end of his brush to get a finer point.

"I mean, when did you start this?" Ambrose insisted.

Geraint looked at him surprised. "As I said, about thirty minutes ago," he shrugged. "I can never get over how you writer types spend so long staring into space. I have to be working. The devil makes work for idle hands, so they say!"

Geraint's hands were anything but idle. He was mixing colours to make at least a dozen shades of green on his pallet. The ground in front of him was strewn with tubes of paint and brushes with different sized bristles. Ambrose looked again at the watercolour on the easel in amazement. In so short a time, Geraint had created an exquisite scene of Chalk Heath Hall, nestling in its extensive grounds. He was dappling the paper with green, building up trees and rolling lawns as he did so. It wouldn't take long, at this rate, before he was finished.

As if hearing Ambrose's thoughts, Geraint sighed ruefully. "Of course, you know what my problem is?" He didn't wait for a reply before carrying on.

"I paint too quickly. Ruthie keeps telling me and, for once, I'm sure she's absolutely right. So unless I die tragically young, there'll just be too many Geraint Templeton originals out there to have any value."

"There," he turned to Ambrose, "what do you think? Does it need a bit of colour? Perhaps a little figure in the foreground, a woman perhaps. Maybe with Edith's beautiful hair, although not, I should say, her rather eccentric choice in clothing."

He busied himself finding the right colour paint amongst the tubes at his feet. A sudden noise startled them both.

"I say there, any chance of some help?" Phyllis called. She was trying to get over a fallen log, teetering on her crutches while holding on to a large wooden painting box. At once Geraint dropped his brush and rushed to her aid, followed by Ambrose.

"Awfully kind of you," Phyllis breathed, looking up at the two men. Ambrose was struck by her makeup. Surely she hadn't reapplied lipstick just to go painting in the woods? She smelled of perfume too. He wondered who she was trying to attract. Ambrose had already noted the lack of ring on her left hand. Perhaps she had her eyes on Geraint, although he had to be a good ten years younger.

"I don't suppose you know where Ruth went?" Phyllis looked concerned. "She's meant to be showing me how to paint trees. Oh what a lovely watercolour!" She turned her attention to Geraint's easel.

"It's nothing. Just a quickie to keep Ruthie happy. She does love it when I do her beloved Hall," Geraint replied with a wink. "But it's dreadful that she's abandoned you. That won't do at all."

Geraint was clearly relishing the opportunity to stir trouble with their hostess. "Why don't we holler for her?" he said mischievously. "I'm sure she'll hear us if we all shout together."

Ambrose was horrified at the thought. Fortunately Ruth's arrival spared him any embarrassment.

"Oh there you are, Phyllis," Ruth sounded annoyed. "I've been looking everywhere for you."

She turned to Geraint. "I should have known *you'd* be involved somehow." He merely grinned.

"Can't blame me, old girl," he replied cheerfully. "I've been as good as gold, painting your beloved Hall for you. There," he indicated the easel, "that'll look lovely in your library don't you think? I even used that Emerald Green you insisted I try last month, though I still think mixing my own colour works fine."

Ambrose could sense Ruth's increasing irritation, but she smiled sweetly. "Well since you don't need my paint, I want it back, please," she replied. "It's expensive, you know."

Geraint ignored her. "And what have *you* been up to? Hiding from your students?" he laughed.

"Not at all. I was just finishing a little study of some mushrooms," Ruth replied. Turning, she found a growing throng of guests listening to their conversation. "Here," she added, showing a beautiful oil painting in autumnal colours.

"That's absolutely superb," Edith said over Ruth's shoulders. "You really must show me how you get that ochre shade."

"And what kind of mushrooms are those?" Margaret enquired. She was admiring the painting from Ruth's left. "Are they a type of ink cap?"

"I really have no idea," Ruth replied, surprised, examining the little grey-white funghi on her canvas. She could clearly sense the forthcoming inquisition from Geraint. How could she possibly not know about the mushrooms in her own back garden? For once she appeared glad to see her husband.

"Frank, darling, don't we have a book on mushrooms in the library?" she called to him.

"That's right, dear, in the natural history section, right next to the maps. Now I do hope the writers have achieved as much as the artists," he beamed at Ambrose and Margaret. "But it will be dark soon so can I suggest we all go back to get ready for dinner? Don't forget, this is the last time you'll be cooked for until Saturday!"

The group started gathering its belongings and walking towards the house. An autumn fog was rising from the river beyond the woods. It curled and swirled upwards, like steam. The sunlight filtered through the misty air, silhouetting the trees. The afternoon was turning from late summer to early winter. It was wonderfully atmospheric, as Ruth said, but chilling to hands and feet.

Ambrose was faintly aware of other guests tagging along at the rear as they moved out of the woods. With a wry inward smile, he realised he hadn't done any writing at all that afternoon. He must produce something to justify being there or people would begin asking questions.

Chapter Five

Ambrose sat at his bedroom desk with the curtains open. He could just see the driveway between swirls of mist. He felt silly writing in his dinner jacket, but he was trying to jot down a plot that had been going round his head for months. Dinner would be early, to leave time after for the first 'sharing session'.

Since his school days, Ambrose had loved to write, scribbling stories in his exercise book when he should have been doing arithmetic. He'd been telling the truth earlier, for the local newspaper had published several of his short stories, under a pen name of course. He'd learnt very quickly it wasn't wise telling colleagues he was a writer. Now he longed to write a full-length novel.

He got so little free time, though, that lately even short stories were impossible. Now this week gave him chance to write, made it necessary in fact, as a reason for joining the house party. Yet, even now, alone in his room, he found it difficult to settle. He was too aware of other guests coming and going, of the chatter of voices. People would calm down in a day or so, he told himself. It was like taking the local Boys Brigade to camp. They were always too excited to sleep on the first night.

The gong sounded in the hallway below. Sighing, Ambrose put down his pencil and went to dinner. He glanced at the rota pinned on the door to the guests' kitchen, opposite the dining room. He noticed that Edith had already signed up for the following day. It was a chance he shouldn't miss. If James Marshall had been poisoned, and perhaps by Edith, he needed to watch her closely to ensure no one else suffered. Taking the pencil hanging on a string, he entered his name beside hers on the rota. If he saw nothing of use, he would at least have got his kitchen duties done. He'd be able to spend the rest of the week writing and keeping an eye on the other suspects.

As soon as the first course was cleared away, Frank clapped his hands. "I have a few announcements to make," he began, "and so that our meals don't go cold I'll start now, and finish before the dessert."

"Gosh, are we having notices all through the meal? It's like being back at school!" Betty giggled.

Clearly not sure whether she was serious or not, Frank smiled. "We were so fortunate with the weather this afternoon," he continued, "and I know excellent work has been going on in the gardens. After dinner, you are all invited to the library to share what you have been doing. There's no compulsion. If you'd rather sit and listen or look, that's fine. We need an audience. If you'd prefer to go straight to your room to work, that's fine too. This is a house party, not a school. We're all artists and writers escaping from our normal routine, for one precious week of creativity."

"Isn't there anywhere we can work downstairs?" Jack asked. "My bedroom's ruddy freezing."

Frank smiled again, this time, the sort of smile reserved for awkward children. "Of course you can work downstairs. We've divided one of the larger rooms into a lounge and a library. You can work in either," he replied. "I'm so sorry you're finding your room cold. I'll get the odd job man to look at the radiator tomorrow."

"I'll bet I know who that odd job man is," Sheila whispered across the table.

"Poor Frank!" Edith whispered back.

So others had noticed the lack of servants, Ambrose reflected. He recalled Margaret's comments earlier: how Ruth had inherited the house from her father, Edgar Dawson. Before the Great War, the Hall had huge grounds, with romantic walks and a lovely chestnut avenue. Since then, most of the land had been sold off in bits. Now there was only the narrow strip from the front gates to the Hall, and then behind it to the woods and the river.

"I do admire Ruth," Margaret whispered to Ambrose. "She's determined this lovely old house shouldn't be pulled down like so many round here. She and Frank do everything they can to keep the place going. They regularly offer weeks like this, and Ruth runs the market garden too. She did really well in the War, but now rationing is over, her income must have been halved. I'm sure she finds it very difficult to keep her painting going. She's a fine artist, but I don't imagine she makes much out of sales, and I'm afraid Frank hasn't had a lot of luck with his novels lately either."

A loud honk interrupted them. There was a murmur of polite laughter, as if Jack had just cracked a rather poor joke.

"What an unpleasant little man!" Sheila whispered. "I hope I don't have to be with him too often or I'm sure I shall say something I shouldn't."

Fortunately Ambrose didn't need to reply. The main course had been brought in on a trolley. Everyone set about putting dishes on the table and serving the very welcome casserole.

"We're certainly not going to go hungry," Phyllis commented, helping herself to a mound of mashed potato.

For the next quarter of an hour, people were too busy eating to talk, but gradually the babble rose again. Sheila and Phyllis were discussing the problems of first person narrative; Margaret and Edith were talking about the similarities between the artist's and the poet's observation of nature. Ambrose could just hear Christina and Jonathan complaining about the informality of using first names. Even the normally silent Betty was asking about finding a publisher for a poetry collection.

Ambrose joined in the conversation nearest him, about whether the Suez invasion had been a mistake. He felt a little out of place but enjoyed the sense of free expression. It was a very different meal and atmosphere from supper at 'The Copper Kettle', with its stewed tea, slices of doorstop toast and half a dozen bobbies coming off their shifts, smelling of tiredness and wet uniform.

Frank stood up again and 'hemmed' politely. "I'm sorry to interrupt," he apologised, "when you're all beginning to get on so well, but I do have other announcements before dessert."

"I hope it's better than the main course," Geraint said in a noisy whisper. "I can feel my stomach churning already."

Frank had clearly heard, for he stared coldly in Geraint's direction.

"If looks could kill..." Edith commented quietly.

"About breakfast," Frank persisted. "There's no set time. You'll find porridge oats in the cupboards, and plenty of bacon, eggs and milk from the local farm in the pantry. Ruth picks the mushrooms herself every day when they're in season, and they're at their very best just now. Help yourselves. There are two gas rings, as well as the range, so several of you can cook at once."

"You mean we have to cook our own breakfasts?" Jonathan asked. "I haven't done that since I was a Boy Scout." He smiled at the assembled group. "Do me good to learn to fend for myself I'm sure."

"Presumably he has servants," Sheila hissed.

"And a butler!" Edith whispered back. "We're dead common down our way. Have to crack our own eggs."

Ambrose sighed inwardly. He found such talk of 'them and us' wearying. There'd been too much of it when he was a boy, and he'd hoped the last war would end it all. Yet here it was again. The house party was already beginning to split along class lines: Ruth, Margaret and Jonathan were clearly 'old money' (even if some of them had little of it now); while Frank and Geraint were trying to pretend they were too (but clearly weren't). The rest of them were born into 'trade', even if they'd risen through their professions since.

"You really don't mind us helping ourselves to the food?" Betty asked. She giggled slightly and flicked her hair back from her face.

Intrigued, Ambrose watched her. Ever since they came down to dinner the woman had been a little silly, not at all the shy outsider of earlier in the day. She was smoking heavily, too, sharing a packet of cigarettes with Jack, which had so annoyed Jonathan that he'd feigned a coughing fit. Nervousness affected people in different ways Ambrose reflected, but there was definitely something odd about Betty.

"Mind? Not all!" Frank assured her. "The guest kitchen is all yours while you're here."

There was the squeak of a trolley being wheeled out of the Yates' kitchen, at the other end of the corridor. Frank glanced with evident relief towards the sound. "There's just one more thing," he said lightly. "I'm afraid our guest speaker, Thomas Weill, has had to stay in London due to a family emergency. He sends his abject apologies, but he won't be joining us tomorrow."

"Not coming?" Christina demanded. "But he's the reason I booked."

"Me too," Sheila agreed.

"I'll bet he didn't want to drive out here in the fog," Geraint suggested. "The weather report said it was bad in the city already."

"Oh, I'm sure that's not the case," Frank insisted. "It must be an emergency. Thomas wouldn't let anyone down if he could help it."

"Looks like we're the exception," Phyllis suggested.

Jack joined in. "We should have our money back," he declared, rather too loudly.

"It is very disappointing," Margaret agreed, more politely. "Have you managed to find a replacement?"

"No one can replace Thomas Weill!" Christina insisted. She sounded near to tears.

Not knowing anything about the guest, other than that he was a famous novelist, Ambrose kept out of the discussion.

"We do have another speaker," Frank assured everyone quickly. "Equally eminent. I'm delighted to say Charles Coulson has stepped in at very short notice. He'll be talking about writing autobiography, a genre I know several of you are working in. I'm sure even the artists among us will find him entertaining. He has a whole host of amusing stories."

"Who's Charles Coulson?" Christina asked.

"Never heard of him!" Jack agreed. "If you ask me…"

"I have," Sheila cut in quickly. "He's an ex-policeman; written a couple of books about his experiences during the War. They were very popular at one time. I don't think he's had anything published recently, but I may have missed it."

Appalled, Ambrose looked down at his plate. He'd never heard of a policeman called Charles Coulson, but it was possible they'd met. Even if they hadn't, the last thing Ambrose needed was some well-meaning old bobby getting in the way.

Frank was trying to get a word in, but the mutter of concern and annoyance was growing. He glanced urgently towards the door. On cue, his wife entered, carrying a tray of splendid glass dishes, each filled with a delicious-looking swirl. "Summer fool," she announced winningly. "Made with our own fresh raspberries!"

At once there was a pause. "Fresh raspberries?" Christina repeated in amazement. "At this time of year?"

"The last ones from our autumn canes," Ruth explained, setting the tray down on the table.

As the dishes were passed round, the talk began again, but with better humour.

Jonathan looked up from his dessert and smiled. "I'll let you all into a secret," he said mysteriously.

"Oooh, I love secrets!" Betty said and clapped her hands like a little girl. "What is it?"

"Charles Coulson is one of my authors. I can't say how delighted I am that you invited him, Mr and Mrs Yates. It's quite a compliment."

"One of your authors?" Ruth asked him. "I'm sorry. I don't follow you."

"I told you that I run a literary agency and I specialise in non-fiction. Charles is on my list. He was one of the first I signed up, and might I add, one of the most successful. His first book, *The*

One That Got Away, was a best seller. What a strange turn of events, but how pleasant!"

"Well, in that case…" Christina said grudgingly. "If he's one of your authors, I'm sure we'll find Mr Coulson a good replacement."

"Yes, indeed!" Frank declared. "What a coincidence! As they say: It's a small world!" He sounded relieved.

There was a murmur of agreement and several people asked Jonathan about Charles Coulson. Then everyone settled to enjoying the raspberry fool; everyone that is, except Ambrose. Before the last dish had been emptied, the question he'd been dreading came. "Do you know Mr Coulson?" Sheila asked.

She'd spoken quietly but Geraint had heard. "Oh, of course!" he said and laughed. "How embarrassing for you! A fellow policeman. He'll blow your cover!"

Puzzled, the others looked on, though Sheila shook her head at Ambrose in apology. Resisting the temptation to tell Geraint that he was an insufferable little fool, Ambrose couldn't think how to reply.

"We have an illustrious guest already amongst us," Margaret explained. "Let me introduce you to Detective Inspector Paul Ambrose."

"Good Lord!" Edith said in awe. "You mean we'll have two coppers with us tomorrow? We'd better not do anything illegal!"

"You don't look like a policeman," Betty giggled. "You're much too handsome." She was lighting yet another cigarette, much to Ruth's annoyance.

Ambrose stared into his dish in discomfort. Having another policeman at the Hall certainly complicated things. Would he be able to maintain his cover to an old copper?

"A policeman who writes!" Gerald said quietly. "Now that must be a rarity."

"Two policemen who write," Jack corrected him. "That must be even rarer. Mind you, if we have a murder in the library, we'll have plenty of brains to solve it. Not even Agatha Christie had <u>two</u> policemen at once!"

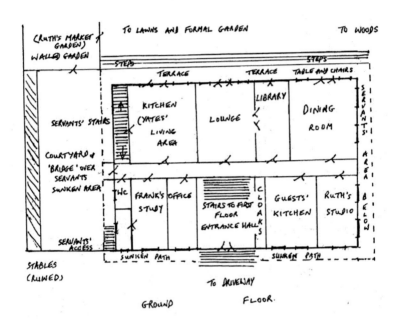

PC Sutton's hand-drawn map of the ground floor

Chapter Six

Ambrose was certain this was the first time, and hopefully the last, that he'd washed up whilst wearing his dinner jacket. In fact, he was now in his dress shirt with his sleeves rolled up and the jacket hanging safely on the back of a chair in the guests' kitchen.

Edith was standing behind him, drying up. Somehow she managed to look exactly the same as she'd done earlier, but just a fraction smarter. She was still all in black, but at least it was a dress, and the red blanket had been replaced with a shawl of a very similar colour. When she stepped forwards, Ambrose noted that she was wearing shoes, rather than boots, but they were functional and flat.

"I'd forgotten," Edith was saying, "that when I signed up for cooking tomorrow, it meant we'd be washing up tonight. There's an awful lot of crockery here."

"Quite," Ambrose replied, handing her yet another plate to dry. It was only now, faced with the enormous amount of dirty dishes, that he realised just how many guests were staying at Chalk Heath Hall this week.

In fact, they'd probably have been there all evening if Margaret and Sheila hadn't taken pity on them. Promising to return the favour later in the week, when it was their turn to wash up, Ambrose was grateful for their help.

"To be honest," Sheila confided. "I'd rather be here than listen to that odious Jack Harper read extracts from his book!"

She was making short work of cleaning the cutlery, having almost pushed Ambrose to one side. Her blue satin trousers and matching jacket highlighted her trim figure.

"I do rather fear," Margaret agreed, "that he's nowhere near as funny as he thinks he is." She was clearly very experienced with a tea towel, despite her upbringing. Ambrose couldn't help but admire the beautiful grey silk dress she was wearing. As ever, she managed to look effortlessly stunning.

"Forgive me for asking," she said gently. "But I can't imagine you signing up for a week like this. You'd think you were spoiling yourself; that you ought to be doing something more practical. Are you on official business?"

The woman's perception was unnerving, but Ambrose was well prepared. "It was a gift from my wife," he replied. "I've been telling her for years that I wanted more time to write, and with my job it's so difficult. She gave me this week as a birthday present. I was really touched." He stacked plates carefully.

"She sounds like a very understanding lady, as well as generous," Margaret commented, smiling.

"She is," Ambrose agreed. He'd told the truth, even if not all the truth. Mary had always encouraged his writing. She'd been delighted at him joining the house party, even if he did have an ulterior motive. And because the force wouldn't pay, she'd bought him one of the Yates' gift vouchers. But at that moment he would far rather have been at home with his feet on the stool and a nice fire in the grate. The guests' kitchen was cold; polite conversation over pots and pans with potential murder suspects was a strain.

The four of them made quick work of the remaining dishes. Sheila was just passing a cloth over the kitchen surfaces when Geraint appeared. He looked pale.

"Gosh, are you having a secret party? It's a good job the only man in here, with all these beautiful women, is a policeman!" he jested, but he didn't sound his usual cheery self. "I'd really appreciate a glass of milk, if there's one going."

Nearest to the refridgerator, Ambrose obliged, assessing Geraint as he did so. Before Ambrose could say anything, however, Margaret intervened.

"Are you feeling alright?" she asked, putting an elegantly manicured hand out to Geraint's arm. He seemed to wobble slightly. Edith stepped forwards with a chair.

"Just a bit queasy, nothing serious," Geraint managed a wan smile as he sat down. "I have a stomach problem and it flares up from time to time."

Ambrose wondered briefly if this was part of the young artist's act. After all, as Geraint had just commented, three of the best looking ladies were in the kitchen. But it seemed genuine. Ambrose felt certain that even Geraint wouldn't feign illness just to get attention. He was less sure about Phyllis Hey's injury, he realised.

"Perhaps you should go to bed?" Edith suggested.

To Ambrose's astonishment Geraint agreed. Then astonishment turned to alarm. Surely the young man couldn't have been poisoned already? While Ambrose was watching? They'd all eaten the same meal, from the same tureens, so how could just one person have been poisoned?

"I'll take him up," Ambrose announced. Realising he was alarming the others, he lightened his tone. "It really wouldn't do for one of you ladies to escort a handsome artist to bed," he joked.

He helped Geraint up both flights of stairs to the attic. Perhaps he shouldn't have swapped rooms earlier, but he could hardly have known that Geraint would be taken ill. "I'll call a doctor," he promised, "as soon as you're safe in bed." If the young man had been poisoned then the sooner he got medical attention the better.

"Nothing to worry about, old boy," Geraint assured him. "It must be Ruthie's cooking. I mean, she feeds us wonderfully but it is all very rich, and I have a bit of a liver problem. Glandular fever when I was at College, you know. I shouldn't have eaten so much, although to be honest, I haven't felt too good for the last few weeks."

"You really should see a doctor," Ambrose repeated.

"No!" Geraint insisted. "It would worry Frank and Ruth and upset the party. I don't want to do that." He saw Ambrose's disbelieving expression. "I'm very fond of Ruth and Frank. I know we joss each other, but they've been good to me. Their house parties keep this old place going and I wouldn't want there to be any gossip about guests falling ill. Not after that last chap, what's his name, the one who died. The scandal would simply ruin Ruthie. Just let me have a good night's sleep. I'm sure I'll be as right as rain tomorrow."

Reluctantly, Ambrose left Geraint to settle down for the night, but he promised he'd come back before the end of the evening.

The others had gone to the library where the night's 'sharing session' was being held. Reluctantly, he joined them. Sitting on the only available chair, right at the back of the room, he found himself squeezed between a rather serious Phyllis and a very unserious Betty.

This close, Ambrose immediately realised the truth behind her giggles. She was drunk. He could clearly smell alcohol on her breath, despite the copious number of cigarettes she'd smoked. "Where on earth did she find alcohol?" Ambrose wondered. He knew the Chalk Heath Arms wasn't far away, but Betty couldn't have got there without being missed. He'd noticed the absence of Gerald and Sheila earlier, but they might have gone to work in their rooms. No one else was missing that afternoon.

Christina was finishing her reading.

"That's as far as I got this afternoon," she announced with a flourish. "Death and violence as usual, but it does sell doesn't it? *Terror Weekly* took three of mine last year, and they pay *very* well." She glanced in Frank's direction. "One has to meet the market, you know. No use writing masterpieces if they're not what people want."

Frank stared intently at the carpet, but didn't reply.

"That was unkind," Phyllis whispered to Ambrose. "Really, the woman is impossible. She coughed or sneezed every time one of the others read. Either she has a very nasty cold, or she's being plain childish. You haven't missed much. Jack Harper's book was quite dreadful, too."

"Really?" Ambrose replied vaguely. He was still concerned about Geraint. Ought he to have called a doctor?

41

Looking up, he was surprised to see that Gerald had agreed to do a reading. The audience were clearly eager to hear something new. It suggested Jack's book genuinely was dreadful and Christina's story not half as good as she thought.

Nervously, Gerald stood rustling his manuscript. "I'm going to read an extract from a short story that I'm writing," he almost whispered.

Ambrose hoped the man would speak a little louder. He was finding it hard to concentrate. Betty was deliberately pushing her leg against his. He tried to move away, without pressing against Phyllis instead. A moment later, he nearly leaped out of his chair when Betty put her hand on his knee. Gently he lifted her arm by the sleeve and replaced it in her own lap.

"It's called 'Jealousy'," Gerald suddenly boomed. Almost everyone jumped. Betty giggled. Gerald pushed his shoulders back and started reading loudly.

"He held her by her long hair, twisting her blond locks between his fingers. This time she wouldn't be able to ignore him. This time he had her full, undivided attention.

"He stared into her deep blue eyes. He watched the way they reflected the light. He thought of the sea, of sapphires. Except, this time her eyes were bloodshot, from crying. He laughed in her face.

"He held the dagger up to the light, watching it glint in the moonlight. One swoop and it would all be over. One slash of the knife and she would be his forever. He brought his arm down, feeling the resistance of her neck against his blade. She screamed."

"I say," Frank jumped to his feet. "Gosh, this is rather different to what you read last time. Perhaps this isn't quite the right, er, *material*, for this gathering." He looked very uncomfortable. "After all, there are ladies present."

"Speaking as one of the ladies," Christina announced, "I think we should hear him out. Surely there should be no censorship here!"

Frank glared at her. He clearly felt stung by Christina's comments. He didn't have time to reply.

"Quite right, I'm sure," Margaret interceded softly, "but I'm afraid you'll have to excuse me. I'm feeling rather tired. I hope to finish my poem tomorrow, so I'll turn in now. Please do forgive me."

Ambrose smiled. With her usual tact, Margaret had given everyone who wanted to leave the perfect excuse. He rose too, seeing the group disperse in front of him.

Glancing back into the room, Ambrose wished everyone good night. It looked like Gerald's remaining audience comprised Christina, Frank and Sheila.

As he walked up the stairs, he became aware of hurried footsteps behind him. Turning, he saw Jack Harper. There was nowhere for Ambrose to hide, so he did his best to smile.

Jack was a little out of breath. "Not used to running, I'm afraid," he gasped. "But with that little minx around, one can't keep still for too long!"

"Little minx?" Ambrose queried.

"Betty what's-her-name. By day, the respectable housewife, by night, the rampant man-eater!" Jack looked over his shoulder, as if worried she was on the stairs behind them.

"I rather think she may have, well, drunk a bit too much," Ambrose said politely.

"You've noticed have you?" Jack snorted. "Well that's why you're a famous detective, no doubt! Still, if I were you, I'd lock your door tonight. Then tomorrow perhaps you can find out where, exactly, she found the drink. That'll give you something to detect."

With another glance down the stairs, Jack ran along the landing, leaving a bemused Ambrose behind him.

Before retiring, Ambrose climbed up to the attic to see Geraint.

The young man answered the tap on the door at once. "Is that you, Mr Ambrose?" he called.

"Yes. How are you?"

"Much better thanks. I'm sitting up in bed reading. See you in the morning."

With a sigh of relief, Ambrose went back down to his own room. He immediately checked his door. No lock. Feeling rather silly, he took the chair from the desk and propped it under the door handle. No one would be able to get in without waking him first. Better to be safe than sorry, he thought.

Chapter Seven

The sound woke Ambrose immediately. Someone was breathing outside his door. He sat up and listened. Was Betty trying to come in? It must be morning by now. Heavy velvet curtains cut out most of the light but a glimpse of sun shone through a small hole. He looked at the clock beside his bed. It was a quarter to seven.

"Huh! Huh, huh!" The breathing went on, too loud for an intruder. "Huh – *huh*!"

Getting up, he pulled a pair of trousers and a sweater over his pyjamas. Bewildered, he moved the chair he'd fixed under the knob, and opened the door an inch. Very carefully he peered out.

A woman was standing a foot away from him, staring through the long window at the end of the landing. First she brought her left hand slowly up to her face, touching her nose. Then she extended it slowly away from her. Counting softly to herself, she did the same with her right hand. Between each gesture, she breathed deeply. "Huh! Huh, *huh*!"

There was a short pause as she stared towards the light. Then the pattern was repeated. "Huh! Huh, *huh*!" Though she had her back to him, Ambrose was sure it was Phyllis Hey.

On the third repeat Phyllis suddenly swept her hands back and clapped them behind her waist. "Huh – *huh*!" Then once again she was staring towards the window, bringing her left hand slowly towards her nose.

Fascinated, Ambrose watched. He could see Phyllis' crutches propped against the wall near her. She was perfectly capable of standing on her own. Though she might need crutches to walk a distance, she was not as disabled as she pretended. Amused, Ambrose closed his door. Then, picking up his toilet bag, he opened the door again noisily, as if he was only just getting up and going to the bathroom.

Phyllis spun round, quickly retrieving one of her crutches. "You gave me a fright," she said, patting her hair into place. "I didn't mean to wake you. I was just doing my Egyptian eye exercises."

"Really?" Ambrose asked. "I haven't tried eye exercises. Of any nationality."

"You should. I do them every morning. They fill me with light and air. This is an ideal place, with that wonderful large window. You could imagine you're on a cliff. Of course, the seaside's the best place for any eye exercise, but we're a long way from the coast, aren't we?"

"We are indeed," Ambrose agreed, managing not to smile.

"See you at breakfast," Phyllis added as he turned towards the bathroom.

"I'm sure you will," he replied politely.

The trouble with a retreat was that it was very difficult to get away from one's fellow retreaters, if there was such a word. Three times he was about to leave the guests' kitchen after breakfast, only to have another guest detain him. If they'd wanted to talk about the weather it wouldn't have been so bad, but Ambrose found literary conversation at eight in the morning a strain. James Joyce's technique in Finnegan's Wake was definitely too much. How Christina could be so earnest over bacon and eggs he couldn't imagine.

Gerald's worship of Raymond Chandler was disturbing too. The man seemed obsessed with crime and violent death, "Fictional of course!" he assured the table several times. Not quite convinced, Ambrose wondered if he should check the knife drawer each day. Having Sheila join in with a gory retelling of a murder case from the News of the World was altogether too much. Going outside seemed the safest thing to do.

Carrying a battered old pencil case (a relic from his schooldays), and a writing pad fixed to a clipboard, Ambrose looked for somewhere to be on his own. The mist was lifting, but the morning was still chilly and he pulled his jacket and scarf tighter. Sitting down on a fallen tree, he considered what he'd learnt about his self-imposed assignment so far.

Not much, Ambrose admitted. It looked very much as though his week at Chalk Heath Hall was going to be an anti-climax. Geraint appeared to be fully recovered. He'd wanted to stay in bed another couple of hours rather than come down to breakfast, but that was probably his normal life style. There certainly seemed no reason to suspect he'd been poisoned last night. All the rest of the guests, even those who'd been present at the earlier house party, were behaving innocently, if eccentrically.

Ambrose might as well take advantage of the opportunity and genuinely use the time to write. Besides, he must have something to produce at one of the evening's sharing sessions.

The tree was hard and the bark uneven. Walking back towards the Hall, Ambrose remembered seeing somewhere more comfortable to sit.

Just below the terrace, an area of formal garden had survived, albeit rather neglected. Going down a broken flight of steps, Ambrose crossed the lawn. In the middle, ancient yew hedges formed a rectangle around a pond, where goldfish hid among the water lilies. Grass paths led around the pond, so a walker could go all the way round and hardly be seen from the house. At each corner of the rectangle a gap in the hedge led to a small private arbour, with two stone benches. In more gracious days ladies in white muslin probably hid there to meet their lovers. Now each arbour was an ideal place for a writer or artist to work.

Ambrose settled down in the corner furthest from the house. Sheltered from the breeze and with the morning sun now breaking through the mist, he was much warmer. In the distance, faint sounds of laughter and chatter came from the library. It sounded as though several people had gone in there to work, but were talking instead. In the gardens it was blissfully quiet, apart from a blackbird throwing leaves around as it searched for grubs.

Beginning to enjoy himself, Ambrose jotted down the ideas that had been swirling in his head overnight. At present they were in no particular order, but he'd found before that a structure would gradually emerge. An hour or more passed without him even looking at his watch.

Then abruptly, Ambrose heard voices coming towards him. In exasperation, he looked up, expecting to find other members of the house party exploring the gardens. The tone suggested anger rather than pleasure, however. Instead of getting up to greet the newcomers, he sat back. If he stayed low behind the hedge, whoever it was might not see him, and he might hear something useful.

As the speakers came nearer, Ambrose recognised Ruth and Frank's voices. They were clearly having a furious argument. "When did you last help with the meals?" Ruth demanded. "I have to do the lot, lay the tables, prepare the lunch, clear it up... If I hadn't thought of getting the guests to cook dinner and wash up afterwards, I'd be doing that too."

"That's not fair!" Frank protested. "Would you like being polite to a lot of idiots day after day? You hide while I sort out everyone's problems. Yesterday was the first time I missed laying the table for ages."

"Only because I nagged you. We agreed we'd share the work, but you're simply not pulling your weight."

"Why should I? These house parties were your idea. I warned you how much work they'd be. If I had my way, this would be the last one."

The couple had paused just beyond Ambrose's arbour. Even if he hadn't been interested, he would have had to stay quiet, or embarrass them by suddenly appearing.

"And how would we pay the bills?" Ruth retorted. "The market garden won't sell much over the winter and you certainly don't earn enough, not nearly enough to pay the heating bill, let alone repair the roof. If I had more time to paint I might earn a bit, but..."

Her husband cut her short. "And why don't you have time?" he demanded. "Because of this bloody house! We would both have time to do the things we want to, if you'd only agree to sell this place, while somebody might buy it. A cottage in the country wouldn't cost a tenth of what we'd get for this, and would be a damn sight more comfortable."

Ambrose's nose was beginning to tickle and he held it firmly. It would be humiliating to give himself away with a loud sneeze.

"Comfortable?" Ruth mocked. "That's all you care about, your own comfort. My family have owned this house for six generations. I'm not going to be the one who lets it go…"

"It's likely to go of its own accord if we don't repair that roof," Frank almost shouted.

"Keep your voice down!" his wife snapped. "We have guests, remember? I shall find the money for that roof, even if you don't contribute a penny. This is my house, and I am not going to sell it! It would break my heart to see it pulled down and rows of nasty little bungalows built instead."

"Look, I know how you feel," Frank replied more gently, "but I think you're wrong, putting a building before our happiness. And I do try to pull my weight. It works better having me keeping the guests amused, while you see to things back stage. When you're with the guests, you seem so jealous sometimes."

"Jealous? What on earth do you mean?"

"Like when you're with Geraint, you're digging at him all the time. I know he can be an exasperating little fool, but he's a very good artist, a tribute to your teaching. You should be proud of him."

To Ambrose's disappointment, the couple began to move away. Fortunately it was only to the next arbour, where they sat hidden from the house. He could still hear their voices, though less clearly.

"He takes too many liberties," Ruth replied. "He's still not returned those paints I lent him, and he can afford to buy materials far better than I can. I've asked and asked him to give them back, but he just smiles. See if you can get them for me, Frank. Please. I need them."

"It isn't just Geraint," Frank insisted. "You seem to resent all the artists we get. The good ones, that is. Like James Marshall....."

His wife cut him short. "Don't talk about him," she begged. Her voice had suddenly hoarsened. "It's just awful. I could tell he wasn't well when he was here, but to die so young!" She sounded near to tears. "I didn't like him I'll admit. He was conceited and arrogant, but I can't bear to think he's dead."

There was a pause. Ambrose wondered whether Frank had put his arm around Ruth and was comforting her. The man's tone when he spoke again was almost fatherly.

"These things happen," he said. "I'm sure Mr Marshall had a grumbling appendix. He shouldn't have gone straight from here to India. Those foreign places are never very clean and India's one of the worst I gather. He was pretty well bound to pick something up, especially when he was so tired, talking until all hours with the other guests. I'll bet he painted half the night when he was there, too. He was burning the candle both ends. I'm sure it wasn't your cooking!"

If that was a joke, it clearly didn't go down well. "It certainly wasn't!" Ruth snapped and stormed out of the arbour.

"I was teasing you," Frank called, following her.

"I'm not in the mood for your jokes," his wife called back. "We've been wasting time. The speaker will be here in a few minutes. Hurry up!"

Her feet sounded on the paving stones towards the pond, then over the grass and up the steps to the terrace. Frank followed her almost immediately.

For some time, Ambrose stayed hidden in the arbour. If he came out straight away his hosts might see him from the back of the house, and realise he'd been listening. After sitting still for so long, though, his knees felt stiff. "Interesting," he thought as he rubbed the life back into his numb legs.

Finally, he risked walking away from the arbour, finding a footpath that led back towards the Hall. As he approached the terrace, it would look as though he was returning from the woods. He heard voices from the lounge, through the open French doors.

There was a small gathering, welcoming the new arrival. "Ah! Our other policeman," Jonathan Prentice said as Ambrose entered. "Let me introduce you to a retired member of your profession, Mr Charles Coulson: one of my most successful authors. Quite a star on my list!"

To Ambrose's relief, he didn't recognise the newcomer. If their time in the force had coincided, they'd been in different patches. Offering his hand, he made polite remarks about being in the same business, and looking forward to hearing some funny stories. "I'd rather you didn't say much about my being in the force, though," he said quietly. "I'm here on holiday."

"Oh yes, quite," Mr Coulson replied. "They never let you rest if they know you're a copper, do they? Always got some problem with their neighbour."

Tall and well built, though going a little to seed around the middle, Charles Coulson looked like a typical retired policeman. About sixty, with closely cropped greying hair, he was quite good looking and could probably still hold his own in a fight. Yet though he spoke genially enough, something in the man's manner suggested to Ambrose he was ill at ease. Perhaps he was finding coming into such an elegant house party unnerving. Knowing he was only a replacement probably wasn't good for his confidence.

"Have you travelled far?" Ambrose asked.

"From the Midlands. Not far really, but a messy drive. You can never get any speed up. It's one city centre after another."

"Yes. We need more fast roads, like the Germans have," Ambrose agreed.

"Ah Mr. Coulson! What a pleasure to meet you finally!" Christina gushed, interrupting their conversation. "I've read all your books." She glanced round, making sure the others had heard. "So entertaining, but so true! Being a policeman during the War must have been terribly difficult. You make everything so vivid. So convincing. Did you keep notes as you went along? Or did you just sit down and remember it all?"

Smiling, Mr Coulson turned away to answer her.

"The woman's latched on to him straight away," Ambrose noted with amusement. He was certain she'd never heard of Charles Coulson before last night. Keenness was one thing. Christina seemed determined to get her money's worth from every minute of the week. Frank clearly found her very difficult. It must be so painful having to earn your living flattering inferior writers' egos: rather like an opera singer having to tell a wobbly chapel choir how good they were, month after month.

Frank was working hard, chatting to each of the guests about their morning's work, and whether it had been fruitful.

"Good job they don't know how he really feels!" Ambrose thought wryly.

Jonathan was being absolutely charming too, making sure everyone had the chance to meet his client. "Such a fortunate coincidence!" he said several times. "I haven't seen Charles for months, and it's so good to meet up like this again."

"That's the sort of agent I need," Gerald said to Ambrose. "He'd soon find me a publisher. Have you got an agent?"

"Not yet," Ambrose had to admit. It occurred to him that it might be worth getting to know Jonathan better. Then he realised that every other writer in the party would probably have had the same thought. No doubt they'd already pressed the manuscript, which they just happened to have with them, into his perfectly manicured hands. It must be as difficult for an agent to have a proper holiday as a doctor or a policeman. Not that this was a real holiday, Ambrose mused, not with a possible poisoner at work.

Chapter Eight

"We're going over to the old chapel," Frank announced. "It's extremely atmospheric," he added.

"That does sound interesting," Ambrose agreed. A ruined chapel would make a good setting for his opening chapter.

Frank continued. "It's not far; on the edge of the grounds, near the Parish Church. There's a path to it through the woods, on the opposite side to where you worked yesterday. It really is a very lovely spot."

"Why's it a ruin?" Jonathan asked. "Did Cromwell knock it about?"

"Nothing so romantic, I'm afraid. It was simply left to ruin after Ruth's ancestor decided to build a bigger church for the whole village. The original chapel's very old though, sixteenth century. I think you'll find it a great place to work."

"Will you show us the way?" Betty asked nervously.

"We'll all go over together, to make sure no one gets lost."

So, carrying assorted easels, paint boxes, writing pads and clipboards, everyone trooped along the path, chattering as they went. To Ambrose's annoyance, Charles Coulson started walking beside him.

"Policing's a lot different now I imagine, to when I joined," he began. "Of course, that was before the War, when we didn't have all your scientific techniques. Mind you, I have my reservations about some of them. What do you think about using photographic evidence?"

"Fine, so long as you don't trust it too much," Ambrose replied guardedly.

"My view entirely! The camera doesn't always tell the truth. I have a good story about that in my second book. Personally, I'm not too sure about fingerprint evidence either. I wouldn't be surprised if that can be forged too."

"Really?"

"If you ask me, nothing's as good as a full confession. My son would be horrified to hear me, but the young don't know everything, do they?"

"No indeed," Ambrose replied, thinking of his own son. "Even if they think they do," he added dryly. "Is your son in the force, too?"

"He is," Charles replied with pride in his voice. "Doing well. Mind you, he has a lot to live up to. We're a police family through and through. Three generations now, and I hope there'll be a fourth." He laughed. "John's little lad loves wearing his dad's helmet, just like I loved my father's. Now he was my sort of copper. Knew everyone on his beat, and was respected by them too…"

And so Charles went on, clearly still very much drawn to his old profession. Since that was the last topic Ambrose wanted to discuss, the conversation was becoming increasingly one-sided. By the time Charles had discussed young sergeants ("What do they actually know?"), women police officers ("Can be good but many aren't") and the increasing use of patrol cars, Ambrose's replies were little more than polite grunts.

Discouraged, Charles moved forward to join Margaret and Edith, who were more interested, or at least more patient.

Sheila replaced Charles beside Ambrose. "How's your plot developing?" she asked. "I'm dying to hear about it. Will you have anything ready for tonight's session?"

"I doubt it," Ambrose replied uncomfortably. "I'm stuck on the middle bit."

"Ah, yes. Middles are always tricky aren't they? You can see how to begin and what sort of ending you want, but getting there's the problem. Nowadays I don't mind not having a definite outline. I like to see how characters grow and where they take me. Why don't you just launch into the first chapter and kick yourself off?"

"Yes, I might try that," Ambrose agreed.

"I find it helps to write a bit of dialogue. It brings my characters to life. How about you?"

"Oh! er... yes..." Ambrose replied vaguely. He always felt embarrassed discussing his writing. Then he saw a way of changing Sheila's focus. "Do you get to the theatre much?"

"As often as I can. It depends on whether I have to work evenings at the library. I managed to get to the Playhouse last week. And I was so glad I did."

"Why was that?"

"They had a new play by a young writer called Osborne," Sheila explained. "Did you see the review in the *Gazette*?"

"It was absolutely damning," Sheila continued when Ambrose shook his head. "But the reviewer had missed the point entirely 'Not at all like dear Mr Rattigan's plays. No structure, just angry ranting...' You know the sort of thing. Wanted a nice cosy evening. I thought the play was brilliant. And it's so good that the Playhouse is willing to take risks."

As she talked, the line of walkers began to stretch out between the trees, with Phyllis bringing up the rear, helped by Jonathan and Geraint while Gerald carried her easel. Edith and Frank were at the front. By now everyone was talking happily, apart from Betty, who seemed to end up alone no matter how often others joined her. Even the complaints about having to carry equipment such a long way were good tempered.

Then suddenly they were out of the trees. The path led on to an ancient wicket gate and a burial ground. As they went through the gate, a surprised silence replaced the chatter.

Moss covered flagstones paved an open area in front of a ruined church, its roofless tower outlined against the morning sky. Broken headstones stood like rotting teeth. Near the gate, an angel wept with one hand across her face, the other pointed towards the clouds. Beyond her, a large stone urn had cracked in half. A marble cross had fallen flat, covered in ivy. Years of wind and rain had blasted the names off many graves. Others commemorated worthies from the village, buried with long suffering companions noted merely as 'Relict', or 'And also his wife'.

"I'll kill anyone who puts that on my grave," Edith joked, but her tone was uncertain.

The doors of the chapel had lost their wood long ago, but its walls still made a broken shelter. Around a tiled rectangle, arched windows gave glimpses of clouds. An empty doorway led towards the new church, across a cobbled yard and a more recent burial ground. They all stood, looking at the ruined gothic building, outlined against the sky.

"There! I told you it was picturesque," Frank said, breaking the silence. "I defy you not to find a painting, a poem, or a story here. I suggest we all scatter, put ourselves in a quiet spot, and see what inspiration we get. Lunch is informal today. Ruth will leave salads and bread out for you in the dining room. I think there's still some summer fool left, too. Go back to the Hall and help yourselves when you feel hungry, and return here for an hour or two in the afternoon if you want. You know the way now. Just make sure you're back before dusk. We don't want any of you wandering around in the woods, getting lost."

"Some chance!" Christina commented softly. "Anyone would think this is Sherwood Forest, not a mile from Chalk Heath."

"I'll bet it was wild once, though," Sheila replied. "You ought to get some nice death and violence here," she added mischievously.

"And you can still get lost, I assure you," Edith said. "I did last time. Took the wrong turning and ended up near an old cabin. I looked for it for the rest of the week and never found it again."

"Ah, the case of the disappearing log cabin," Jack guffawed. "The perfect puzzle for our police duo."

Edith stared at him coldly. She picked up her easel and paint box and went over to the other side of the churchyard.

"This place gives me the creeps," Sheila admitted. "I didn't like it when we came last time and I don't now. Too much death and decay."

"Maybe something dreadful happened here," Gerald suggested.

"Do you think so?" Betty asked in concern.

"Oh yes. A beautiful, neglected woman came here one moonlit night and hanged herself from the bell tower. You can still hear her swinging in the dark," Gerald replied ominously.

"What nonsense!" Margaret said briskly.

"But there is a funny atmosphere here," Phyllis insisted. "Maybe pagan rites used to be held here..."

"Of course they weren't," Charles said firmly. Even so, he glanced around him, as if looking for something.

The atmosphere was affecting others in the party too. One by one, they began finding a place to sit. It was noticeable, however, that they remained within sight of each other.

Ambrose left them to it. He preferred to explore on his own. Going through the stone gateway, he crossed the cobbled courtyard and headed towards the new Parish Church. Solid and very ugly, its front door faced onto the village street. As he walked round the building towards the porch, mouldering flowers and piles of grass gave off a warm, rank scent. The paths were still slippery after the night's showers. Inside the porch, a stone bench looked like a good place to work. Ambrose sat down and got out his pad and clipboard. The air smelt musty though, and the stone seat was cold. After ten minutes or so he got up. He tried the door, thinking he might sit in one of the pews. It was locked.

Walking away from the church to the road, Ambrose saw the pub and telephone box he'd passed on his walk yesterday. Amused, he realised that Frank could have led his guests a far shorter route from the Hall. It was straight up the driveway, left onto the village street, past the village green and then a hundred yards to the church. It would not have been half as an effective a build-up to the ruined chapel, though, Ambrose admitted, nor occupied the guests so long. Once again, he had to admire Frank and Ruth's resourcefulness.

Ambrose looked down the street, away from the church. Every door was shut. The village green was empty. Apart from a woman sweeping the front step of one of the cottages, the other side of the street was silent too. He recalled coming to the village as a lad a couple of times with his mates in the holidays. They'd caught the bus from the railway station, bounced on the top deck across the heath and got off at the post office. All afternoon they'd lolled around on the green drinking pop out of a bottle and eating doorstep sandwiches their mothers had packed. It was a summer treat.

Old Chalk Heath was a sleepy place even then, but a generation or so before, the village was thriving. In those days, it had several shops, three pubs, a village school and busy farms either side of the main street. Now there was just the post office, one pub and the church. "Sad, but I suppose that's progress," Ambrose thought. The new town had grown up around the railway station; that was where people wanted to be. They might like to come out to the Chalk Heath Arms for a summer evening's drink, but Old Chalk Heath would be a dead place to live.

Ambrose returned the way he'd come. He found it difficult to find a place in the churchyard, all the most comfortable corners and walls having been taken while he was away. Finally, he settled down inside the chapel itself, near to a cross in the grass that presumably indicated where the altar had once been.

It took him several moments to think how to begin writing. Charles Coulson seemed to be having difficulty settling too, for he wandered into the ruined chapel, and stood for some time at the far end as if examining the memorials set in the grass. It seemed odd to Ambrose that their guest speaker had come with them in the first place. Surely he wasn't expected to work along side the paying guests? Couldn't he have rested at the Hall, or gone to the library to prepare his talk? Perhaps he thought he should mingle with his audience?

Ambrose managed to ignore the man's presence sufficiently to begin his first chapter. To his surprise, as soon as he did so, he thought of half a dozen possibilities.

Leaning back against the wall, Ambrose stared ahead of him, picturing the opening scene. Yes, a ruined chapel would be ideal.

By the time he'd written for an hour, his back was complaining about the hard wall behind him. Stretching, he looked up. Through the broken window beside him, he could see some of the others at work in the churchyard. Edith was sketching in the far corner. Betty was curled up against a tombstone like a sleepy dormouse. Geraint was feverishly painting quite close to the chapel, so close that Ambrose could see the sketch of trees and wicket gate he was working on. At Ruth's insistence Geraint was trying to develop his skills with oils. "Galleries want oil paintings, my dear," she'd advised him at breakfast, "they never value watercolours properly." Though the different technique slowed him down, it looked as though Geraint would soon become equally proficient in either medium. "The man's a pain, but he's probably the most talented here," Ambrose admitted.

As he watched, Charles appeared and stood beside Geraint, asking him a question that Ambrose couldn't hear. Geraint's reply was inaudible too, but brief. As if dissatisfied, Charles turned and crossed to Betty. She barely looked up at him, intent on what she was writing. Her face was blotched and red, as if she'd been crying. "Definitely unstable," Ambrose thought. Charles also appeared worried about her, for he lingered several moments while she carried on writing. When she didn't reply, he stared ahead of him, apparently watching someone who was out of Ambrose's view. Then Charles moved out of sight, only to reappear a few moments later, heading towards Edith. Mingling with one's audience was laudable, Ambrose reflected, but the man's behaviour looked more like nervousness. He couldn't settle to work himself and was interrupting those who could.

Finally, Charles attached himself to Christina, who was sitting on a flight of steps. Since they led to an angel, devoutly praying towards the sky, it was an appropriate place to seek inspiration. "Trust Christina to get the best spot!" Ambrose thought wryly. Rather to his surprise, however, after a brief conversation with Charles, she invited the man to sit down beside her. "Getting her money's worth, as usual!" Ambrose added, and returned to his own writing.

For the first time in months, he had both the ideas and the time to put them down, and for another hour or so Ambrose stayed quietly on his own, writing. Only the stiffness of his back and the fourth blunt pencil stopped him. Surprised, he glanced at his watch and found that it was after midday. Through the window he saw Christina and Charles leaving through the wicket gate, still talking. Of the others there was no sign. Even Geraint and his easel had gone.

Alarmed, Ambrose gathered up his pad and pencil case and hurried out of the chapel. He and Edith had to be in the kitchen at four o'clock, ready for their cooking instructions. If he wanted to come back to the chapel to work, he needed to go for lunch now.

As he left, Ambrose nearly bumped into Margaret, who was coming from the direction of the newer church.

"I'm glad to see someone else is still here," she greeted him. "I was so engrossed I didn't realise how late it was."

"The others have all gone to eat I imagine," Ambrose replied.

"I hope they leave us some food. I rather fancy one of Ruth's delicious salads. Let's cut back along the road. We'll catch them up easily that way."

Laughing, Ambrose joined her. "Did you get a lot of work done?" he asked.

"Drafted two poems and worked out a third. I found a quiet place under a tree in the new churchyard and thoroughly enjoyed myself. I'm working on a cycle of poems. It started as an autobiography in prose and insisted on becoming a family history in poetry. Whether it's *good* poetry isn't for me to say, but I'm enjoying the writing. And you?"

Ambrose had surprised himself. "I managed nearly all my first chapter, in rough of course," he explained.

"Excellent." There was a companionable pause as they walked side by side down the driveway. "Can I ask your opinion?" Margaret said at last.

"I imagine so," Ambrose replied, wondering what was coming.

"I saw you sitting in the chapel watching people, as you often do. Did you think our speaker was behaving oddly?"

Ambrose avoided answering her question. "What do you mean?" he asked.

"I thought his whole demeanour was very strange," Margaret said. "I couldn't work out why he was here in the first place. Surely he didn't need to spend the morning with us? If he wanted to do some quiet writing, he could have stayed more comfortably at the Hall."

"I wondered that," Ambrose admitted. He was intrigued that Margaret had been having the same thoughts. The woman was clearly observant and thoughtful. She might be a useful ally, someone who could help him to watch the five suspects on his list without others noticing. She might, for instance, keep an eye on the others, while he watched Edith in the kitchen...

"And what was the man up to while we were trying to work?" Margaret continued. "I got the impression he didn't want to be left on his own, as if he was afraid of something."

"Or someone..." Ambrose suggested.

Chapter Nine

Ambrose felt slightly nervous. He held the telephone handset firm, ready to slam it down quickly if needed.

As soon as he heard Winters' voice, Ambrose cut in: "It's me; Ambrose. Are you on your own? Just answer yes or no."

"Clear, sir," DS Winters replied cheerfully. "Ginny's out shopping. I'm off duty for another couple of hours. I didn't realise you're that scared of her!"

Ambrose could almost hear Winters grinning down the telephone.

"You know half the Station is afraid of your wife," Ambrose replied, grimacing. The last time he'd called Winters at home, Ginny had shouted at him: "You make my man work, work, work! I never see him. Then you ring him here!" She hadn't let Ambrose speak to his colleague. Winters didn't even know about the call until the next day.

"Maybe you should tell her you choose to do overtime," Ambrose insisted. He had to admit, he did have sympathy for Ginette Winters. Coping with four young children in a foreign land must be very difficult, particularly with a husband who was hardly ever there. Yet Ambrose needed to be able to speak to his Sergeant at home when the job demanded.

"Trouble?" Winters asked, bringing them back to the job at hand.

Ambrose had left lunch before any of the other guests. He'd given the excuse that, as one of today's cooks, he needed to do as much writing as possible before meeting Edith in the kitchen. Checking no one was watching, he'd walked up the main drive to the village phone box.

"No. I just need information. Sorry to trouble you at home but can you track down a Charles Coulson for me? He's written two books about being in the force during the War. He's turned up here as a guest speaker. I've never heard of him. Even if he was in a different patch I'd have known the name, surely."

"Charles C·o·u·l·s·o·n did you say? Rank?"

"Sounds like Inspector. I haven't had chance to look at his books yet, though."

The phone had begun to beep and Ambrose urgently pushed more coins into the slot. "Do it on the quiet please," he added. "There's also a fifth name to add to your list of suspects: Edith Greenwood. Art student from Chalk Heath. Probably from the wrong side of the rail track and on a scholarship. Could be the Women's Education Trust. If you get something, post it to me here. It should arrive the next morning. I'll say I'm expecting a report."

"Very good, sir." There was a brief pause, as if Winters was considering how to frame his next remark. "Have you found any concrete evidence of foul play, sir? Something I might check on further?"

"Nothing exactly," Ambrose had to admit. "But I'm even more convinced of it. Just keep digging for me. While you're at it, see if there's any gossip about Sheila Butterworth and Gerald Thompson. They seem to disappear from the group at the same time."

Winters laughed. "Never! Isn't she chief librarian at Jenners Park?" he asked. "Mind you, she could be a dark horse. She was a Section Leader in the Women's Auxiliary Air Force and she still goes to France for her holidays. Fluent apparently. Not your average librarian. Gerald Thompson's married, though, with two children, and wouldn't say boo to a goose I gather. I can't imagine him having a steamy affair. I've got some more background stuff on all the names you gave me, sir. I'll post it to you today."

The minutes were clicking away too quickly. Reminding himself to bring more coins next time, Ambrose hurried on. "Thanks, I knew I could rely on you. Everything alright while I'm away?"

"Fine. It's been pretty quiet. A couple of drunks on Saturday night, and a Bentley stolen from outside the Conservative Club. The owner wasn't pleased, but if you will leave the keys in the ignition…"

"Thank you for holding the fort," Ambrose said awkwardly. "It's appreciated."

The final coin dropped. With a brief farewell, he put down the phone.

"Well now," Ambrose thought afterwards. "Sheila Butterworth gets more interesting by the hour."

Walking briskly down the village street, he cut through the parish graveyard to the older church behind. Finding his earlier spot inside the ruined chapel, he settled down with his pad and pencils, as if he'd been working there for some time. The other guests arrived soon afterwards, through the wicket gate from the woods. "Hard at it," Frank called across cheerily. "That's what I like to see!" Christina Wright was the last to arrive, out of breath. Without speaking, she sat in a corner, and began writing furiously. She seemed unusually animated and a little flushed. Over the lunch break something had happened that had lightened her normally sour expression.

For the next two hours everyone was quiet, working hard. The only one not to return for the afternoon was Charles Coulson. Presumably he'd decided to stay at the hall to prepare his talk for the evening. Despite his concerns, Ambrose was soon absorbed in his own writing again. Suddenly Edith was standing beside him. "Sorry to disturb you," she began, "but we'd better go back to start the dinner. It was an awful rush last time I did it."

Amazed to see the church clock showed half past three, Ambrose got up. Together they walked the quick way back to the Hall.

Ruth was waiting for them, armed with menus and instructions. "It's quite an easy meal. Wild mushroom and beef stew with fresh bread, apple pie and custard for dessert. Just leave the meat out of some of the stew mix to make a separate casserole for Edith. All the ingredients are on the table."

At once Ambrose was alarmed. He didn't like the thought of one of his suspects eating a separate meal, but without voicing his suspicions there was nothing he could do. In any case, the girl would hardly try to poison everyone beside herself, surely? The idea was ridiculous. He would watch her very carefully though.

The basket on the table seemed to have a whole forest of wild mushrooms. First Ambrose had to wipe and peel them, then slice the larger ones, while Edith prepared enough potatoes and carrots for an army. Neither of them had much idea what they were doing or how to do it. Every time Ruth 'popped in', she had to show them how to hold a peeler properly or avoid boiling something dry. Cooking for fourteen would have been a challenge for a trained chef. In an unfamiliar kitchen, with a total lack of skill, it was turning into a nightmare. There was so much to do and so little time to do it in. The onions made their eyes run, the pastry went sticky, the apples caught at the bottom of the pan. Ambrose would appreciate his wife's cooking forever afterwards.

Watching Edith was impossible. Having stayed at the Hall before, she knew where utensils were kept, and darted around the kitchen, her hands often out of Ambrose's view. If she'd emptied a whole beaker of arsenic into the stew he wouldn't have seen. Getting the meal ready in time became a far more urgent concern.

All the other guests were relaxing in their rooms or taking quiet walks around the grounds. As Edith said, it hardly seemed fair that she and Ambrose were slaving away in the kitchen and paying for the privilege. "Why can't we just have egg and chips?" he grumbled. "And why does everything have to be so...." he fumbled for the right word. 'Prissy' came to mind but he decided 'fussy' was more polite. "I mean, why do we have to put everyone's lemonade in fancy little decanters? Why can't we just plonk a big jug on the table?"

Edith laughed. "They're not decanters," she replied. "I called them that last time and Ruth corrected me. Apparently a decanter's for port or sherry. We have individual *carafes*, crystal of course." She glanced at the clock. "Oh Lor! We've got to fill all those yet. We'll never be ready in time!"

It was six o'clock and they hadn't even found the cutlery, never mind laid the table. The dinner gong would sound in under an hour. When Margaret came into the kitchen, panic was settling with the steam. "Do you need a hand?" she asked.

"Do we ever!" Edith said. "Ruth pops in, but she usually spends the time sorting out something we've done wrong."

Taking off her shawl, Margaret looked for an apron. "What needs doing first?" she asked.

"You wonderful lady!" Impulsively Edith hugged her. "Could you lay the table and see to the drinks? The carafes are in the sideboard in the dining room and the labels are out ready. The lemonade bottles are on the cold slab in the basement. You'll need Paul to carry them up." Ambrose almost started at the unexpected use of his first name. He still hadn't got used to the week's informality.

With Margaret's help they stood a chance of being ready in time. While Edith tried to persuade the apple pies to cook, Ambrose carried the bottles through to the dining room.

"Leave this lot to me," Margaret instructed briskly. "I'll pour the lemonade into our carafes and find our place names. Really, there's doing things properly and there's making work. Poor Ruthie! She does like to impress," Margaret sighed.

Smiling, Ambrose returned to the kitchen. Ruth looked in on them for one last time. "You seem to be coping wonderfully," she enthused. "I'll be with the others in the lounge if you need me. I'm enjoying listening to our guest speaker."

Edith muttered something inaudible and shook a tea towel vigorously.

Ambrose could feel sweat trickling down his nose when Margaret came back into the kitchen. Edith's face was bright red, but Margaret was too tactful to remark on either. "The table's laid," she said. "I've also set glasses and a jug of lemonade on the sideboard, like Ruth did yesterday. People may want a drink before dinner. Now if you don't mind, I'll go up and change."

In alarm Ambrose looked at the clock. It was half past six. It would take him at least five minutes to put on that silly bow tie. "Oh Lor!" he muttered. "Can you spare me too?"

Grimly Edith nodded. "You'd better change," she said. "If I keep my apron on, I can probably stay as I am. We can't leave this custard."

"I won't be more than ten minutes," Ambrose promised. He could hear footsteps going into the dining room already.

Running up to his bedroom, he grabbed his evening suit. Mercifully the tie behaved itself. He was back in time to take over the custard spoon, while Edith snatched five minutes to do her hair.

They managed to serve the meal to time. Just as the dining room filled with hungry, chattering guests, Edith finished draining the boiled potatoes. Margaret had set out the cutlery immaculately and the carafes of lemonade stood neatly on the table. Each person's place was marked with its copperplate label. After a brief clamour of "I'm here," and "This is me" everyone sat down and looked towards the kitchen expectantly. As tired as if he'd completed a double shift on a Saturday night, Ambrose carried the tureens to the table.

For the first few minutes there was little sound apart from the clattering of knives and forks. Then Geraint looked up. "This is excellent!" he remarked though a mouthful of stew. "I've got my appetite back."

There were murmurs of agreement. Ambrose's tiredness turned to relief. "Well done, us," Edith whispered to him.

For a few moments they managed to sit at the table together and eat some of the meal themselves. After the heat of the kitchen both were thirsty and took long drinks of their lemonade straight away. Charles Coulson looked hot too and had half emptied his carafe. Ambrose was surprised to see a second carafe on the sideboard, the word 'speaker' written in Ruth's beautiful copperplate. She must have known how much Charles would need.

Fetching the extra carafe, Ambrose lent over Charles Coulson's shoulder, to pass him the lemonade. Ambrose had the distinct impression the man was nervous. Coulson cleared his throat and shuffled the notes on the table in front of him. Christina was sitting beside him, and to Ambrose's surprise, touched Charles' sleeve under the table in a gesture of reassurance. Charles smiled slightly in response. "It's hot in here, isn't it?" he whispered and loosened his tie.

Clapping his hands for silence, Frank got up as Ambrose seated himself again. "Now the first pangs of hunger have abated," he said grandly, "I'll introduce our guest speaker, Former Inspector Charles Coulson, of Her Majesty's Police. Some of you have already met him, and found how entertaining he can be. Now we have chance to hear more of his stories, and how he came to write them."

"So, I was right, he *was* an Inspector," Ambrose thought. "Funny I've never heard of him." He couldn't stay to listen to Charles' talk, however. Edith was whispering, "The apple pies are burning!" Together they went back into the kitchen and rescued the dessert.

They could hear bursts of laughter from the dining room. As Frank had promised, Inspector Coulson was an entertaining speaker. When Ambrose returned to fetch the stew plates, he found everyone enthralled, turned towards Charles and barely noticing as their plates were taken away.

"I borrowed a tractor," Charles was saying. "It was the only way of getting through the snow. We tied a 'Police' sign on the back and that was our patrol car for nearly a month. Not that there were many break-ins. The thieves couldn't get through either. We shipped milk from the farms to the villages and post back to the farms. We even took the midwife out on her rounds. One night, she delivered a baby on the back. Tried to get Mum to the hospital and babe couldn't wait. Mum decided to call the little boy Noel, it being Christmas. Still, could have been worse, we were on a *Massey-Harris* tractor!"

Everyone laughed, but Charles was looking hotter than ever. He seemed to Ambrose to be in increasing discomfort, though he was too practised a speaker to falter in his delivery. The clenched hand pressed against the tablecloth betrayed how much self-control was needed.

Ambrose was intrigued, even a little worried. He lingered, taking longer to stack the plates. Frank had opened the French windows and the room had cooled down, but Charles was sweating. He'd loosened his tie further, and his hair was sticking damply to his forehead. "We coped with floods too," he was saying. "One year, there was a torrential downpour and the drains got blocked…" He paused, as if forgetting what he was going to say. "As I said, water gushed up in fountains. The square in front of the Police Station was flooded. So we found some barrels and put planks on them to make a bridge." He mopped his brow, wiping his mouth with his handkerchief afterwards. "The children had great fun running across. Then our daft rookie had a go and fell flat in the water. We had to sit him in the sun to dry off. He was making the windows of the Police Station steam up."

There was more laughter.

"We need the serving spoons," Edith hissed from behind Ambrose. "I can't find any in the kitchen. We'll have to wash the ones we used earlier."

Reluctantly Ambrose picked up the pile of plates and went back into the kitchen. Edith was urgently cutting slices of apple pie.

"Take your time," he reassured her. "Everyone's happy enough." In confirmation, a gale of laughter came from the other room.

"Sounds like they're all enjoying themselves," Edith said wistfully. "I would have liked to hear him."

"He doesn't look very well," Ambrose remarked. "I think he might finish early."

Not too quickly, so they didn't interrupt the speaker, they set dishes of apple pie onto trays and ladled custard into jugs. Then, when they heard a pause in the laughter, they carried everything into the dining room. "Sorry folks," Edith announced. "The custard's gone a bit thick while it waited. Just fish the skin off."

"I love custard skin," Jack called in reply. "We used to fight over it at school."

"Me too," Geraint agreed. He seemed in unusually good spirits.

Ambrose glanced towards Charles Coulson and began to feel alarmed. The man was definitely unwell, becoming worse. His face was flushed and he was breathing heavily but so experienced a performer that he was managing to keep talking. As the heavy custard jugs were passed around he stopped with evident relief and sat down. Christina whispered something to him in concern and he shook his head. His carafe was empty and she poured some of her own drink into his glass. Charles drank greedily, and sat back with his eyes closed. Then he got up again, holding the table edge for support.

"Do you mind if I ask a question?" Jack interrupted. "You said we could."

"Of course. Ask away," Charles replied. Clearing his throat, Charles looked towards the French windows rather than at the group, as if he longed to run away from them all. His shoulders seemed to have sunk, making him look smaller, and the cheerful smile was becoming strained and pale. "I'm sorry. I've forgotten your question?" he said vaguely.

"I haven't asked it, that's why!" Highly amused, Jack honked several times. "My question is this: how did you gather all your stories? Did you write them down at the time, thinking you'd write a book later? Or did you just remember them afterwards? I'm recording things as I go along. When I'm staying overnight I often sit in my bedroom and go through the day's happenings. I find it best to make notes while things are fresh...."

Jack's interruption meandered on, turning into one of those queries that don't really need an answer. Everyone had turned to look at him when he spoke but as he rambled, eyes began to move towards the view outside, or to stare downwards in embarrassment. On the far side of the table, the dessert dishes had suddenly become very interesting, and there was a lot of whispering as they were passed around.

Only Ambrose continued looking in Charles' direction. The man's face was losing its colour and going very pale, with a blue tint around his mouth. He was bent forward over the table, and rubbing at his left arm as if it ached. Ambrose wondered if he should alert Ruth or Frank to their speaker's illness. From Frank's expression, though, it was clear he too was worried. Ruth was too busy examining her apple pie and praising the cooking to notice.

It was Christina's gasp of alarm that warned Ruth and the rest of the table. Charles was swaying as he stood. His face was ashen grey now, his eyes unnaturally bright and staring ahead in a panic-stricken gaze. Suddenly he flopped back into his chair, as if his legs had buckled under him.

"Are you alright?" Jonathan called.

"No," Charles replied faintly. "I feel - very - odd." He pulled at his tie until it was almost torn from his neck. Desperately, he stood and turned towards the window. "I can't breathe."

Leaping up, Ruth opened the French doors wider. A cold draft blew into the room, making the voile curtains flap.

Everyone at Charles' end of the table began to move to give him room or to help him towards the terrace. Only Betty stayed in her place, looking frightened and bewildered.

Instead of going outside, though, Charles turned back to the table as if he'd lost all sense of direction. He was clutching his left arm tight and grimacing in pain. His whole face seemed to be dragging downwards. "Heart attack or stroke!" Ambrose thought in alarm. Urgently putting down the custard jug, he moved round the table towards Charles.

"I'll be all right," Charles managed to say, his professionalism trying to return. "It's just a bit of indigestion."

"You don't look all right," Geraint said in concern. "You'd better sit down. It's probably a touch of what I had earlier. It doesn't last long."

Ambrose crossed to lend a supportive arm. Suddenly Charles' legs buckled. With a cry of pain, he clutched his chest. "Oh!…" he said in a terrified whisper. His words were strangled in his throat. Pitching forwards, he fell across the table.

Betty screamed. Christina leapt forward to help him up. Ruth rushed back from the French windows. "Give him some air!" Frank shouted.

"Someone call an ambulance!" Ambrose ordered, cutting through the babble.

"I'll go!" Ruth said, running out of the room. Her lips seemed to be moving in a silent prayer.

Together, Ambrose and Frank lifted Charles from the table, straightening him up so that he could breathe more easily. His mouth had gone completely blue, and there was a frightening gurgle in his throat. Urgently Christina grabbed his hand and began rubbing it, as if that would bring the circulation back.

An appalled silence settled on the room. Everyone stood in their places, unsure how to help. Ruth's footsteps echoed on the tiled floor, down the corridor, towards the telephone in the office.

"Is there anything we can do?" Margaret asked softly.

Ambrose shook his head. Charles' breathing was becoming more and more laboured, his whole skin going grey. He suddenly looked very old.

"Oh, my God!" Frank whispered. "I've seen that look before. Where the Hell is Ruth?"

They could hear feet running back along the corridor. "She must have got through by now," Christina said. Her voice had gone tight and small.

"Help me get him onto the floor," Ambrose suggested. "If we prop him up with some cushions he'll breathe better."

They were lifting Charles down when Ruth came bursting back into the room. "I can't get through!" she shouted. "I've tried and tried. There's something wrong with the phone."

"It was all right this morning," Frank shouted back.

"Well it isn't now. I think someone's rung us and left their phone off the hook. I keep hearing noises in the background."

"I'll go up to the phone box," Sheila offered at once. "I must be the fastest runner here."

Not waiting for a reply she dashed from the room, pausing only to kick off her high-heeled shoes.

For an eternity they waited while Ambrose and Frank struggled to keep Charles breathing. The gurgling in his throat was getting deeper and more irregular, his skin going greyer with every minute. Then there was silence.

"He's gone," Frank whispered.

"Don't give up," Ambrose insisted. "Help me roll him onto his front."

"What for?" Frank whispered, but he did as Ambrose had asked.

Quickly Ambrose turned Charles' head to one side, to free his mouth and nose, then stretched the man's arms out in front of him. Kneeling astride his body, he placed his hands either side of Charles' ribs. Rhythmically he pressed forwards and back, compressing and releasing, so that air was drawn in and expelled in gulps. "Artificial respiration," Ambrose gasped between movements.

He was still trying to bring Charles' breathing back when Sheila returned, her stockings torn and her jacket missing. "An ambulance is coming!" she called from the door.

Frank and Ambrose glanced at each other; both knowing it would be too late.

Chapter Ten

The bell rang across the night. At first only a faint sound, it quickly grew louder as the ambulance crossed the heath and headed along the lane towards the village. Ambrose looked up, but the rhythm of his movements didn't alter. Squeeze and lift. Squeeze and lift.

To his relief, Charles moaned, and a great breath jerked from his chest. Urgently Ambrose pressed again. Frank felt for a pulse. Softly, so that the others wouldn't hear, he whispered, "You've got it going…"

In stricken silence everyone waited as the bell grew louder. Speeding through the village, it turned sharply, coming down the driveway. As Ruth ran towards the front door, tyres skidded on the gravel outside.

Wearily Ambrose got up as two ambulance men hurried into the room. "Looks like a heart attack," he said.

They bent over the contorted figure. "Let's see what we can do," the younger man replied. "You were quick, sir! How did you get ahead of us? Nice outfit, by the way."

Ambrose realised he knew both men: Tom Abbiss and Fred Plummer. They'd attended a couple of murder scenes he'd investigated, and been called as witnesses when the cases came to court. "I was already here," he admitted.

Stretching his back, he looked around the room. Frank stood up also, just as his wife reappeared in the doorway, her face flushed and anxious. Betty had flopped back into her chair, her breath coming in deep gulps. The others remained in their positions around the table. Though she stood upright and controlled, Christina was near to tears. In concern, Sheila put a hand over Christina's in a gesture of comfort. Even Geraint's face had gone pale.

"Charles is in good hands now," Frank said calmly. "I suggest we leave the ambulance men to it and go into the lounge out of their way."

Like obedient children, the guests trooped towards the door. Suddenly there was a cry of alarm from Sheila. Betty was swaying as she stood. Urgently, Sheila and Margaret put their arms around her and held her from falling. "Let's get her out of here," Margaret advised. "She'll be better where she can't see."

The others stepped aside. "Come on, dear," Margaret said. "There's nothing we can do, and the ambulance men need to be alone with Mr Coulson."

No one else spoke. Following the group surrounding Betty, they filed out of the room and headed down the corridor.

Ambrose didn't join them. With professional interest he watched as the ambulance men attended to their patient. Tom Abiss glanced up at Ambrose and shook his head. "Doesn't look good," he admitted.

"Nah, he's probably a gonner," Fred said phlegmatically. He turned to Ambrose. "Heart attack you reckon? Sounds about right. Heavy meal and a weak heart. Not a good combination."

Moving so he wouldn't interrupt their work, Ambrose waited for the right moment. "Can you do me a favour?" he asked as Fred wrapped a blanket round Charles' legs. "Can you check there's nothing suspicious?"

In surprise Tom looked up. "Certainly sir," he answered. "We'll have a look in the eyes and mouth. They can tell you a lot." He smiled slightly, beginning to understand. "But not here? Out in the van, out of sight."

"If you would. You might spot something that fades before the doctors see him."

"One of us'll ring you at the station tomorrow," Fred promised.

Ambrose thought for a moment. "I'm not sure when I'll be back," he replied. Officially he was on holiday. Besides, the week's retreat might still continue. People could demand their money back if it was cancelled; Ruth and Frank would want to avoid that. "Ask for DS Winters," he instructed. "I'd rather you didn't speak to anyone else." Realising how odd that must sound, he explained, "You know what Chalk Heath's like – gossip gets around."

"It does indeed," Tom agreed with a knowing wink.

Fred had the stretcher ready for lifting. "We'll be off now," he announced. "Been a busy night already and the pubs'll be turning out in an hour or so."

Ambrose left them to it. He heard their feet pass along the corridor; their steps slow and measured, as they gently moved the stretcher outside. Then there was the sound of doors being shut and an engine revving up. Once more the ambulance bell clanged, rapidly receding up the drive.

For a moment Ambrose stood in the hallway wondering what to do next. He needed to think quietly and he wouldn't be able to do that if he joined the others. So, as if he was clearing the last of the meal away, he picked up several dessert dishes and went back into the kitchen.

"It can't be," he told himself. "We all ate the same meal, from the same pot." He paused as he set the dishes down on the kitchen table. "If the man was poisoned, why aren't the rest of us ill? How could anyone add something to his dinner, without being seen? It would have had to be done at the table, in front of everyone."

Telling himself not to be ridiculous, Ambrose put a stack of dishes into the sink. The pair preparing tomorrow's dinner should wash them up, but no one had appeared from the library. If he made a start he could gain a few more moments' quiet.

"It has to be a coincidence," Ambrose told himself as he turned on the tap. A shuddering passed along the pipes and a spurt of cold water shot out, drenching the front of his dinner jacket. Cursing, he found a tea towel and mopped himself up. As he did so, an uncomfortable idea began to niggle. If Charles *had* been poisoned, Ambrose himself would be a prime suspect.

"Who would I look at first?" he admitted as he wrapped an apron over his suit. "The person who cooked the meal. That would look good in the *Gazette*: 'Police Inspector questioned after death of famous writer.'" Even if Charles' illness was due to natural causes, if he died there would have to be an inquest, and that could make a good story itself. The Coroner might comment on the delay in calling an ambulance. It must have taken twenty minutes before they'd got through; it would have been even longer if Sheila wasn't such a good runner. It certainly couldn't have helped…

"Now that is odd," Ambrose thought. "Why was the phone out of order when it had been working earlier?" "Someone's rung us and left their phone off the hook," Ruth had said, or words to that effect. "I keep hearing noises in the background." That sounded as if someone had left the Hall connected to another phone, blocking the line. It could be an unfortunate coincidence. These things happen. It would take a while for the switchboard operator to realise and several hours for an engineer to check. But there was the question of Charles' odd behaviour too. "As if he was afraid to be left alone," Ambrose mused.

For several seconds he stared ahead, recalling their guest speaker's manner and whether he'd been trying to avoid anyone in particular. "No, he talked to us all," Ambrose conceded, returning to the washing up. "He must just have been nervous. I would be with a crowd like this, asking questions. Plus he'd know he wasn't the first choice of speaker…"

Still the niggle persisted. "But why didn't the phone work?"

Coming to a decision, Ambrose moved quickly. The dinner plates sat on the side in a pile, so there was no way of knowing exactly what Charles had eaten. There was some of the casserole left, however, and Ambrose hadn't had time to eat much of his own meal. What would be more natural than for him to take something to his bedroom to eat later? Serving a liberal helping of the beef and mushroom casserole, he added some of Edith's vegetarian casserole and placed a saucepan lid over the food. Then he put the plate on a tray and set cutlery and a cruet beside it.

Afterwards, he went cautiously into the dining room. No one was around yet, though voices came from the room next door. People had recovered enough to talk to each other. Uneaten apple pie and custard remained in Charles' dish and fortunately hadn't been moved before he collapsed. One of Charles' carafes had the dregs of lemonade left in it and there was a crust of his bread left. Wrapping the bread in the man's napkin, Ambrose put it in his pocket, then picked up the carafe, Charles' glass, and the remaining dessert and took them to the kitchen.

Adding them to his tray, he turned the label on the carafe round in case he should meet anyone in the hall, and placed an upturned dish over the dessert. Still no one came out of the lounge. Picking up the tray, he set off to his bedroom.

The tray just fitted onto his dressing table. Long ago Ambrose had learnt that the best way to hide something was to leave it in plain view. In the morning, or that night if possible, he would have to find a way of giving his samples to DS Winters before the food went bad.

He barely managed to get back into the guests' kitchen before Edith appeared. "Sorry! There must be lots of clearing up still," she said. "You should have called me." Glancing at the apron over Ambrose's suit, she smiled. "You started the washing up on your own? You silly man!"

"Well, it needed doing," Ambrose replied. "And I was glad of a bit of quiet."

Emptying a tray of dishes, Edith nodded. "Yes," she agreed and sighed. "It's been pretty grim in the lounge. People are very upset. Jonathan says Charles is more like a friend than a client, Christina is in tears and Betty's had to go to bed to recover."

"Really?" Ambrose asked. He doubted if everyone's concern was altogether genuine. Apart from Christina, none of the guests had shown much interest in Charles during the morning.

"Betty's the sort to find any shock difficult," Edith chattered on, "but I was surprised Christina was so upset. Apparently she and Charles got friendly over lunch. He'd been very encouraging and given her lots of useful advice." Scraping the rest of the casserole into the waste bin, Edith paused. "Funny isn't it?" she added. "If Charles hadn't keeled over, those two might have hit it off together." She smiled ruefully. "There I go, matchmaking as usual. But it would have been a nice ending to the week, wouldn't it?"

Ambrose presumed that Charles had a wife at home, but there was nothing to be gained from saying so. He watched the girl put the last scrapings of her own casserole into the bin too. Whether intentionally or not, Edith was making a good job of removing evidence. "Ruth and Frank must be very worried," he remarked.

"Yes, it's rotten luck for them. I mean, someone being rushed to hospital from one of their Special Weeks. There was enough gossip about James Marshall dying."

Interested, Ambrose tried a little casual probing. "So I heard," he agreed. "Did you know him?"

"He was here the last time I came, and we had a couple of sessions with Ruth together. Way ahead of me of course. James was already one of her students, you see, and very good too. Could easily have got into art school, but his parents paid for him to have private lessons. Jenners Park College would have been beneath them and they wouldn't let him try for London. Their blue eyed boy might have been corrupted."

"Whereas you've had to settle for Jenners Park?" Ambrose asked, smiling.

Edith had the grace to laugh. "I must sound like a bitter old hag," she admitted. "But it did get my goat. I mean, James had everything: money, a big house, a doting Mama and Papa, and then God gives him this wonderful talent. I'd have given my right arm to be as good as he was. Not that that would have helped either of us. I wouldn't have been able to paint with my left arm and I doubt if the other one would have stopped him dying somewhere in the middle of India."

"I gather you rather liked him," Ambrose commented.

Edith nodded. "I was a bit smitten. He was arrogant and bossy and terribly, terribly 'upper class', but I really admired his painting. He was engaged though, to a sweet girl who kept phoning him and turned up on the last day in a snazzy little sports car. I wouldn't have stood a chance. That's life," she ended philosophically.

"Hey, you two," a voice called suddenly from the door. In surprise, they both spun round.

"You don't have to do the washing up as well as cook," Frank remonstrated. "And certainly not tonight."

"It's easier than talking in the lounge," Edith said honestly.

Wearily Frank lent against the kitchen table. "Yes," he agreed. "Rotten business isn't it?" He glanced at Ambrose. "If Charles doesn't recover it'll be pretty awful for us, won't it? Will there be a post mortem?"

"And an inquest," Ambrose nodded. "There'll be no way of avoiding it. Still, let's hope it doesn't come to that. Doctors can do wonderful things nowadays."

"It's selfish of me," Frank admitted, "but I can't help wishing the man had been taken ill somewhere else. He could have been. It sounds like he's had a heart problem for years."

"He seemed ok to me," Edith objected.

Frank shook his head. "He told Ruth he had to avoid fatty foods. Said it was something to do with his heart. To be honest, I don't know much about the man. He wrote asking to be put on our list of guest speakers. We booked him at the last minute, when we heard Thomas Weill couldn't come. Ruth's rung the number he gave us, but no one answered. We'll have to try again in the morning. Maybe his wife has gone out, if he has one."

"The phone's back on?" Ambrose asked in surprise.

"Yes. Odd, isn't it? The very worst time and our phone goes on the blink. Sod's law I suppose. Fortunately you all witnessed Ruth trying to call for help." Frank cleared his throat uncomfortably. "I'll have to get back. Come and join us," he invited. "Whoever's on tomorrow's rota should be doing the washing up, not you. I'd say leave it till tomorrow, except that we'll need the stuff for breakfast."

"I'm sure the others will help," Edith replied, hanging her apron back on the door hook.

"We've been talking about what to do with the rest of the week, whether to cancel or go on," Frank continued.

"And what does the majority want?" Ambrose asked.

"Most want to carry on. We need your votes, though."

As they entered the lounge, faces turned towards them expectantly. "I've found them," Frank announced. "Doing the washing up! We can't let them do that, can we? Not when they cooked."

"I apologise profusely," Jonathan said, getting up. "I believe I should have been out there with Sheila. We're on the rota tomorrow, aren't we my dear?" He looked across the room.

Frank smiled. "We'll all help tonight," he promised. "Sit down a bit longer. We haven't heard what Paul and Edith think about carrying on or cancelling. Paul first."

Ambrose found everyone's eyes on him. He was conscious of a sense of personal disappointment. He'd been enjoying having the time to write, even if events had proved distracting. "I suggest we carry on," he replied. "We've all booked holidays, or had to make arrangements at home. It would certainly be difficult for me to come again later."

"Edith?"

Flushing slightly at having the final vote, Edith nodded emphatically. "I had to, well, I'll be honest…" She tailed off in embarrassment, but found courage again. "I had to get a grant to pay. I don't think they'd transfer it to another week. It's either carry on, or not at all, for me."

There was a perceptible sense of relief in the room. A decision had been made. "Right then; we have a majority wanting to stay," Geraint announced. "You don't have to give anyone their money back, Ruthie."

"That has nothing to do with it," Ruth replied huffily. "We just want you all to have the best possible week while you're our guests." Even so, she looked relieved as she moved towards the door. "I'll go and make us all a strong cup of coffee. I think we all need it."

Chapter Eleven

"I'm sure it's what Charles would want," Christina said, putting the percolator back on the table. "He'd say our writing, or our painting, are the most important things." Her eyes had gone very bright and her voice shook a little. "So long as we don't hurt others," she added. "I talked to him a lot this morning and he was adamant about that. He told me off in fact, only gently, but he made me see how selfish I was being, hogging the sessions, not caring about other's work."

A deep flush was spreading across her face, but she carried on speaking. "If anyone else feels I was doing that, I'm sorry. Truly I am. I didn't mean to. It's just that I want so much to write, and to do well..." She was almost crying but speaking through her emotion. "I'm making a fool of myself, aren't I?" she asked. "But Charles has made me see so many things. He told me how he felt he was on borrowed time, after his heart attack. That he needed to get his books out quickly. I'm glad we're carrying on, so we can show him how much he inspired us."

Phyllis laid a comforting hand on her arm. "Tell you what," she suggested. "Let's all paint or write something to send to Charles in hospital. He might like that."

"He would indeed," Jonathan agreed. "I know Charles pretty well. He's a thoroughly nice man. He found a whole new life after he retired and often told me how privileged he felt. I'm sure when he's better, he'd hate to think he'd spoilt our week."

Ambrose began to feel annoyed. "Bloody hypocrites!" he thought. "They hardly knew him this morning! Now they're his best friends."

"Right!" Sheila said briskly. "Thanks for the coffee, Ruth. Now to the washing up! Anyone feel like helping?" She looked across the room. "How about it, Jonathan, 'my dear'? And you two, Gerald, Geraint? You can both wield a tea towel."

"Not me, darling," Geraint called, leaning back in his chair. "I'm on tomorrow night. Ruthie can't afford two lots of broken pots."

Slowly the atmosphere was easing. Everyone was still shaky, but a steady buzz of chatter began to come from the kitchen, punctuated by the occasional clatter. Those who were not helping with the washing up drifted back to their rooms, or settled in corners to calm down. Frank glanced in Ambrose's direction with a relieved expression. He'd managed to reassure his guests. There was an air of expectation, of waiting for news, but no one expected the hospital to ring until morning. Christina began a long letter to Charles, wishing him a speedy recovery. Ambrose settled down to polish the work he'd done earlier in the day.

"Maybe I over-reacted," he told himself.

In which case, the tray of food on his dressing table was going to prove embarrassing. It could also alert a potential attacker that he was suspicious. He must either eat it, which didn't sound a good idea, or get rid of it as soon as possible. But how? The question grew more insistent, interfering with his writing. He must think of an answer, but his head ached with the effort. He needed fresh air.

Packing up his pencil case and clipboard, Ambrose went out onto the terrace. It was too cold to sit down, however, the mist hanging damply around the tables and chairs. After a few moments pacing he had to go back into the dining room. To his surprise, he found someone waiting for him.

"Can I have a word?" Jack asked quietly. "With you being a policeman..." The brash, noisy bonhomie had gone from his manner. Instead, he appeared rather ordinary: tired and anxious, the sort of man you'd meet on a train and instantly forget.

"Of course," Ambrose replied, puzzled. "What is it?"

"Sheila was talking while we were washing up. She said something that worried me. I think we ought to pass it on, but she and Gerald know the Yates and they don't want to cause any trouble. I don't know them well, though, and I think we should. Say something that is. It's about the phone."

Immediately Ambrose was interested. "What about it?" he prompted.

"When Sheila ran up to the box, she found the receiver off the hook. That might be why the line was permanently engaged. It could have been a coincidence. Sheila wants to think so. But if it wasn't, someone may have deliberately jammed our line, so that we couldn't call an ambulance for poor Mr Coulson."

Frowning, Jack paused. 'The other two say I'm being melodramatic. But supposing someone *wanted* Mr Coulson to be ill, and you lot, I mean the police, found out? I'd feel awful if we hadn't told you. Do you think I'm right to be worried?"

Ambrose smiled. "I'm not sure," he admitted, "But I'm glad you told me. You never know what details could be important."

In a gesture of relief, Jack pushed his hand through his thinning hair. "I feel better now," he said. "I think Sheila may come to you herself after she's thought about it. Don't say I've already seen you, please. It'd sound like I'm telling tales."

"Of course I won't," Ambrose promised. He liked this quieter, more hesitant man better than the over-jovial salesman they'd seen until then. It must be awful having to hide your real self so often that it becomes a habit. "Leave it with me," he added. "I'll get a colleague to make enquiries, see if any local children play around the box and could have left the phone off the hook."

Reassured, Jack nodded. "I thought you'd know what to do," he said. "Thanks for listening."

Ambrose wished he'd kept his car, instead of letting his wife drop him at the Hall. At the time he'd decided Mary would enjoy having the car to herself, and it might put his son in a better temper being able to sit in the front. Now, without either car or private phone Ambrose felt trapped. He would have to walk up to the village and call DS Winters from the box, no matter how dark and late it was. Fortunately he'd brought a good torch with him.

A few moments later, Ambrose was coming down the stairs after fetching his coat and some change ("Take more coins this time," he'd reminded himself), when Margaret met him. "Going for a walk at this hour?" she asked curiously.

"I've developed a headache," he said truthfully.

"So have I," Margaret replied, and wrapped her shawl closer around her. "I suppose it's with all that's happened. Do you mind if I come with you? I'd rather have company."

Since he could hardly say anything else, Ambrose replied, "Not at all," and held the door open for them both.

Side by side, they walked up the driveway. Within minutes the mist swallowed the glow from the porch. Two ornate lamps marked the route to the front gates, but they cast no more than faint pools of light onto the gravel. Ambrose shone his torch ahead of them, picking out bushes and the lower branches of trees lining the drive. Their feet scrunched on gravel but otherwise the night was silent. Suddenly something thin and white ran in front of them. Margaret yelped in surprise. Even Ambrose felt his breath come sharply.

"Stoat," he suggested. "Made me jump, though."

Margaret laughed. "It frightened the wits out of me," she said ruefully. "Silly isn't it? I've walked in darkness deeper than this, with far more dangerous animals around, and not been so scared. It's just that…" She paused as she sought the right word. "There's a rather odd atmosphere this week."

They were near one of the lamps and Ambrose turned to consider the woman's expression. She looked very serious. "Yes," he agreed guardedly. "I thought it was just me, not being used to this sort of place. But you've been here before, haven't you?"

"Several times. I knew Ruth when she was a girl. But I haven't been on one of her retreats till now. It's a strain, isn't it? Especially with our poor speaker being taken so ill. And of course, everyone's trying *so* hard to impress everyone else."

"Aren't they just?" Ambrose agreed.

"It isn't just the showing off I'm finding difficult," Margaret added. "I don't pretend to be psychic, but living in India does make you more sensitive to the way people behave. Someone's out of place here."

"Edith and I certainly are."

"No, I don't mean being unused to dressing for dinner. I mean wrong, unpleasant, maybe even wicked. The weird thing is I can't tell whom. Everyone appears so nice on the surface, a bit irritating perhaps but nothing more. Yet I find myself wishing the week had been abandoned, for everyone's sake."

In surprise, Ambrose glanced at Margaret again, but her face was shrouded in shadow. "I thought you were enjoying the time to write," he commented. "You seem to have done a lot."

"I would rather be safely at home!" The woman's sudden vehemence startled Ambrose. "There's been a shadow over this place," she continued, "ever since that poor artist died. It's just gossip I'm sure, but..."

Margaret opened her hands expressively. "I don't know what it is," she admitted.

"You sound as if you're afraid of something."

"Something or someone's wrong," Margaret repeated. "Betty's frightened too. I know you think she's a silly woman, but she was genuinely ill this evening. When I took her upstairs she was sweating and giddy and kept going hot and cold. I suggest you keep an eye on her."

Remembering how he'd had to barricade his room the night before, Ambrose wasn't inclined to get any closer to Betty than he could help. All the same, he was alarmed. Could Betty have been poisoned too? Surely not. She was sitting nowhere near Charles Coulson at the dinner table. It must be her imagination. "I don't think she's exactly stable," he replied cautiously.

"And nor would you be if you'd had her life!" Margaret replied quickly. "She lost a child three years ago and a brother soon afterwards. Since then she's nursed her mother and the funeral was only in July. This week is more a convalescence than a holiday."

"Betty told you all that?"

"I got her talking tonight, in her room. Her husband bought her this week to help her recover. He thought it was a better remedy than the tablets her doctor's prescribing."

They'd reached the main gates. A lamp on the pavement cast a pale glow above them. In its warm yellow halo, Margaret looked younger, her dark eyes and hair taking on subtle shades of brown and gold. Ambrose suddenly imagined her living in India, looking quite beautiful in a sari.

He risked another question. "You mentioned James Marshall a moment ago," he began. "I heard he died of heat stroke. Is that common?"

"Not for someone who was born over there. James Marshall was Raj. My own parents were government officials. They taught me to treat India with respect, as I'm sure Mr Marshall's parents would have done. Only new arrivals trudge round during the middle of the day."

"Then why should he die from the heat?" Ambrose persisted.

"He probably didn't. 'Heat stroke' is a convenient label when doctors don't do a proper examination, and why should they have done one for poor Mr Marshall? Who would have paid the bill? I gather he was on a train and didn't have a lot of money with him, or if he did, it had disappeared. His family were the other end of the country. They were lucky to hear of his death, never mind give him a funeral. Such things happen. It's a big continent and it's not like Chalk Heath. Unfortunately the gossipmongers here don't understand that."

Still they lingered under the lamp. How could he get to the phone box without her knowing?

Margaret herself solved the problem. "You go and have your drink," she invited. "I won't delay you any longer."

"But…" Ambrose protested, then stopped. Margaret had assumed he was heading to the village pub. He might as well let her continue to think so. "I'll walk you back first," he replied.

"Your torch would be useful," Margaret admitted. "I don't think there are any tigers here, but I've discovered stoats can give one quite a fright. See me to the lamp half way along, if you'd be so kind. I don't think anything or anyone will leap out at me between there and the front door."

Ambrose laughed. Even so, he walked Margaret all the way to the front door, before he turned back towards the phone box. To his annoyance, DS Winters wasn't at the Station when he called. "He's out on a job, sir," the duty sergeant explained. "Can I take a message?"

"Ask him to ring me on this number at nine o'clock tomorrow morning," Ambrose began. Pausing, he changed his mind. Winters could still be asleep at that time, after a busy night shift. "Make that eleven," Ambrose corrected himself and dictated the number on the dial in front of him. He would have to find a way of getting there for eleven and hope no one else was using the phone.

Feeling relieved, Ambrose went back into the fog. Car headlights were approaching through the mist, moving slowly down the lane. Since most of the cottages near him had their bedroom lights on by now, Ambrose wondered who might be coming into the village so late. Standing on the pavement, he waited for the car to pass.

As it grew nearer, the unmistakable shape of a police squad car emerged. It passed him, then stopped suddenly and reversed until it was level. "Well now," a man said. "Isn't that lucky?"

He knew that voice. "It is indeed," he replied.

DS Winters grinned broadly. "I was just coming down to the Hall to see you."

Ambrose leant in to speak through the car window. "Ha, 'ill met by moonlight'," he quoted.

"Pardon sir?"

"Sorry, I'm in a literary mood. I left a message at the station for you to ring me tomorrow. This is much better."

"Why don't you sit inside for a moment, sir?" Winters invited. "You look frozen."

"I thought you'd never ask!"

Ambrose climbed in the passenger side, closing the door quietly. The squad car was warm, a faint smell of bacon sandwich and tea lingering about the upholstery. After standing in the mist for so long, it felt like heaven.

"What did you want to speak to me about, sir?" Winters asked.

"I've got some samples I need you to take to the lab as soon as possible. Our speaker was taken ill this evening, and it sounds like one of the guests may not be well either. I need to know there was nothing funny in the meal." Ambrose didn't add that he'd cooked it.

"Ah," Winters said softly. "I have some news."

"Oh?" Even as he asked, Ambrose knew what Winters was about to tell him.

"Your speaker died in the ambulance. He never made it to the hospital."

Ambrose let out a long slow breath of concern. "Do they know what from?" he asked.

"Not yet, sir, but Tom Abbiss rang. He said you'd asked him to get in touch if they saw anything suspicious. They didn't. It looked like a genuine heart attack. They did think he'd had quite a bit to drink, but I suppose that was the wine with the meal."

Puzzled, Ambrose shook his head. "The place is TT," he replied. "Mrs Yates is strict Methodist. We're not even allowed to bring alcohol in ourselves. You told me that yourself before I came here. Are they sure?"

"Apparently. Your man must have been having a quiet tipple in his room before dinner."

For a moment Ambrose sat in silence, considering this new idea. He hadn't noticed a smell of alcohol, but he'd rolled Charles onto his front to give him artificial respiration. He wouldn't have smelled his breath.

"Being as it's a sudden death, there'll be an investigation," Winters continued. "And with what you told the Super about that artist chap earlier, I imagine he'll let you do it. Officially that is. He asked me to drive over to you, anyway."

Ambrose nodded. "Give me twenty minutes," he instructed. "You can sit here and have a quiet fag if you want. Then drive down to the Hall and say you need to speak to me privately. Ask to come up to my bedroom. We'll chat a suitable time, then I'll give you a tray of samples to bring down to the car. Hopefully no one will see you, but if anyone does, I'll say the hospital wanted to check our dinner for food poisoning." Smiling ruefully, Ambrose paused. He could just imagine Geraint's laughter: "Our policeman chef investigated?" he would say, or some such remark.

Winters nodded. "Very well, sir."

"I'll break the news that Charles Coulson is dead, as if you've only just told me. As soon as you're back at the station, take the samples to the lab and ask them to test for anything harmful. Sorry to be a bit cloak and dagger, but I'd rather keep things as quiet as possible. We may have a poisoner amongst us."

"If there is, you'd better take care yourself," Winters pointed out.

Getting out of the car, Ambrose smiled. "I shall watch what I eat," he promised. "See you in twenty minutes."

As he walked back down the drive, it occurred to him that Charles Coulson had probably taken care what he ate too.

Chapter Twelve

Ambrose could hear voices talking softly at the front door. He listened as footsteps came up the stairs and along the hallway to his bedroom. He waited for the tap on his door.

"Sorry to bother you, Paul," Frank whispered. "But there's someone to see you. A colleague: DS Winters. He said you'd know him." Frank came into the room, his brow creased with worry. "I thought I'd better show him up here. When a policeman calls, it's usually bad news and some people are still in the lounge. I'd rather…" He tailed off miserably.

"You'd rather they didn't overhear." Ambrose completed the sentence for him. "Yes, that's fine."

With a sly wink, Winters greeted Ambrose as if they'd met for the first time that week. They paused as Frank left them to talk in private.

Winters made himself comfortable on the window seat and looked round the room. "Bit…er…tatty, isn't it?" he commented. "Not what I imagined."

"Faded gentility," Ambrose corrected him. "It's all the rage."

"Reminds me of places in Italy: all airs and graces and rotten plumbing." Winters laughed. "It'd give my Ginny a surprise though. She thinks everything English is neat and boring." He glanced towards the tray on the dressing table. "Are those the samples?"

Nodding, Ambrose lifted the covers, revealing congealed stew and solid custard.

"Nice," Winters commented dryly. "Was that your dinner?"

"Mainly, plus whatever was left over in the tureen. I'm afraid I've no idea which plate Charles Coulson ate from. He wasn't taken ill until dessert. We'd already stacked the dishes by then."

Winters paused, considering how to word a question tactfully. "With respect, sir, if you've eaten that stuff and you're still ok, is the lab likely to find anything? Wouldn't you be ill too?"

Ambrose sighed slightly. He knew Winters was too intelligent to accept orders blindly, but he did have a habit of asking awkward questions. "You'd think so," Ambrose conceded. "I helped cook the meal so it ought to be ok. If it isn't, I need to know."

"Ah," Winters said, smiling. "That could be interesting."

Ambrose chose to ignore the comment. If the situation wasn't so tragic, it could indeed have its funny side. "So if the lab says my meal's clear," he continued, "we have to work out whether something was added to just the victim's food, although I don't know how. We served ourselves at the table from big bowls."

"Quite, it would be tricky to poison just one person like that. I take it you still think there may have been foul play?"

"Yes. Coulson was frightened. There's a funny atmosphere here too."

Winters raised an eyebrow. He wasn't given to feeling atmospheres.

"I'm not the only one to feel it," Ambrose insisted. He changed the subject. "What do we know about Coulson himself?"

"No one at the station recalls the name. He must have been in a different patch. I've left a note for WPC Meadows. She'll ring round tomorrow."

"He told me he'd driven here from the Midlands. Our hosts have a phone number, but there was no answer when they rang. I'll get the number from them and his address. If the Yates can't make contact tomorrow morning, you'll have to ask a local officer to inform the next of kin."

"Will do." Winters looked out the window. "You forget how dark it is out here," he remarked. "This place'd give me the creeps. I suppose it's nice and quiet though for work." He glanced at the pad and pencils on the desk. Winters was about to ask what Ambrose was writing, but changed his mind. "Is it possible

Coulson's only, what do they call it, a pen name?" he said instead. "I mean, if I was telling stories about the blokes I'd worked with, I wouldn't want to be recognised."

"His agent should know," Ambrose agreed. "He's here too as it happens. I'll ask him tomorrow." He put his jacket back on. "OK, that's long enough. I'll come with you downstairs and carry the tray as though I'm returning stuff to the kitchen. If no one's about, you take it from there. Oh and I nearly forgot. Can you get in touch with the telephone exchange and find out why the line here wasn't working when we tried to call an ambulance?"

"Gosh, that wouldn't have helped," Winters nodded.

It was almost eleven o'clock. By then most guests had gone to bed. Fortunately the few who were still in the lounge stayed there and Frank tactfully remained out of sight. It seemed safe to pass the tray over.

"Dig up everything you can," Ambrose instructed as Winters left. "I'll start some discreet questioning here." He watched his sergeant go out into the mist. As he did so, he suddenly felt he was being watched. He turned round quickly but no one was in sight.

Uneasily Ambrose shut the door, then began to return upstairs.

"Psst! Paul..." There was an urgent whisper from below. Frank was standing at the foot of the stairs, beckoning. Intrigued, Ambrose turned and walked down towards him.

"Was it about Charles?" Frank asked. "Come in, please. We need to know what's happening."

Frank led the way down the corridor, away from the dining room, and opened a door. Ambrose found himself in a second, larger kitchen. Cluttered and cheaply furnished compared to the rest of the house, it felt lived-in and warm. This clearly was where the Yates lived for most of the year and where they fled when the paying guests became too demanding.

"How is Mr Coulson?" Ruth asked. Her voice shook.

"He didn't make it to the hospital," Ambrose replied gently. He watched the couple's reaction.

Frank sighed and rubbed his eyes. "I expected it," he admitted. Gently he put his hand on his wife's arm. She'd begun to cry, silently.

"He seemed such a nice man," she said. "And now we'll have so much trouble..."

"There needn't be," Frank assured her.

"But there will be! The papers will say the Hall is jinxed, like they did when my father died. No one will want to come on our weeks anymore."

Frank looked up at Ambrose, seeking reassurance. "We can't get a reply from Mr Coulson's home," he said. "Maybe his wife doesn't answer the phone at night. That's if he's married. I have absolutely no idea if he lives alone. If we still can't get in touch in the morning, what do we do? We need your advice."

"Presumably he gave an address?" Ambrose asked.

"It's in Nottingham. We can't just pop in. Could you get a police officer there to call?"

Pulling herself together Ruth cleared a pile of magazines and invited Ambrose to sit down on a wooden chair. "We'd be so grateful for your help," she said. "Mr Coulson's clothes and papers are in his room. It doesn't seem right to pry, but should we look through them? There might be something about his family."

"There could be valuables too," Frank agreed. "Would you witness that we haven't taken anything? Or should we just lock the room?"

Ambrose had intended to question the Yates first thing in the morning. Now he found himself being interrogated by them. It gave him an unexpected opportunity. "Tell you what," he suggested. "I'll go up there and do a quick search, then I'll lock his room and keep the key. That way no one can accuse you of anything improper."

An expression of relief came to Frank's face. Getting up, he fetched an envelope from the sideboard. Popping out into the corridor, he selected a key from a hook on an ornate board. A dozen or more keys hung from it, each with a card bearing its name.

Going back into the kitchen, Frank said, "This is Mr Coulson's letter, with his address on, and this key fits all the bedroom doors that have locks. Most don't, so we don't bother with keys normally. The guest speaker's bedroom does have a lock fortunately. We have a spare key, of course. I can give you that too if you'd prefer."

Ambrose considered the offer and decided against it. He'd like to see if anything in Charles' room was moved after his search. "I'll trust you," he replied. "But keep your spare key out of sight, just in case."

"Do you think one of the guests might steal something?" Ruth asked in alarm.

"I don't think anything. But I'm always careful," Ambrose replied. "I presume you'll want to break the news at breakfast, rather than now?"

"That would be better," Frank agreed. "Most people are in their rooms. Some will be asleep already. I'll put a notice up asking everyone to meet in the guests' kitchen at 10.00. Even the ones who like to sleep in should be around by then."

Nodding in agreement, Ambrose took the key and letter. He went upstairs to the speaker's room on the first floor.

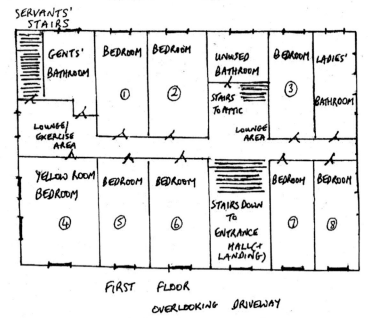

SERVANTS' STAIRS

GENTS' BATHROOM

BEDROOM ①

BEDROOM ②

UNUSED BATHROOM

STAIRS TO ATTIC

BEDROOM ③

LADIES' BATHROOM

LOUNGE/ EXERCISE AREA

LOUNGE AREA

YELLOW ROOM BEDROOM ④

BEDROOM ⑤

BEDROOM ⑥

STAIRS DOWN TO ENTRANCE HALL (+ LANDING)

BEDROOM ⑦

BEDROOM ⑧

FIRST FLOOR

OVERLOOKING DRIVEWAY

BEDROOMS:
1. SPEAKER   2. EDITH   3. SHEILA
4. GERAINT THEN D.I. AMBROSE
5. PHYLLIS   6. CHRISTINA   7. MARGARET   8. BETTY

PC Sutton's hand-drawn map of the first floor

Clothes lay on Charles' bed, as if he'd changed hurriedly for dinner. His desk was covered in papers. A wooden pencil case was placed across them, to stop them blowing away in the breeze from the open window. Mist was seeping between the flapping curtains, making everything damp to the touch. Shivering, Ambrose tried to shut the window. At first the sash stuck. Pushing hard, Ambrose managed to move the window an inch. Suddenly it dropped with a crash. "No wonder Charles left it open," Ambrose thought. "He must have meant to close it after dinner when he'd have more time to fight with it."

The window was just above the terrace. No one could climb up easily from there. Besides, with the door unlocked, what would be the point? Turning back, Ambrose prepared himself for an unpleasant few minutes. Though he'd had to go through a room emptied by death many times, he always disliked doing so. This time there was a special poignancy. He was looking through the possessions of a fellow writer, not to mention a fellow copper.

The papers on the desk included a draft of that night's talk. Notes for another talk lay beneath them. Headed "*Memories of a Rural Bobby*", it seemed to be intended for a women's meeting, Town Women's Guild perhaps. On the floor, a page of writing lay where it had been dropped or blown by the wind. "*The Burglar who helped himself*" was written across the top, crossed out and changed to "*The Thief who stayed for Tea*". Three paragraphs of anecdote followed, with several phrases crossed out and rewritten. The man clearly amended his work many times before he used it. Perhaps, Ambrose mused, Charles Coulson also found writing didn't come easy.

Carefully, Ambrose replaced the papers. He would hate to have someone looking at his own unfinished writing. He'd want to call out "It's only a draft!" Charles Coulson wouldn't get the chance.

Ambrose began to feel angry. He hadn't particularly liked the man, but he didn't deserve to be cut off before he was ready. No one did. Particularly not by someone he thought was a friend, or at least a fellow writer or artist, if that was indeed what had happened. "Keep an open mind!" he told himself firmly.

Methodically he began going through the dead man's pockets, taking out any valuables: some loose change, an expensive-looking fountain pen, a silver cigarette case (empty) with the words "In appreciation of twenty years' faithful service" engraved on the back, and an old fashioned fob watch. That too bore an inscription: "All my love, Peggy". Whoever Peggy was, her memory was valued, for the watch had stopped. A finger was missing from the dial.

Turning to the chest of drawers and the wardrobe, Ambrose examined the contents. There was nothing of value in either. The shirt collars looked well worn, and the cufflinks were white metal not silver. Either their guest speaker was of a mean disposition or he'd not been doing too well financially.

Ambrose couldn't find any sign of a hip flask or bottle of spirits. Like many secret drinkers, Charles must have got rid of the evidence. Ambrose did find some tablets in the bedside cabinet, one lot in an enamelled pillbox and a second in a bottle. The handwritten label was illegible. Ambrose could just make out "Take as directed" but the name was a mystery. A typical doctor's handwriting, Ambrose sighed. He'd give it to WPC Meadows. She might be able to get something from the label. She was good at such things: she'd had practice reading Ambrose's own scrawl.

Where was the man's diary? It could be invaluable. Ambrose checked all the drawers and pockets again. There was definitely no diary. The dead man must have had it on him when he went to hospital. Hopefully, Winters would find it amongst his effects. Otherwise, apart from the letter there was no source of identification: no name tags sewn into shirts, no invoices, no signed books; not even a business card.

Wrapping the valuables in one of the victim's handkerchiefs, Ambrose locked the room behind him. It was nearly midnight before he managed to get to bed. He slept fitfully, dreaming of clanging bells and custard that wouldn't set.

Frank's notice the following morning was as good as an announcement. A group gathered in the kitchen long before ten o'clock, immediately drawing their own conclusions.

"Such a shame!" Phyllis Hey said several times.

"How awful!" Betty repeated.

"He seemed well in the morning," Margaret agreed. "When he began the talk he was fine, too."

"Shows how quickly it can get you," Gerald agreed.

"In the midst of life, etcetera...." Geraint remarked, shrugging his shoulders.

Everyone seemed chastened. There was no talk of critical theory over the washing up; Jack's bray of a laugh was missing. Jonathan and Edith were still eating their breakfast, but they too were quiet. There was nothing unusual about anyone's reaction, Ambrose admitted.

Prompt on ten, Frank came in. "Thank you all for coming," he began, looking tired and strained. "I'm afraid I have some bad news. Mr Coulson died on his way to hospital last night. His heart gave out, despite the best efforts of Paul here, and the ambulance men afterwards. We will of course be sending our condolences to his family, and if any of you wish, I'll arrange for you to be informed about his funeral. I'm so sorry such a sad event has cast a shadow over your week. However, as some of you remarked last night, I'm sure Charles would want you to go on with your work, and to enjoy yourselves. He was that sort of man."

It was a pretty speech, Ambrose thought wryly, though he doubted whether Frank had any idea what Charles would or would not have wanted. The others would have known even less, but everyone asked to be added to the condolence letter and to know when and where the funeral would be held. It seemed to Ambrose that only Christina and Jonathan felt any genuine sense of loss. For the others, it was the reminder of their own mortality that saddened them. Betty in particular was depressed by the news, but for herself, rather than for a man she hardly knew.

"I suggest we have a quiet morning," Frank said finally. "Do whatever helps. If you have a one-to-one period scheduled, Ruth and I will squeeze it in tomorrow."

Ambrose was pleased. He had a session booked with Frank himself. "I'm as bad as the others," he thought afterwards. "A man's dead and I'm worried I won't get my money's worth." He found he felt irritated at having to trace the dead man's family. It would be another couple of hours before he could get back to writing. "For god's sake, you're a policeman, not a famous novelist!" he told himself crossly.

Talking to Jonathan proved easier than Ambrose had feared, for he lingered to wash his breakfast things. "I'm sorry," Ambrose began in a friendly manner. "You must be feeling it more than most of us. You've lost a client."

Jonathan nodded. "It is a blow," he admitted, "financially, apart from my personal feelings. Charles had given me his third book and I'd started trying to place it. That work's wasted now. No one will take an autobiography posthumously, however amusing it might be. They want a living author to promote it."

"You said last night Charles was a friend," Ambrose remarked. "I suppose you get quite close to your writers."

"Not to all of them." Jonathan smiled wryly. "Some can be very demanding. I liked Charles though, and we saw quite a bit of each other, especially when his first book came out. Perhaps 'friend' was an overstatement, but we had an excellent working relationship, despite..." He left the sentence unfinished.

"Despite what?" Ambrose prompted.

"Well, he had a drink problem and it affected his work at times. That's not unusual in a writer, and I gather it's a bit of an occupational hazard for you policemen."

Ambrose bridled. He never allowed himself to drink too much and was scornful of those who did. "Not as often as the newspapers suggest," he replied.

"My apologies," Jonathan replied softly. "I gather I touched a nerve."

"I don't remember a Charles Coulson," Ambrose remarked, changing the subject. "Was that a pen name?"

Finishing the washing up, Jonathan looked round for a tea towel. "Probably," he replied, "but he never told me any other. His postman certainly knew him as Coulson, and so did his bank, but that's not uncommon with writers. They like to keep their two lives separate."

"So you can't help trace his family?"

"Why? I thought Frank said…"

Ambrose shook his head. "Don't tell the others. It will only upset them. At present we can't contact the next of kin. We hoped you'd be able to help."

Staring into space for a second, Jonathan considered the question. "He lives alone," he replied, "Has done since his wife Peggy died."

"Which is why no one's answering the phone," Ambrose thought.

"You could try his neighbours," Jonathan continued, "but he moved there less than a year ago. The people at his previous place might know more. I'm afraid I don't have that address to hand. It'll be in the files at my office, but I gave my secretary the week off. I could drive back and see if I can find it…"

"No one would expect you to do that," Ambrose replied.

Jonathan nodded in relief. "Don't think me callous," he said, "But I've come here as a writer rather than agent. I value every hour here."

"Of course," Ambrose agreed. "I have the same feeling."

"With you being a policeman, I imagine you do."

They parted in the hallway, Jonathan to the library and Ambrose to the Yates' private kitchen.

"We'll have to get a local officer to call at Charles' home," he advised Frank. "He lived alone, but his neighbours might have a contact address. Now if you don't mind, I'm going to go up to my room to work for a while." As he went upstairs he realised he'd sounded grumpy. "But I *am* supposed to be on holiday," he thought in self-defence.

By dinner time Ambrose was feeling better tempered, two whole chapters completed in draft. After all, he admitted, he'd come expecting to work on a case, even if it was a different one. He sat down next to Christina and let her talk about Charles.

"He seemed to need someone to talk to," she explained. "I got the impression he was very nervous, that we frightened him. I mean some of us are pretty high powered or at least very intense." She glanced towards Geraint and Edith talking animatedly on the other side of the table. "And I needed to talk to someone too. He was very understanding. Mind you, he gave me quite a ticking off. Said I was trying too hard, and making myself seem unpleasant. Whereas he knew I wasn't really, just caring too much about my writing, hating teaching girls who can't appreciate good literature. He said it nicely though, and we found we had a lot in common. I wish he hadn't died like that."

There was a wistfulness in Christina's voice that Ambrose found touching. "Did he tell you much about himself?" he asked. "You said he knew he had a heart problem."

"Yes. He'd been told by his doctor that he had to take things easy, but it was difficult he said. He was too used to being busy and active. He was very careful what he ate, and he never touched alcohol, though he used to be quite a drinker, like a lot of police he said."

"Are you sure of that?" Ambrose asked in surprise.

"What? That he said a lot of policemen drink heavily? I'm sorry, I didn't mean to offend you."

"No, that Charles never touched it."

Christina nodded. "Yes. That was one reason he came here, because it's tee-total. He said his hosts were offended sometimes when he wouldn't accept the wine they'd provided. He didn't like having to explain about his health."

For a while after dinner, Ambrose sat at his desk trying to make sense of what Christina had said. He wanted to have a third chapter ready for Frank's session with him, but it took him nearly half an hour to settle to his writing again. Then he became so engrossed that he jumped when Frank tapped on his door and whispered, "It's DS Winters again, Paul. Shall I show him in?"

With a sigh Ambrose returned to the normal world. Putting his drafts away in the drawer, he got up to let Winters into the room.

"Lor! It's cold out there," Winters said. "It's not much warmer in here either." He glanced at the counterpane Ambrose had wrapped round his shoulders as he worked.

"They're teaching us how to starve in a garret," Ambrose replied and cleared the only chair so that Winters could sit down. "Apparently it's the 'done thing' for struggling writers! Have the lab replied?"

"Not yet, sir. I marked the samples high priority but they said it'd take a day or two, especially when they don't know what they're looking for."

"Any news on the people I listed?"

Winters tore two pages out of his notebook and passed them over. "Here's some background info on the locals, sir. Meadows looked up Mr Coulson and Mr Prentice, and this is a summary of what she found." Smiling, he glanced at the next page. "Got a few bits of gossip too. You were right about Edith Greenwood: Art student, lives on a farm in Millbrook. Miss Greenwood's very bright though. Went to Chalk Heath Grammar, got an award to go to the Jenners Park Art School. This year she won a bursary from the Women's Educational Trust. They only give one a year 'to a young woman of outstanding promise'. She may have a bit of a chip on her shoulder. Millbrook's a rough area, and I'll bet some of the other students don't let her forget it."

Ambrose had guessed Edith came from a poor background. He liked the girl but if James Marshall, and now Charles Coulson, had been poisoned she had to be a prime suspect. She'd certainly had the opportunity. A sense of the unfairness might have given her motive. Both men must have seemed privileged and successful, perhaps beyond their merits. "Anything on the other names?" he asked.

"A bit." Winters rubbed his hands to warm them. "Tell you what, sir, judging by the stuff you gave me last night, they don't serve real food here, and I've not had my break yet. How about I drive us both to Mucky Mick's for some fish and chips? We can talk there."

"What a sensible suggestion!" Ambrose replied, picking up his coat.

Mick's Van, or Mucky Mick's as it was affectionately known, was still open, the light from its front spilling out onto the misty lay-by where it was parked. A night-watchman from a local building site and two Gas Board Repair men were being served. "Evening, officers," Mick said cheerfully afterwards. "You're in luck. There's plenty left. I can throw in some scraps, too."

Mucky Mick's fish and chips were famed at the Station. Cooked in real dripping and too hot to eat until well blown on, they were a treat on a cold beat. That night they seemed better than ever. Sitting on the wall in the lay-by, warming their hands on the newspaper wrapped food, Winters and Ambrose chatted between mouthfuls. "Did Meadows find Coulson's family?" Ambrose asked.

"We got a Nottingham lad to go round this afternoon, but there was no one at home, and the nearest neighbour didn't have a key. Said he lived alone. There's another neighbour we can try, a Brigadier Barrington, but he's visiting his sister in Weston-super-Mare at present. If he doesn't come back soon, the local lot will have to break in and see what's there."

"There's a nice bit of gossip about Gerald Thompson. Apparently he's married to a real dragon. Always quarrelling with her neighbours, you know the sort. The talk is, she hardly lets him out without her. The one thing he does go to on his own is the Jenners Park book club, and guess where that meets?"

"Jenners Park Library," Ambrose suggested.

"Got it in one!" Winters laughed as he finished his food. He rolled the newspaper into a ball and aimed it at the waste bin a few feet away. It sailed in perfectly.

Ambrose did the same. To his satisfaction, his wrapper also went in. It was a matter of honour. Any officer from Chalk Heath station must be able to deposit their used wrappers in that bin, without getting up from the wall. Rookies had been known to come back night after night to practice.

"Did you pick up Coulson's effects from the hospital?" Ambrose asked.

"Nothing of interest. Twenty quid in his wallet but no paperwork."

"Wasn't there a diary?"

"If he kept one, he left it behind."

Ambrose was bewildered. "He must have kept one," he insisted. "He'd need to know when he was booked for talks. It wasn't in his room though. Something else is odd. According to his agent Coulson had a drink problem."

"That'd explain what the Ambulance men said."

"Yes, except that the woman he talked to before he died is adamant that he never touched alcohol. His doctor had told him not to."

Winters gave a derisory snort. "How often have you heard that, sir? 'I never touch a drop, honest guv.' Sounds like it's no wonder the old guy keeled over. It's not my place to tell you what to do, sir, but if it was me, I'd enjoy the rest of my week off."

The shutter on the van slammed shut. Mucky Mick's had closed for the night. "I'd better get back before I'm locked out," Ambrose said, standing up. "You may be right, but I'll still watch what I eat."

As the police car crunched quietly over the gravel towards the Hall, Ambrose was surprised to see lights blazing from the porch. A figure was leaving the Hall, walking towards a car parked near the entrance. He recognised Dr. Walford.

Getting out quickly, Ambrose ran towards him. "Trouble?" he asked.

Dr Walford looked at him in surprise. "Can't think why they called you out, Inspector," he said. "The man's sick, that's all. Not sure what with, but nothing to panic over. Someone thought it might be jaundice but it's probably just a virus."

"I'm staying here," Ambrose explained. "Who's sick?"

"One of the guests; young man with a fancy name."

"Geraint Templeton?"

"That's it. Collapsed on the stairs and gave everyone a fright."

Alarmed, Ambrose ran into the Hall.

Chapter Thirteen

Geraint was sitting up in bed, his face frighteningly pale. Yet he forced a smile. "Come in," he invited. "Just about everyone else has had a good look!"

"I gather you've been ill again," Ambrose remarked. He glanced round the room, checking to see if there was anything unusual: a poisoned cup of cocoa or mouldy chocolates perhaps. The top of the bedside cupboard was empty, apart from an alarm clock and a rather racy novel. "Are you feeling any better?"

"A little, thanks. I feel an idiot, to be honest."

"What happened?"

"I gather I slid elegantly down the stairs and landed in a heap in front of Betty. Knowing Betty, I'm sure she screamed most impressively. I remember Sheila mopping my fevered brow and Ruthie all upset, but not a lot else until Frank and Jonathan got me up here. And a long way it was, I might add. You did well to change rooms."

"How are you feeling now?" Ambrose asked in concern. He was no doctor, but there seemed to be something strange about the young man's colour.

"Heaps better, thanks. I perked up as soon as the cold air up here hit me. It must have been the heat downstairs. The doctor's been. Nice enough man, but not a lot of use. Just told me to go to bed earlier and eat my greens."

Ambrose smiled. "Helpful," he replied. "Is he coming back?"

"Tomorrow. He wanted me to go to the hospital, but what for? I've been overdoing things, that's all. Burning the candle at both ends as Mummy would say. Besides, who wants to hang round a hospital at this time of night? It would be full of people bleeding from orifices. Not at all nice." With an exaggerated gesture, Geraint waved the image away. "I'll be fine after a good night's sleep."

"It would be best to have a check-up," Ambrose advised. "If you're passing out it's something more than Ruth's cooking." Or mine, he could have added.

"I've got a virus or something equally dull. I've been feeling a bit off for a couple of weeks: sick, headachy, you know. It's made me pretty drowsy and forgetful, too. Not my usual scintillating self at all. And before you ask, I haven't been hitting the bottle. Like Ruthie, I have a deep suspicion of the demon drink. I left that to my dear old Papa and it certainly didn't do him any good."

"Do you want me to change back with you for the night? You'd be nearer help if you needed it."

"And have you brain yourself on these beams every time you stood up? Dr Walford would have to sleep in here with you to keep patching you up. No, I'll be fine," Geraint repeated. "Thanks for the offer, though."

There was nothing more Ambrose could say or do. He couldn't force Geraint to go to the hospital. Clearly Doctor Walford had failed earlier. Ambrose wished the young man's room was not so far away. Jack's room was probably the nearest, just the other side of the corridor. If Geraint cried out in the night, Jack might hear. Ambrose decided to ask Jack to check Geraint was safe before he settled for the night. Fortunately Jack was a good deal more sensible than he appeared.

"Goodnight, then," Ambrose said reluctantly.

As he went back down the stairs Ambrose was still worried. Something wasn't right. As Margaret had said, it might have been better for them all if the week had been abandoned.

Ambrose slept badly that night. He had barely lain down when rain began to hammer against his window. A drainpipe nearby made a noise like an old man gargling. The sash frame rattled. Far down the corridor, something was banging. The old Hall seemed alive.

Ambrose's mind kept turning over and over. Thoughts jumbled on top of each other: his next chapter, Charles' death, Geraint collapsing, Winters' visit. His head began to pound. He wished he still smoked. At least that would have helped him relax. In desperation, he stuffed some cotton wool in his ears and pulled the blankets around him. They smelled damp.

At last he fell asleep.

He was running up an endless flight of stairs. It was very dark. Only a chink of light shone ahead of him but he couldn't reach it. His feet kept slipping backwards. He fell on his knees. The walls were closing in on him. He had to get his wife towards the light but she was too heavy. The air was being squeezed out of his lungs. Bombs were falling above. They would both be crushed. He could feel the bricks cutting his flesh as they landed on him. Urgently he shouted for help.

With a jolt Ambrose woke. For an instant he couldn't think where he was. He was shivering but covered in sweat. Slowly his mind cleared. He'd been dreaming. It was dark and airless because he'd pulled the blankets over his head. In disgust he threw them off his face.

By now, he only had a faint memory of his dream but he knew it well. It had stayed with him for more than fifteen years and he was probably stuck with it for life. It was always the same, although sometimes he got Mary out, as he'd done in real life, and sometimes he didn't. Those times, he woke the whole house, shouting in terror. Fortunately that didn't happen often. He always felt a fool afterwards.

Yawning, Ambrose sat up against his pillows. He realised he felt very alone. Normally he had a team supporting him when he investigated a case. This time he was on his own and he wasn't even sure there was a crime.

By morning the rain had eased, to become a chilling, soaking drizzle. Ambrose looked out of his window and decided he would need the warm sweater Mary had packed. "I'll bet that place is cold even in summer," she'd said. "Sensible as ever," Ambrose thought.

He'd barely finished dressing when there was a quiet tap on his door. In surprise, he opened it to find Betty outside. After a bad night, the last person he wanted to see was Betty Williams. "What is it?" he demanded. Immediately he regretted his grumpiness.

"I'm sorry to disturb you," Betty whispered, "But I need to speak to you. We could sit over there." She nodded towards the armchairs on the landing. "Don't worry. I'm not going to be silly or anything." A deep flush spread up her face. "There's something I think you should see. I've lain awake all night worrying about it."

Warily Ambrose nodded. "If it's important," he agreed and headed towards the chairs.

As soon as they'd sat down Betty passed him a sheet of paper. It had been torn into four pieces, and then carefully stuck together again with strips of brown sticky tape across the back. A message was written on the front, in capital letters: "IF YOU WANT TO KEEP ME QUIET, YOU KNOW WHAT YOU NEED TO DO. G.T."

"It could be nothing," Betty said, "Perhaps it's just a bit from someone's story, but it looks like a threat, doesn't it?" Her voice shook.

"Where did you find this?" Ambrose asked.

"In a wastepaper basket, in the library."

Seeing Ambrose's bewilderment Betty continued, "I was working there yesterday, feeling really low. I suffer with my nerves, you see, and it can make me feel horribly down. Everyone here seems so clever and their work's so much better than mine. Even Henry doesn't think I'm any good. Henry's my husband, though he was very kind paying for me to come here. He bought me a gift token you see."

"So did my wife," Ambrose admitted. Trying to bring Betty back to the note, he smiled. "We're both rather out of place, aren't we?" he added encouragingly. "I can understand how you feel."

Betty looked up at him in gratitude. "I felt everything I'd written here was useless," she explained, "so I tore all my poems up and threw them in the basket. Then Phyllis came in and saw what I was doing. She said she liked my poems. I didn't expect her to be so nice. I mean, I'd thought she was, well, rather demanding. But she was lovely to me yesterday. We had a long talk about how being sensitive makes you want to write or paint, but makes you hurt too. I felt so much better, I agreed to take the basket upstairs and stick my poems together again. Phyllis fetched a roll of sticky tape for me."

"And you found this amongst the pieces?" Ambrose prompted.

"Yes. There were some other screwed up pages. I realised it wasn't my handwriting and ignored them. But this was in pieces so I thought it was mine. I stuck it together, then realised it wasn't. By then I'd read it. I kept asking myself 'who's G.T.?' It does sound like a threat, doesn't it? I couldn't go to sleep for thinking about it. So I thought I should show you. You're a policeman. You can tell me what to do about it, even if you are on holiday."

"Give it to me," Ambrose advised. "It may be nothing, just someone's story as you say, but it could be important. I can't see why at the moment, but it's certainly odd."

"Thank you. I thought you'd understand."

"I wouldn't mention this to anyone else. You never know…"

"I told Margaret," Betty replied. "She said I should speak to you. She won't tell anyone else, I'm sure. Thank you again. You've been very good all week, ignoring things." She gave no further explanation. She didn't need to. Ambrose merely nodded.

"See you at breakfast," he said.

Nodding, Betty got up and went towards the stairs. Then with her hand on the banister, she hesitated. "I don't like it here," she said softly. "Funny things keep happening." She seemed about to say more, but stopped. "See you at breakfast," she said instead.

Chapter Fourteen

By the time everyone had drifted in and out of the guests' kitchen for breakfast, the rain had started again. Puddles collected on the terrace. Damp seeped into every room, through gaps in window frames, under closed doors. Ruth lit a fire in the lounge but it spluttered and smoked, rain spattering down the open chimney onto sodden coal. She held a screen against it to draw the flames upwards, but that only made the room smokier. Like children, guests stood at the windows looking out wistfully and asking, "Do you think it'll clear soon?" There would be no chance of a walk that morning.

Ambrose had hoped to go out himself. He wanted to find the mysterious cabin Edith had mentioned. It might make a good setting for his next chapter. He would get soaked if he went now. It must be in the woods towards the river and his bedroom was so cold he might not be able to dry his mackintosh afterwards. Reluctantly he gave up the idea.

Several of the other guests went back to their rooms after breakfast, "To have another nap," Jack suggested with a honk. Those who had appointments with Frank or Ruth found quiet corners to work in until they were called.

Having booked a session with Frank, Ambrose settled in the library. He began to correct the chapter he'd written in the churchyard. Within minutes though, his brain had returned to work mode. Staring into space, he tried to make sense of the note Betty had found. GT could be Geraint Templeton or Gerald Thompson. Both were on the original list of suspects. Could one of them know there was a murderer and be blackmailing him (or her)? But how did Geraint's illness fit in, unless that really was a virus?

Ambrose watched Geraint surreptitiously. He was unusually quiet, sitting near the French windows painting the view across the lawns.

"After last night's little drama" as Geraint himself put it, the young artist was not on form. He seemed to be struggling with his painting.

Phyllis was also near the windows finishing a sketch she'd started yesterday. When Geraint muttered in exasperation for the fourth time, she got up and looked over his shoulder. "Trees are the very dickens, aren't they?" she commented. "Mine often come out cotton-woolly."

"Are you saying mine are?" Geraint asked in an aggrieved tone.

"No, of course not. It's just that you seem to be having trouble getting them as you want. You're working in a different medium, aren't you? That's always difficult."

"Ruthie wants me to keep going with the oils," Geraint replied, "but I feel like I'm starting all over again."

"Then you're doing very well," Phyllis commented, smiling winningly. "It took me far longer to change from pen and ink to gouache." She touched his hand as if accidentally, bending her head close to his.

Ambrose watched Phyllis flirting with Geraint beside the window. The young man was enjoying her attention, sick as he was. Not that he was particularly attracted to Phyllis, Ambrose decided, just that he liked being flattered.

Jack crossed the room and joined them. "Filthy morning!" he commented. "Did you hear the rain last night? I'll bet there are leaks all over the place. Do you reckon Ruth puts silver buckets under them?" He guffawed loudly.

"There's a puddle in the porch," Jonathan agreed, looking up from his writing. "Ruth was mopping up first thing. She went quite red when she saw me. It must be the maid's day off, again, or..." he broke off as Frank appeared at the door.

"Phyllis," Frank invited affably. "Do you mind seeing me rather than Ruth? She's busy at the moment. I'm afraid art's not my strong point, but I might be able to offer some useful ideas. Then I'll chat to Gerald. Sorry to keep you waiting, Paul, but we're running late."

As soon as Phyllis and Frank had gone out, Jack laughed. "You've got a conquest there," he teased Geraint.

"Where?" Geraint asked, bewildered.

"Our Phyllis of course. She's got a crush on you. Haven't you noticed? If we hear your bedroom door squeaking we'll know what you're up to!"

"I'm sure our young friend has better fish to fry," Jonathan responded. "I'll bet he has half a dozen pretty young things, all expecting him to pop the question."

"Which I never do," Geraint replied, laughing. "They think they can turn me into a sensible husband. I'd hate to disappoint them."

"Very wise, my boy," Jonathan agreed. "Who'd want a Betty Williams hanging round their neck?"

"Who'd want any woman hanging round their neck?" Jack asked. "Stay fancy free, that's my advice."

In annoyance Ambrose looked back at his writing. The three men continued talking at the window but he tried not to listen. He found their conversation disagreeable. He didn't particularly like Phyllis but he felt she and Betty deserved better. Besides, they had no idea who Phyllis really was. For all they knew, she could have had an important role in the war, been in Communications, or served as a driver, like his own sister. She reminded him a lot of Gillian in fact. "Poor Gill" he thought for an instant; hard and flirty outside, but inside still grieving for the fiancé killed at the Front. He wondered whether Phyllis too was mourning for someone she'd lost. It would explain a lot.

Ambrose was considering what to say when Geraint carried on. "Let's not be too hard on the ladies," he said gallantly. "They do brighten a place up!"

"And they serve such excellent teas at our cricket club," Jonathan added.

Ambrose had had enough. "Really?" he began sarcastically. "Is that *all* you think women are for?" He was just about to get very angry indeed, when Frank interrupted tactfully from the door. He must have been listening for the last couple of minutes at least.

"Well as it happens, Ruth's brewing up right now. Gerald, are you ready? I'll see you, Paul, at ten forty-five if that's ok. We've just got time for a quick chat before the morning break."

Ambrose frowned. He'd been saved from starting an argument, but he still felt irritated with the others' attitude. And he'd hoped for more than a quick chat with Frank, but clearly that was all he was going to get.

At least the delay meant he would have chance to speak to Margaret first. Since she'd directed Betty to him, Ambrose felt he could talk to Margaret safely about the mysterious note. It was worth checking what she thought of it. She knew a number of the guests, and their hosts, far better than he did.

For the past two days Margaret had worked in the guests' kitchen, rather than in her own room or with the others in the lounge or library. She found the kitchen warmer she said. Hopefully she would be there now. Picking up his writing, Ambrose went to find her.

As he'd hoped, Margaret was sitting at the table with her back to the door, politely discouraging others from joining her. She looked round with a smile though as Ambrose entered. "Too much idle chatter," he said by way of explanation. "I can't concentrate. Do you mind if I join you? I'll go to the far end."

"You're welcome," Margaret replied and seemed to mean it.

For ten minutes they wrote in silence. Ambrose wasn't sure how to start a conversation. As if reading his thoughts, Margaret looked up. "Did Betty show you the note?" she asked.

"Yes. Before breakfast."

"Is it blackmail?"

"It could be," Ambrose agreed. "I'll pass it to our lab and see if they can get anything from it. What did you make of it?"

"Obviously that it could have been written by either Geraint or Gerald. It's their initials. To be honest, though, I really can't see it. Since it was found in the library yesterday, it must have been meant for someone on this retreat. What secret could any of us

117

have, that'd be worth Geraint or Gerald blackmailing us? If it was addressed *to* a G.T., it would make more sense."

"Why?" Ambrose asked, intrigued.

"Gerald's always writing about blood and death. Maybe there's something unhealthy in his mind. Of course, he's having an affair with Sheila too."

Ambrose raised an eyebrow. "I know you've noticed," Margaret continued. "It would be quite a scandal: Sheila would lose her job at the library, and from what I've heard, Mrs Thompson isn't the sort to treat adultery lightly. But would Geraint blackmail him over that?"

Ambrose smiled. "I doubt it," he replied. "He'd probably laugh and wish Gerald luck. Geraint's too clever to take risks. Blackmailers usually end up as the next victim. Besides, he doesn't need money. He's got loads."

"There's nothing about money in the note," Margaret reminded him. "'You know what to do' it says. Perhaps there's some sort of deal between Gerald and Geraint: 'I'll keep quiet about your whatever, if you keep quiet about my affair.'"

Staring ahead of him, Ambrose considered Margaret's suggestion. Talking to her was like talking to Winters, he realised. They could bounce ideas off each other. "But what could Geraint have done?" he asked. "What would be worth blackmailing him about? He seems to get away with most things. And I doubt very much if Gerald's capable of threatening anyone. In my experience, people who write about violence are usually scared stiff of it in real life. No, I don't think the note was between Geraint and Gerald, either way round."

Margaret nodded. "I can see why you enjoy your job," she commented. "There's a kind of intellectual pleasure in it isn't there? Like doing crossword puzzles. I agree: the note's probably nothing to do with either Gerald or Geraint. My grandfather was an army chaplain. He used to put 'D.V.', God Willing, at the bottom of every announcement. Perhaps 'G.T,' is some sort of code; not a signature at all."

"We're also assuming 'G' stands for Gerald or Geraint." Ambrose pointed out. "It could just as easily be Georgina or Gertrude. Perhaps one of the other lady guests has a middle name we don't know about?"

"Not me, I'm glad to say. My middle names are Elizabeth and Sarah. Maybe it's just a bit of someone's story. Perhaps it'll turn up in the read-round tonight. That would be an awful let down," Margaret replied.

Ambrose smiled and glanced at his watch. "Talking of which, I'd better get back to the library," he replied. "I've got a one-to-one with Frank in five minutes."

In fact, Frank was already waiting for him. Presumably he hadn't had much to say to Gerald. "Ah! There you are!" he said cheerfully. "Just the man I want."

Trying to put all other thoughts from his head, Ambrose followed Frank. Judging by the bells on the corridor wall next to the door, Frank's study had once been part of the servants' quarters: the butler's pantry perhaps.

The room was dark, with one small window looking out onto the drive. Now it was lined with bookcases, every shelf stacked with novels and poetry collections. Ambrose was interested in a small table against the wall. "Probably eighteenth century," he noted. It looked as though it could barely support the weight of paper on it. The oak desk by the window was covered too. Perched on the top of opposite bookcases, busts of Milton and Shakespeare glared at each other. From the other wall, a portrait of Dickens scowled towards the door.

"The great writer's study," Ambrose thought wryly. He wondered how much of it had been posed for effect. Certainly the copies of Frank's own novels had been carefully placed, centre stage. Near them, a framed newspaper cutting showed a younger and happier Frank shaking hands with a bearded gentleman. "Someone I should know?" Ambrose wondered. He did recognise the photograph of Millicent Kendrick though. "To my mentor, with grateful thanks," the inscription said. Beneath it, "Partners in crime!" had been added with a flourish. Nowadays, Milly Kendrick was doing a good deal better than her mentor.

"Splendid!" Frank said as soon as they were sitting together. "I'm really enjoying your drafts. You create a great atmosphere. I particularly like your description of the ruined chapel." He took his glasses off, and taking a little blue cloth from his desk, polished them vigorously. "Our little walk proved fruitful for you, didn't it?" he continued. "I hope you can get as much from our river walk this afternoon, providing the rain stops of course."

Glancing down at Ambrose's manuscript, Frank read cursorily. "I like the piece about the woodland as well," he added. "So observant, but then, you're a policeman. One would expect that." Putting his glasses back on, he replaced the cloth.

Ambrose grunted in acknowledgement. He felt acutely embarrassed. It was a long time since anyone had analysed his work. He was more used to having to assess others. Also, his writing was so personal it had taken him a long time to agree to give samples to Frank to read.

"You have an interesting style too," Frank continued. "Quite brief. I suppose that comes from writing reports so often. No long meandering sentences for you." The glasses seemed to be irritating him, for he took them off again and stared at the lenses intently. "I'm not sure I've got to know your characters yet," he went on, "but it's early days, and they really do come alive when they're talking." More rubbing with the little blue cloth.

Ambrose wondered if Frank found the situation as embarrassing as he did. "Thank you," he said vaguely.

There was an awkward silence. A smell of hot buttered scones was coming from the kitchen, reminding them it was nearly time for the mid-morning break. "Good dialogue is so important isn't it?" Frank remarked suddenly. "So many writers make their characters talk too artificially."

And so the session went on. Ambrose barely got a word in. He never got chance to ask the questions he'd so carefully prepared. By the time the session was up, he wasn't sure whether to feel encouraged or downhearted. Frank had said a lot of nice things, but it was difficult to decide whether they were his 'stock comments' or actually personal to Ambrose. The man would make a good politician, Ambrose decided. He could talk for fifteen minutes and say almost nothing.

Scenting coffee, the others had come down from their rooms when Ambrose returned to the lounge. To his surprise, Ruth pulled at his sleeve and motioned that she wanted to speak to him in private. "It's pretty much stopped raining now," she said aloud. "Paul, would you help me open the French doors and straighten the chairs out? People might like to sit outside later."

"Of course," Ambrose replied, wondering what Ruth really wanted.

"I think I've found Mr Coulson's coat!" Ruth whispered as soon as they were outside. "There's one in the lobby that I don't recognise. I'm sure it doesn't belong to any of the guests. I don't want to go through the pockets on my own in case people say I've helped myself. Would you see if you know whose it is? If you don't, would you take charge of it?"

"I should have thought of looking in the lobby myself," Ambrose admitted. He was annoyed at the oversight.

Quietly they slipped past the others, who were far too engrossed pouring coffee to notice them.

The coat was hanging in the middle of a rack, surrounded by jackets and scarves belonging to members of the group. With its astrakhan collar it looked expensive, but the cuffs were worn, and one of the buttons didn't match the others. It certainly fitted Ambrose's image of Charles Coulson: of a man who'd done well in the past but had made little money lately. Ruth turned the collar inside out. There was no name-tag.

Making a sudden decision, Ambrose carried the coat back into the lounge. "Does this belong to anyone here?" he asked loudly. "It was hanging on the rack but I haven't seen any of us wearing it."

"It must be Mr Coulson's," Edith suggested.

"How awful! To think it's been there ever since…" Betty broke off, unable to speak.

Ambrose laid the coat on the table. He was puzzled. He ought to have noticed it earlier himself. Why had no one else spotted it either?

It would be interesting seeing others' reactions if he examined the coat in front of them. "I'm going to empty the pockets," Ambrose said aloud. "It should confirm this is Mr Coulson's."

Everyone crowded round. Carefully Ambrose laid the items on the table: a folded handkerchief, a fountain pen with a gold band, an envelope, a change purse and a diary.

Ambrose opened the purse straight away, it held several coins, including a couple of florins. It looked as if nothing had been touched. If Coulson's death was suspicious, robbery didn't seem to be the motive. Frowning, Ambrose turned to the diary.

Charles Coulson's name and address were written on the flyleaf but the 'Personal Details' page was blank. Ambrose had hoped to find next of kin entered there at least. Quickly he flipped to the end of the book, checking whether there was a section for addresses and notes. If there was, it had been torn out, for a couple of pages seemed to be missing. He glanced at the daily entries to see if there were clues there, but Coulson's notes were cramped and difficult to read. It would take a long time to decipher them all Ambrose realised. It would be better to pass the job onto WPC Meadows.

The envelope was addressed to Charles Coulson Esq. It contained a postal order for three shillings and six pence and a note: "Dear Mr Coulson," Ambrose read aloud. "Thank you for sending me a copy of *The One that Got Away*. I looked for it everywhere but my local bookshop said it was out of print. I do so admire your writing and I wanted to give a copy to a friend. Yours sincerely, Barbara Masters."

"Oh dear," Margaret said softly. "This is so sad!"

There was something else in the coat, something heavy that seemed to be tucked inside the lining. Turning the coat over,

Ambrose found an inner, concealed pocket, and pulled out a small silver flask. Undoing the stopper, he sniffed the contents. "Vodka," he said, "or something similar." His mouth tightened as he replaced the stopper.

Betty gave a little cry and Christina looked bewildered and upset. "But he assured me he didn't drink," she said.

"I'm afraid that's what alcoholics do," Frank replied. "They won't admit they have a problem even to themselves. Mr Coulson had a heart condition and vodka won't have done it any good."

Ruth nodded sadly. "It's such a shame, but that's why I don't serve alcohol here. Yet another good writer throwing their talent away."

"I'll take charge of these items," Ambrose said quietly. He'd have to ask Mr Coulson's doctor, when they found him, about the alcohol. He couldn't help but feel there was something odd about the way the flask had turned up now.

"Seeing that coat's ruined my morning," Sheila said brusquely. "If you don't mind, I'm going for a walk in the garden. A bit of light rain will do me good."

Ambrose decided he would go out too, as soon as he could. He needed to think. "I'll put this safely in my room," he announced, picking up the coat.

As he went out towards the stairs, Ambrose was surprised to find Ruth following him.

"Something's going on," she said softly. "I'm pretty certain that coat wasn't there yesterday."

"It is a little odd," Ambrose replied carefully.

He began to go upstairs. On an impulse, he turned back to Ruth. "Edith mentioned a cabin in the woods," he remarked. "Can guests use it?"

"Do you mean the old sleep-out?" Ruth asked.

"I don't mind what it is, so long as it's quiet. I can't concentrate with so many people about."

"It's not very nice," Ruth warned. "My father built it before the war, for Travellers who helped on the farm. Frank did it up as a studio for me, but it's too damp."

"Sounds just the place for a spooky setting," Ambrose replied cheerfully.

"You'll get soaked walking there. The grass hasn't been cut."

Ambrose began to wonder if Ruth was putting him off. "You don't join the police and mind getting wet," he pointed out.

"No. I imagine you can get very wet on the beat," Ruth agreed, smiling. "Come with me and I'll find the key."

They walked towards the Yates' kitchen, Ambrose still carrying Charles Coulson's coat. Ruth examined each key on the board in the corridor until she found one tagged 'Sleep-Out'.

"Lock up after you, please," she asked, passing the key to him. "A stray Tom cat got in once. The place stank for months afterwards. We've had tramps too. And with this being such an awful week..." She left the sentence unfinished.

"I feel so silly," she added suddenly. "I can't think how I missed that coat earlier."

"Don't worry. We both did," Ambrose reassured her.

Except he didn't believe for one minute that the coat had been there yesterday.

Chapter Fifteen

The rain had finally stopped, though the sky looked threatening. Sheila Butterworth came back just as Ambrose was leaving. "Lovely weather for ducks!" she said cheerfully, shaking her umbrella on the front steps.

"Did you have your usual run?" Ambrose asked.

"Too wet," she replied. "No point in slipping and twisting my ankle. So I walked briskly up to the village and bought a couple of cards at the post office. It's not too bad if you keep under the trees."

Ambrose turned up the collar of his mackintosh and walked towards the formal gardens. His footsteps showed on the damp lawn as if in snow. A fitful sun was coming out, but everything was still soaked. Droplets shone on the branches of the yew hedges, spattering onto the paths. The benches were too wet for him to sit down, so Ambrose walked towards the pond. Thinking intently, he stared at the goldfish swimming between the water lilies. *Was* that coat there yesterday?

Heading into the furthest of the arbours, Ambrose perched on the arm of a seat. It was almost dry. He had brought the diary out with him. Shielding it from the damp, he tried to read the scrawled handwriting. He still couldn't make out much from the entries, but the name 'John' was mentioned several times. Unfortunately, there seemed to be several different Johns; either that, or one lived in Cardiff and London simultaneously. Neither John seemed to have any connection with the police force.

He was concentrating on a note when he heard steps coming towards him. Urgently Ambrose pushed the diary into his pocket.

"It's all right, sir," DS Winters said, smiling broadly. "It's only me. Mrs Yates said I might find you here."

"Did she now?" Ambrose replied grimly. Clearly Ruth knew all about his private thinking-place. "She doesn't miss a trick, does she?" he said out loud. The woman reminded him of nougat: all pink and sweet on the outside and hard enough in the middle to break your teeth on. "I'm afraid you'll have to walk round with me. The seats are soaked."

Winters joined him and they walked side by side around the formal gardens. "I thought you'd like to know. The lab's analyzed the contents of the lemonade bottle that was in front of the speaker," he began. "Seems your chap liked to spice up his drinks with Vodka. He must have added it from a pocket flask, when no one was looking. Not enough to do you or me much harm, but if he had a heart condition it wouldn't help. The poor chap must've caused his own collapse."

Ambrose frowned. "Sounds like it," he agreed. "We found a small hip flask in his coat pocket."

"Well, there you are!" Winters said confidently. "Case solved. Natural Causes."

Once again, Ambrose frowned. "I dunno," he admitted. "It doesn't feel right. As I said, Mr. Coulson told me he wasn't drinking, and I believed him, and so did one of the women he talked to. She's adamant he knew alcohol could be the death of him."

"Maybe it was deliberate, then?"

"There are easier ways of doing yourself in, and more reliable ones. Plus, why do it in public?"

They walked in silence towards the lily pond. "Where was his coat?" Winters asked suddenly.

"Hanging on the rack in the lobby."

Winters only just managed to prevent a smile. Ambrose saw it and was thoroughly annoyed. "I know, hiding in plain sight," he commented.

"No criticism meant, sir," Winters assured him hurriedly. "It's just a bit ironic."

"It's more than ironic. It's downright odd. I'll swear that coat wasn't there earlier. So does Ruth for that matter. Unless, of course, this place is rotting my brain."

They stood watching the fish. It had begun to drizzle and both men pulled their mackintoshes tighter. "It sounds like you're not enjoying it much, sir," Winters commented. "I thought that with you being a writer, it might be your sort of thing."

"I'd rather be back at the Nick." Seeing Winters' raised eyebrow, Ambrose explained, "I don't think anyone's enjoying it much. It would have been better if the rest of the week had been cancelled."

"Why wasn't it, sir? I mean, with the speaker dying I'd have thought you'd all be off home by now."

"According to the rather vocal majority, 'poor Dear Charles' would have wanted us to carry on," he adopted a fake sanctimonious tone. "More importantly, I don't suppose the Yates wanted to give us our money back either. But at least everyone would have parted friends."

"And they're not now?"

"You could cut the atmosphere with a truncheon."

"Maybe it's having someone drop dead in front of them, sir," Winters suggested. "It's not often a speaker dies mid-flow: it's usually the audience and they die of boredom!"

Ambrose smiled. It was good to be in company he understood. "Perhaps we need a speaker to keep us in order," he admitted. "As it is, it's like being at a Union meeting, all 'them and us': them who's got 'Class' and us who hasn't." He laughed, aware he sounded edgy. "There's a men versus women thing developing too. The women say the men aren't doing their kitchen duties. The men say they shouldn't have to. Some of the blokes are being deliberately messy or downright patronising. The kitchen's not for real men, you know the sort of thing. Our Mary'd give them what for. Or we could let your wife lose on them for five minutes. That would sort them all out."

Ambrose saw Winters' face and changed the subject abruptly. "Any more luck tracing Coulson's next of kin?" he asked.

"None at all. He seems to have kept himself to himself. No church connection or clubs we can find. He hasn't registered at the local doctors' or dentists'; probably went back to where he used to live or he registered in his real name. The Brigadier from next door still isn't home yet. It looks like we may have to break into the house and see what's there. That'll alarm people though, so we're holding off a bit longer."

Ambrose pulled the diary from his pocket. "This might help," he said, handing it across. "Coulson talked to me about a son called John, who followed him into the force. Ask Meadows to go through this and see if he's mentioned. Tell her the family's served in the force for three generations and Coulson himself was probably an Inspector in a rural patch. The surname won't be Coulson, so if there are any Johns with surnames listed here, she could try ringing them."

Nodding, Winters took the diary and put it safely into his inner pocket. "Anything else, sir?" he asked.

"Yes. Take this note back to the station and see what the handwriting expert makes of it. I don't suppose there'd be any use checking it for fingerprints. It was torn up in a waste-paper basket, then glued back together by one of the other guests, so there'll be nothing but smudges."

Turning his back so that there was no chance of being seen from the house, Ambrose handed over the paper Betty had given him. "I'd keep this one to yourself," he warned. "At least for a while."

Surprised, Winters glanced at the note. Then he read it again. "Bit odd, isn't it?" he commented. "'IF YOU WANT TO KEEP ME QUIET, YOU KNOW WHAT YOU NEED TO DO. G.T.' Sounds like blackmail."

"My thought entirely," Ambrose agreed. "But what about? Like I said, it was given to me by one of the guests. Probably the dowdiest woman you'll ever meet, so I really doubt it was aimed at her. She found it in a waste paper basket and brought it to me this morning. Now you know why I think something's going on here."

"Blimey, sir! Some tranquil Retreat!" Adding the note to the diary, Winters turned to go.

"Have you found out anything more about James Marshall, sir? You haven't mentioned it."

"Nothing I can pin down. Mind you, if the week Marshall was here was like this one, I'm not surprised someone got poisoned."

Smiling, Winters returned to his car.

Ambrose didn't go back to the Hall but headed down the path to the woods. Ruth had given him directions but the path forked different ways. He wasn't sure which route to take. There were no buildings in sight, nothing but dripping trees. Even the river seemed to have disappeared. His trouser turn-ups caught on the long grass until they were soaked. Heavy droplets from the trees went down his neck. Twice he slipped on the muddy path. If he didn't find the cabin soon, he'd have to return to the Hall to dry off, *if* he could find his way back that is. Then suddenly, the sleep-out was in front of him: an old wooden cabin, roofed with corrugated iron that looked as though it had been recycled from a bomb site.

"Edith must have stumbled on it in the same way," Ambrose thought. Having taken so long to find the place, he might as well go inside.

The path to the cabin had been covered with gravel, but clearly it wasn't used much for weeds were growing through the stones. Taking the key from his pocket, Ambrose put it in the lock. To his annoyance, it turned a little way, then stuck. He tried again. The door wouldn't open.

Vexed, Ambrose peered through the dirty window. A couch and small table filled the far wall, while to the right of him an area had been set out as a kitchen. Everything looked dusty and unused. Behind the cabin was a small shed. Judging by the faint smell it was a field toilet. Though likely to be damp, as Ruth had warned, the cabin would make a useful quiet retreat. Ambrose decided it would be worth asking for the correct key.

He was about to turn from the window, when he paused in surprise. Inside the door there was a faint muddy smear. Someone had left footprints and then tried to wipe them away. The building had been entered recently.

"Curiouser and curiouser," Ambrose said to himself. He wondered if Frank had changed the lock and not told Ruth. Or had someone else done so? A connection between recent events at the Hall and this lonely cabin seemed unlikely, but it was all very odd.

The sun had gone behind an ominous cloud. Among the trees the light was fading. Ambrose looked up apprehensively. If he didn't want to get caught in another shower, he'd better find his way back at once.

The paths through the woods deliberately meandered, providing pleasant walks for the gentry of the last century. Ambrose realised he could use the rougher tracks between them. It took him far less time to walk back to the Hall, just ahead of the next storm.

Ruth was busy laying the table for lunch. Ambrose returned the key to its hanger. He'd have to ask her later for the correct one.

Lunch that day was particularly trying. Everyone was bored with the rain and despite the new central heating the Hall was cold. Frank was talking about lighting a fire in the dining room that night.

The discovery of Charles' coat had left an air of depression. People had begun to forget what had happened, "and now the whole sad business is back with us" as Phyllis said. Christina repeated several times that Charles had assured her he no longer drank, as if she felt personally insulted by the hip flask in his pocket. "I don't like people lying to me," she insisted.

"Never believe a writer or an artist, my dear," Jonathan advised her. "I'm afraid I learnt that from experience. Running an agency isn't half as glamorous as you think."

"I never thought it was glamorous," Edith commented tartly. "If you literary agents are anything like the galleries, you're more interested in making money than helping writers."

"Is that sour grapes, sweetheart?" Jonathan remarked.

Edith glared but didn't reply.

Frank intervened. "The forecast's much brighter for this evening," he promised. "We should be able to walk up to the village along the road, even if the woods are too muddy. And if the rain does start again, we'll open up the games room."

"You have a games room?" Sheila asked, perking up.

"In the basement, darling," Geraint announced cheerfully. "Table tennis, darts, skittles, playing cards, there's even a set of draughts. Ruthie won't usually open it up for Retreats. Says it distracts us too much."

"I think we'll make an exception today," Ruth replied. "In the circumstances."

"I didn't even know you had a basement," Betty said nervously.

"Oooh yes, full of ghosts and ghoulies," Jack teased. "A perfect setting for a murder. How about it, Gerald? Cue for one of your long-drawn-out deaths?"

"I think that's in very poor taste," Sheila replied. "Especially with what's happened."

The Yates were working hard to keep the atmosphere from becoming fractious. "There's quite a big area below us," Ruth explained. "In my grandfather's day there would have been a cook, kitchen maids, boot-boy, general handyman, and at least one scullery maid all working away down there."

"And never seeing the light of day," Margaret said quietly. "Thank goodness we've moved on."

Once again the conversation faltered. Everyone returned to their food.

"Would you mind passing the salt, my dear," Jonathan asked Edith, with exaggerated politeness.

With an equally exaggerated flourish, Edith slid the saltcellar across the table to him.

"I was reading an essay about creativity this morning," Frank announced. "By the critic Joshua Tarrant. It made some very good points. According to him, creativity is what distinguishes us from the animals. It's what makes us human."

"And less than human when it's suppressed," Ambrose mused. "An interesting thought. I don't think the Nazis had much time for creativity."

"They loved music," Margaret pointed out. "I'm sorry to say."

"Only a certain sort," Phyllis joined in. "Wagner for instance."

A discussion was getting under way. Ambrose saw Frank and Ruth glance at each other in relief. The peace didn't last long sadly. The topic turned to music and how few women composers there were. "You try writing music with twelve children round you," Sheila remarked. "Besides, there's good evidence that Mendelssohn's sister wrote some of 'his' finest pieces. Not to mention the female writers who had to pretend to be men to get published."

"I'm afraid I find few women really creative," Jonathan replied, smiling, "unless you count flower arranging."

"That's nonsense!" Edith retorted.

"Don't glare at me like that, sweetheart. I'm merely stating a fact. Look in any history of art and it's full of men. If a woman's mentioned, she was somebody's mistress or muse."

Jack honked and there were several embarrassed giggles. Edith exploded. "You arrogant…!" She couldn't risk saying more. Snatching her blanket shawl from the chair, she stormed out of the room.

There was a stricken silence. "Oh dear," Ruth said. "I think I'd better go and talk to her." She turned to Jonathan. "Do try to be a bit more tactful," she pleaded. "We have to get on until the end of the week. And we could have such a nice time together."

"What did I say?" Jonathan asked. He seemed genuinely bewildered. "I merely told the truth."

"Some things, even if true, are best left unsaid, don't you think?" Frank commented quietly. Ambrose couldn't have agreed more.

For several moments everyone ate in silence, though several of the guests had lost their appetites. Sheila was clearly having trouble not exploding at Jonathan herself. Betty looked near to tears and Margaret and Phyllis both had their heads down. Even Jack and Gerald seemed embarrassed. "Young girls are so prickly nowadays," Jack remarked, but he made no comment in support of Jonathan.

Finally, Ruth returned with Edith. "Sorry I went off alarming," the girl mumbled. Then she sat down and without looking at anyone, ate a bit more of her meal.

The matter was allowed to drop, everyone finding an excuse to examine their plates or look out the window. Geraint resisted the temptation to make some witty remark. Wisely he turned instead to Phyllis and asked how her painting was getting on. Though she studiously avoided looking in Jonathan's direction, Edith was calming down.

Gradually normal conversation returned. Frank managed to get another discussion going, this time on the safer subject of landscape gardening. Then Gerald wanted to know more about the basement area. Ruth promised him a tour after lunch was finished.

"Jack's right," Gerald enthused. "It does sound a great setting." That set Margaret recalling the house she'd lived in as a girl. "I used to love playing hide and seek in the kitchen," she admitted. "There were all sorts of cupboards you could hide inside until Cook chased you out."

"Did you live in a big house like this?" Edith asked, at last emerging from her silence.

"Bigger I'm afraid. A monstrous ugly place; freezing even in summer. You needed a cardigan just to go down the corridor. We slept in our dressing gowns."

Edith smiled. The atmosphere eased. Even the weather co-operated by brightening up.

Phyllis glanced outside. "Must catch the sun while we've got it," she said. "Do you mind if I leave now?"

Margaret also got up. "Me too," she said. "Thank you for another lovely lunch, Ruth."

One by one the guests excused themselves and left the table.

Ambrose went upstairs to fetch his pullover. "Lord, what a crowd!" he thought. "Give me half a dozen straightforward thieves any time."

Almost all the guests were irritating in some way, he reflected. Phyllis was using her bad leg to get attention, and that annoyed Sheila, who was the sort 'to get on with things whatever'. Betty annoyed everyone, especially by ringing home so often, fussing about her children. Even Geraint's charm was wearing thin, trying to be ever-so-dashing still, when he was obviously unwell.

Jack was the prime candidate for victim of the week. Half an hour in his company was more than enough. His honking laugh could be heard all over the house. Margaret and Ruth clearly found his stories in very poor taste. If their looks could kill, the undertaker would be busy.

As he walked back down, Ambrose saw Margaret and Geraint talking softly at the foot of the stairs. They stopped immediately they saw him.

"That young man is not well, even if he won't admit it," Margaret said to Ambrose after Geraint had gone upstairs. "I'll have a word with Ruth. See if she can talk some sense into him. He should be home, seeing his doctor." She turned down the corridor, towards the Yates' private room.

Ambrose wondered if that really was what they'd been talking about, but it was true Geraint looked thinner and paler than yesterday. Perhaps Margaret genuinely was concerned. "Is he being given something regularly," Ambrose mused, "so that he gets sick but doesn't collapse until the week's over? Is there a poison that kills long after you've taken it? No one would suspect murder then."

As soon as Ambrose had the thought, the idea grew. Was that what happened to James Marshall? If it was, Geraint must be protected at once. They could all be in danger, too. A determined poisoner could kill again and again, if it would stop them being caught.

Then Ambrose came to a full stop. "It couldn't be what killed Charles Coulson," he admitted. "He died suddenly."

Still the idea wouldn't go away. He must find out. WPC Meadows had been on a course a few weeks ago: 'How to identify common poisons' or something like that. She'd always been interested in poisons and was a bright young woman. She would go far in the force so long as she didn't offend too many people. She should be on afternoons this week. If he described Geraint's symptoms she might be able to identify what was causing them. He would ring her from the office.

Frank was seeing people individually in his study and hopefully Ruth would still be talking to Margaret. If not, Ambrose would have to find an excuse for needing privacy. He could say he was ringing DS Winters to check on the post mortem perhaps.

As he approached the office, however, Ambrose could hear someone already using the phone. He sighed. Betty Williams. The office phone was supposed to be available to them all, but only if really necessary. But Betty kept hogging it. Ambrose would have to go up to the village.

"If Frank asks, say I won't be long." he said to the group in the lounge. "I'm just going to call home."

He'd got to the point when he didn't really care if they believed him.

Chapter Sixteen

Two young girls were squeezed into the telephone box. As Ambrose approached they almost fell out the door. "No hurry," he said affably but they shrieked with laughter. Shouting, "See you," to each other, they ran home. Clearly the public phone box was a highlight of Old Chalk Heath. He wondered if they'd even been calling anyone.

PC Higgins answered the phone. "What is it Guv?" he asked cheerfully. "Thought you were on holiday."

"I am," Ambrose replied. "But I've got a question WPC Meadows might answer. If she's there, can you fetch her?"

He heard Higgins call down the corridor, "Pauline! The D.I. wants to talk to you. Take it in the duty office."

There was the sound of hurried footsteps and the extension being picked up, then Meadows' voice. "Can I help, Sir?" she asked.

"Is anyone listening your end?" Ambrose asked.

Meadows' tone faltered in surprise. "People are coming and going, but no one's in here at the moment."

"Fine. You went on a toxins course recently?"

"Yes, sir. Very useful. Thank you for letting me go on that."

"No thanks needed. I did it so you could answer questions like this. Is there a poison that acts slowly, without killing until later?"

There was a pause, while Meadows considered her answer. "Several, Sir. They have a chronic effect, damaging vital organs. Arsenic's the classic one. Antimony's another."

Staring out the window, Ambrose was conscious of a sense of unreality. The village pub was closed but several men were walking around the back. He would much rather be investigating a breach of the licensing laws than one death and an illness that might or might not be natural. "But how can you give arsenic to one person and not others?" he asked, "if you're all having the same food and drink, and all eating together?"

"It'd be difficult. You'd…" Meadows stopped suddenly. "Half a mo'…"

"How ya' doing, darling?" a voice asked in the background.

"Fine, thank you," came the reply. "And please don't call me 'darling'."

"Alright, darling, won't do it again."

Ambrose sighed, recognizing PC Vernon. The man was a good copper but despite being one of the younger ones, old fashioned. To him the WPCs were 'a nice bit of skirt' or 'that woman' depending on their prettiness and willingness to flatter him. Ambrose had spoken to him several times. Clearly he would have to do so again. He'd have to speak to Meadows too. She would be wiser ignoring the banter, than tackling it head on. That only made Vernon and his sort worse. In the background, Vernon was telling a dubious joke about some underwear stolen from a washing line, deliberately embarrassing his female colleague. After the unpleasantness at lunchtime, Ambrose found the overheard conversation depressing. Things should have changed with the war, and yet the old prejudices dragged on…

"Sorry sir," Meadows said afterwards. She sounded irritated, but recovered herself quickly. "Where was I? Oh yes, it'd be hard to poison someone if everyone's eating together. You'd have to be good at sleight of hand: drop a dose in a drink while no one was watching, that sort of thing. It'd be easier administered some other way."

"How?"

"Can you leave it with me, sir? I've got an idea but I need to check my facts. You're at Chalk Heath Hall aren't you? I can cycle over."

"Just put some notes for me through the door," Ambrose replied. "Make sure the envelope's sealed."

"Right you are." Meadows' tone suggested surprise, but she made no comment.

Ambrose changed the subject. "Could you decipher the diary I sent?" he asked.

"Just about. DS Winters has suggested a couple of leads."

"Oh?"

"It sounds like the son is married to a Carole and passed his Sergeant's exams this year. I'm working my way down the list of recent promotions. I haven't managed many calls yet, I'm afraid. We've been pretty busy."

Ambrose would have liked the enquiry to be given higher priority, but there was no reason why it should. "Anything I ought to know about?" he asked instead.

"A Domestic up at Heath Farm and a smash and grab at the car showrooms. All under control, sir. We've got a lad for the showroom job already."

"Fine," Ambrose said. "See if you can find time to trace Mr Coulson's next of kin, though. There's a family somewhere wondering why Dad hasn't called."

After he'd put the phone down, Ambrose paused. Slow poisoning could indeed have killed James Marshall and be making Geraint ill. But how did Charles Coulson's death fit in? There was still no proof that was foul play. Having the office phone out of order at exactly the right (or wrong) time was certainly odd, as was Sheila finding the village phone off the hook. But no one could have walked up to the box and back just before dinner without being seen. People were milling round in the entrance hall waiting for the gong.

An idea was niggling at the back of Ambrose's mind, but wouldn't form. He'd told the other guests he was going to ring his wife. Why not actually do so? Mary had a knack of seeing things he was missing. Besides, she would be wondering how he was getting on.

She answered his call almost immediately. "Hello, Love. How's it going?"

It did Ambrose good to hear his wife's voice, sensible and warm as ever. For the first few moments they talked trivialities: whether his room was comfortable, what the Hall was like, how many guests were staying. Mary was far too careful to mention the real reason Ambrose was there. A nosy telephone operator could be listening in. "Are you managing to get any writing done?" was all she asked.

"Quite a bit," Ambrose assured her. "More than I expected."

"What are the other writers like?"

"Lots of egos banging together. Still, the discussions are useful and the food's excellent. We have to help with the cooking though. My speciality is lumpy custard."

"You'll have no excuse for not helping me now," Mary laughed.

Ambrose paused, wondering if anyone was listening. "Remember that idea for a plot I had?" he asked guardedly. "I can't work out how to get my character out of the house without being seen."

"Is there a back door?"

"Yes but they'd still have to walk up the main drive. They'd almost certainly be seen by someone."

"Then you need another route, don't you? Preferably one hidden by trees, so they're blocked from view."

As soon as Mary spoke, the fuzzy idea at the back of Ambrose's mind became brilliantly clear. "You lovely lady!" he said. "Of course. It's always good to bounce ideas off you."

"I make a good wall."

There was a companionable silence between them. Then Ambrose saw his money running out and had to insert more pennies urgently. "How's Joe?" he asked.

"Fine." Mary paused, seeking the right words. "Don't be hurt at what I'm saying, Love. He's far better behaved when you're not around. I've heard a lot of policemen have the same problem. Perhaps boys feel they've got to establish themselves and you're 'The Authority'. So they have to rebel against you. Do you see what I mean?"

Ambrose sighed. "Yes," he agreed. "But it doesn't make it any easier." There was another pause between them.

"Thanks for letting me have the car," Mary said more lightly. "I took Joe to his practice last night. It was a trade-off, to get him to do his homework."

"He'll expect a lift next week too," Ambrose warned.

"I can take some ear plugs. Anything to make his teachers happier. They're calling themselves 'The Tramps' by the way. Joe and his band that is. Not the teachers."

Ambrose smiled. They chatted on until his money ran out. Then he put the phone down and looked at his watch.

"All right," he thought. "Suppose whoever left the phone off the hook didn't use the front door or the drive way? I found paths to the sleep-out. Is there a similar cut through from the church? One that ends near the terrace?"

Turning his collar up, Ambrose set off briskly up the main road, timing himself as he did so. The way through the churchyard was open and he found the wicket gate beyond the ruined church easily. Apparently that was rarely locked either for the padlock was rusted. It had taken him less than five minutes to reach that point.

Retracing the route Frank had brought them, Ambrose looked for a rougher, unofficial path off it. After a few yards he found one to the left. It headed towards a wall, presumably the boundary wall around the Hall grounds. Ambrose was obviously using a well-known short cut.

The path led straight to a gap in the wall. Fallen bricks had been moved to either side to make the way through easier. As he looked through the gap Ambrose could make out a path directly in front of him. It was paved with moss-covered slabs. For a few seconds Ambrose stood, visualising the layout of the gardens. Hoping he was right, he turned left along the paved path. Almost immediately, the rear of the Hall was ahead of him. If he walked straight on, he would reach the steps to the terrace in under a minute.

Stepping back into the shelter of the tree, Ambrose looked at his watch. He'd taken seven minutes to get there from the phone box, and he hadn't known the way. Could someone have used that same route the night Charles Coulson died? It would be a lot quicker with a bit of practice, especially if they could run, like Sheila.

By the time Ambrose had doubled round the Hall and returned by the front door, he was thoroughly chilled, not just by the damp air. He was sure of it. One of the people he ate breakfast with, worked next to in the library, had deliberately prevented the ambulance reaching Charles Coulson in time.

Taking off his jacket in the hallway, Ambrose considered what to do. He would have liked to write a report of what he'd discovered, but to disappear to his room now might arouse suspicion. Steadying himself, he rejoined the others in the lounge.

"Oh yes, do show us round!" Christina was saying.

"A glimpse of life below stairs," Sheila enthused. "That could give us lots of ideas."

Puzzled, Ambrose glanced around the group. Frank seemed to have issued an invitation that was being eagerly accepted by the women.

Even Margaret was interested. "I'd love to see what you've done with it all," she agreed.

The men were cooler until Gerald said, "Any new setting is welcome. I was thinking of doing something period."

"Have I missed something?" Ambrose asked.

Frank smiled. He looked pleased with himself. "I offered to lead a tour below stairs," he explained, "And got quite a few takers. Do join us. I just need to go and warn Ruthie."

"I have to hand it to him," Jonathan said afterwards. "Our host knows how to keep his guests amused. Personally I've no desire to see how the skivvies lived, but I could do with a walk, and it's cold outside."

141

Ambrose hesitated. He didn't particularly want to see 'Below Stairs' at any grand house. If the clock was turned back a century, he would probably find his ancestors cleaning boots down there or wringing the sheets. As a writer though, he might find such a visit useful, if not in the novel he was working on, for a story later. Besides, he needed to be part of the group, joining in the activities.

"I'll just pop upstairs and change," he said. "The grass is pretty wet. Tell Frank I'm coming."

In his bedroom Ambrose grabbed his exercise book and opened it towards the back. Drawing a rough sketch of the Hall and the grounds he added the two routes to the phone box, one via the drive, the other via the woods, and the times it had taken him to walk them. Then he wrote a note of his conversation with Meadows. Returning the page to the chapter he was writing, he laid the book open under his pencil case. If someone did come into his room they would think he'd merely paused while working on his novel.

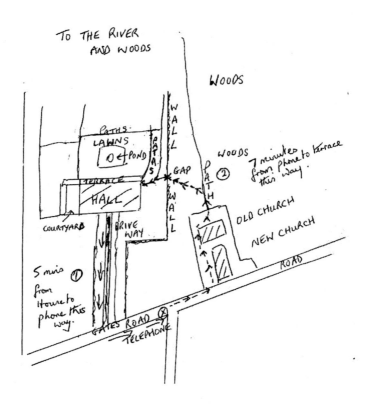

Ambrose's map of the Hall and grounds

Changing quickly, Ambrose pulled on a sweater and returned to the lounge.

"Are you coming with us, Geraint?" Phyllis was calling from the door. "Frank's taking us now. It'll be quite an expedition!"

"I've seen down there lots of times, but I'm sure you'll find it fascinating," Geraint called in return. "I'll stay here on my own. I'll enjoy a bit of quiet."

It was just like going on a school outing, as Jack remarked, only more exciting. They trooped towards the front door together.

"Follow me," Frank called gaily, leading them round the front of the house into the courtyard next to the derelict stables. The East wing was the least attractive side of the Hall. Tucked into the wall, a narrow flight of steps led down to a plain wooden door. "The servants' entrance," Frank explained unnecessarily.

"One mustn't see the *servants* coming and going," Edith mocked, as she helped Phyllis over the rough ground.

"There's another entrance inside the house, from our kitchen, which used to be the old dining room," Frank continued. "But it would have been a bit of a squash taking you that way. We'd have disturbed Ruth too." He headed down the steps, brandishing a large old key, like the ones Ambrose had seen on the rack near the servants' bells. "Let me open the door first. Take care on the steps. They can be slippery."

"I wish I'd changed my shoes," Christina whispered.

"And this corridor's far too narrow for my crutches," Phyllis agreed. She turned to Ambrose with a winning smile. "Do you mind giving me a hand?"

"Women!" Jack muttered under his breath.

"Come along," Frank called, as if chiding a difficult class. It would probably be easier herding cats, Ambrose thought.

The steps led into a large empty kitchen, lit only by transom lights. It took a while for Ambrose's eyes to adjust to the gloom. To his left, he could just make out the internal stairs from Frank and Ruth's kitchen. A large oak table sat in the middle of the room, as if abandoned, and a stone sink ran along one wall. "Does the house still shake when you turn on the taps?" Margaret asked, in her melodious tones.

"'Fraid so," Frank smiled. "Something to do with air in the pipes. We don't use this place much. Ruthie washes her plant pots down here but it's very cold in winter. That's why we have our kitchen, and the one for guests, upstairs."

"It must have been horrid for the servants," Sheila remarked. "Stuck down here all the time, freezing."

"There was always a good fire then," Frank assured her. They trooped across to examine the old range with its black leaded ovens and copper pans and kettles. "Those were the days!" Christina said. "It's like a museum."

They glanced into a laundry, again with stone sinks. "The housekeepers' room's next," Frank continued, the perfect guide. "After that, the cold store and wine cellar are on the right. Don't stand in the doorway together or you won't see much. The windows are small and half blocked by the terrace."

As they peered into the housekeeper's room, Ambrose saw what Frank meant. Even when the house was built the windows below stairs had only been half-lights, looking onto the flagstones around the house. Now they appeared to be trapped in a concrete tunnel. Ambrose shuddered, reminded of another dark, cellar like place. He had to control a desire to walk straight up the stairs and away.

"How odd!" Gerald exclaimed. "That's why you can't see these rooms from outside."

"The Hall was a convalescent home during the War," Frank explained. "The military extended the terrace right across the back. Ruth reckons the view across our woods saved many a soldier's life."

"Why didn't you take it all down again?" Margaret asked.

"It'd be a big job and our guests like sitting in the open too."

They went down a corridor. "Ruth served as a volunteer here you know," Margaret whispered to those around her. "So did her mother. They moved into one of the cottages on the main street, and came back to their old home every day to help with the nursing."

"Gosh!" Sheila whispered back in admiration. "Quite a lady!"

Frank was leading them on, past a couple of doors he didn't offer to open.

"Ah, the secret rooms," Jack commented with a honk. "Linked direct by tunnel to the river."

"And used by smugglers still," Jonathan suggested, taking up the joke.

"Nothing more interesting than extra bedrooms," Frank replied. "Ruth and I use them when we have a full house. As soon as we get the attic finished we'll go up there."

Intrigued, Ambrose wondered whether Frank and Ruth slept separately. It was none of his business of course, but it might say something about their relationship. More significantly, it suggested how much they needed the income from their guests. They surely wouldn't deliberately harm a speaker, or a guest for that matter. The least hint of impropriety would affect their bookings.

The party moved on. "And now the Games Room!" Frank said with a flourish. He opened a door and everyone crowded to peer inside.

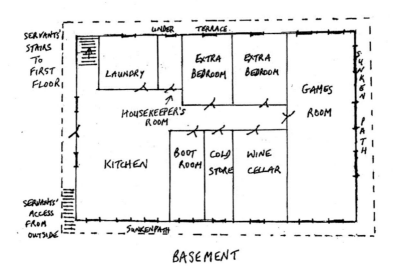

PC Sutton's hand-drawn map of the basement area

Chapter Seventeen

There was a dartboard, pub skittles, packs of cards, a cupboard full of board games and table tennis. "Brilliant!" Sheila said taking up a bat. "Who's for ping pong?" Within minutes everyone was sitting with games or throwing darts while Christina and Sheila hit the ball with aplomb.

Ambrose saw his opportunity. "Fancy a game of crib?" he asked Frank.

"Just a few hands. Ruth'll have my guts for garters if I stay too long." Finding a cribbage board and a pack of cards, they sat down at one of the side tables.

After they'd played for a few minutes, Ambrose risked the question he'd wanted to ask, ever since Jack told him about the village phone. "Think back to the night Mr Coulson died," he said softly. "Did anyone phone the Hall just before dinner?"

Frank looked down at his cards. "Yes," he whispered. "They said 'Sorry, wrong number' and I put the phone down."

"Did you recognise the voice?"

"No. It was muffled, like they had a bad cold."

"Could you tell if it was a man or woman?"

"It's odd," Frank admitted, "but no I couldn't."

"Why didn't you mention it before?"

"I assumed it was genuinely a wrong number, only…" Frank paused, a worried expression on his face. "It's been bothering me. Why should the phone work then and not an hour later when Ruth dialled 999?"

"It might have been a coincidence," Ambrose said carefully.

"You don't think it was or you wouldn't have asked me," Frank replied, equally softly. "Have your lot traced Mr Coulson's next of kin?"

Ambrose shook his head. "Not yet."

"What should we do? Ruth's frightened and I can't say I'm happy. Something funny is going on."

"Do just what you're doing," Ambrose advised. "Keep everyone occupied. Things will be sorted out in a day or so."

"I hope you're right," Frank said miserably. He looked at his watch. "I'd better help Ruth now," he added, getting up. "Sorry not to finish the game."

Jonathan took Frank's place and proved an affable companion. On his own he was pleasant, witty and urbane, meticulous when the points were counted after each hand. There was none of the arrogance he sometimes displayed in a group. He won by eight points but rather to Ambrose's surprise, didn't make anything of the fact. "Another game?" he invited. "Canasta perhaps?"

Ambrose could see what Ruth meant about the games room being a distraction. He shook his head. "Thanks, but I really ought to do some work," he said. "I've hardly written anything today, and I have a one-to-one with Frank after dinner."

He was just getting up to leave when Ruth appeared in the doorway. "Your daughter's here to see you," she said.

"But…." Ambrose began in surprise. He managed to stop himself in time, just before he said 'I don't have a daughter'.

"I didn't expect her," he said instead.

"Come upstairs our way," Ruth invited. "It's quicker."

Intrigued, Ambrose got up.

"You must be very proud," Ruth remarked.

"Of course," Ambrose replied vaguely. He wondered what she was talking about.

"I imagine any father would be pleased to have his child follow him, but having a daughter in the police force must be unusual."

"It is," Ambrose agreed.

"She's waiting outside on the terrace," Ruth continued. "Pauline isn't it? I couldn't persuade her to come inside. She didn't want to embarrass you she said, her being in uniform and you on holiday."

"She's very considerate," Ambrose replied, managing not to smile.

WPC Meadows was walking up and down to keep warm. "Sorry sir," she said, flushing deeply. "I hope I haven't offended you."

Ambrose shook his head. "I'm not offended," he said. "Just a bit surprised."

They walked down onto the lawns together, where they couldn't be heard from the house. The young policewoman could just about be his daughter, Ambrose reflected, if he and Mary had married earlier. It was an odd thought. "What's it all about?" he asked. "I told you just to drop an envelope through the door."

Meadows was ill at ease, aware that she'd exceeded her duties. "Yes sir," she agreed. "But I found something important in my notes. DS Winters said you didn't want people here to know you're making enquiries. Mrs Yates got quite upset when she saw me in uniform, so I had to tell her something. I'm very sorry if…" She bit the skin on her lip nervously.

"Go on." Ambrose replied kindly.

"You asked if someone could be made sick but not die until later. I knew that sounded like arsenic, but I couldn't see how it could be given if you all ate together. But it could, perhaps even accidentally."

They walked on, into the formal gardens. "How?" Ambrose asked, intrigued.

"Well, what with this building being so old, it got me thinking. So I looked it up. Until quite recently, arsenic was used in wallpapers and paints. There's even a theory that Napoleon was poisoned by his wallpaper. Arsenic produces a lovely green you see…"

Ambrose cut in quickly. "Paints, you said?"

"Yes, sir. Watercolours especially. It's being withdrawn now because a lot of artists lick their brushes. In the past they must have ingested quite a bit of arsenic. It will have made them sick, even sent them mad. Van Gogh cut off his own ear and you don't do that unless you're loco."

Ambrose smiled. "Tell me the symptoms," he said.

They walked on, pausing at the lily pond and then crossing to the path around the outer edge.

"General weakness, skin rash sometimes," Meadows listed, "memory loss, stomach complaints. Chronic arsenic poisoning can easily be mistaken for food poisoning. It's the slow effect on the liver that's the real killer."

"Watercolours," Ambrose repeated reflectively. "Now that is interesting. The person concerned is an artist." In fact, both potential victims were artists, he realised.

"See if he has an old tube of Paris or Emerald Green in his box," Meadows advised. "If he has, ask where he got it. Either he's poisoning himself without knowing, or someone is very clever."

Ambrose nodded. Pausing, he considered how to word his next instruction. "I'd rather you didn't record this conversation until I say so," he said.

"Right you are." Though her tone suggested surprise, Ambrose knew Meadows would keep his confidence. "Is there anything else you want me to do?" she asked.

"Go and see DS Winters. Tell him I'd like him to call at the Chalk Heath Arms tonight. They're probably staying open after closing time. Say I don't want him to shut the place down, there's little enough to do round here as it is. He's just to turn up and remind the landlord we're watching him. I'll happen to be there and we can have a word afterwards. Got that?"

"Yes, sir."

"Right, off you go then." Ambrose shook his head, still amused at the girl's resourcefulness. "If you so much as mention pretending to be my daughter down the Station...." He didn't need to finish the sentence.

"Of course not, sir." Flushing deeply, Meadows turned to go. Then she paused awkwardly. "I realise I shouldn't have asked to see you, but if there's someone here using arsenic..." She tailed off but the warning was clear. "They kept stressing at our course that poisoners get very confident. They often don't stop at one. I started thinking. Sorry, if I over-reacted."

"Your concern is appreciated," Ambrose said more gently.

After Meadows had gone, Ambrose returned to the terrace, thinking. He glanced through the lounge windows, looking for Geraint, and saw him sitting beside the hearth, looking away from the gardens. The others were still down in the games room. Voices and the sound of bouncing table-tennis balls rose eerily from beneath the terrace. Softly Ambrose went back into the house, entering the dining room through the French windows.

He went up to the first floor landing. There was no one about. As silently as he could, he continued up the stairs to the attic, to the room that he'd been given when he first arrived.

Going in quickly, Ambrose shut the door behind him and looked round. He was surprised by the untidiness around him. The bed was unmade and the floor covered in cast-off clothes. For so fastidious a young man, it looked worrying. Perhaps it was an indicator of how unwell Geraint was feeling. The air was cold, a draft coming from the window and the radiator was still not working. Geraint's offer to exchange rooms had been more generous than Ambrose had realized. As a regular visitor, he must have known how cold it could be up here in bad weather.

An easel stood beside the window. Paints and brushes were scattered on the window ledge and on an artist's box lying open on the floor. A jam jar full of water stood beside it. Despite Ruth's encouragement to change to oils, in his spare time Geraint was still working on his first love: watercolours. Taking a pencil from his pocket, Ambrose pushed the tubes aside so that he could read their labels. Vermillion, Burnt Ochre, Primrose Yellow, Emerald Green...

There it was.

152

For a moment Ambrose stood looking at the tube, wondering if he should remove it. Doing so would prevent further harm to Geraint. But if the paint were poisoning Geraint, Ambrose would be tampering with evidence. Besides, Geraint would notice and he was one of the original suspects in the James Marshall death, Ambrose reminded himself. It was best not to alert him to being watched.

Carefully Ambrose pushed the tubes back into their original order. It would be chancing his luck to use the main stairs again. Someone might appear in the hallway or come up to their bedroom. Turning left, he found the entrance to the servants' stairs. Quietly he went down them to his own room. He hadn't realised his Yellow Room was directly under Geraint's.

Until then, Ambrose had hardly used his camera: just taken some snaps of the Hall for Mary and a few studies in the gardens. Now he was glad he'd brought it with him. With the camera under his jacket, he paused on the landing to hear if anyone was coming into the hallway below. Then he returned to the attic via the back stairs.

Once safely inside Geraint's room again, Ambrose posed half a dozen photographs of the tubes of paint. He focused as closely on the Emerald Green as his camera would allow. Afterwards he pushed the tubes back to where he'd found them, so Geraint wouldn't notice any change. People were beginning to move about below him, returning from the games room. It would look less suspicious if he appeared to be taking views of the grounds from the attic windows. A door was open opposite Geraint's room and Ambrose peered inside. Damp and urgently needing repainting, it was clearly unused but the view from the window over the gardens was worth taking. Next to it, another door was open revealing someone's bedroom. Ambrose recognised the sports coat on the bed as Jack's. His portable typewriter stood on the desk near the window and a pile of notes had been laid out carefully beside it. Everything was unexpectedly neat for so loud a man. Once again, Ambrose wondered how much of Jack's behaviour was a learned pose.

As if merely exploring, Ambrose continued down the corridor. To his right was a bathroom, distinguishable by the glass panel above the door and a sign saying 'Ladies Only'. The Gents Bathroom was nearby, next to Jack's room. Ambrose imagined awkward meetings in dressing gowns if both bathrooms were used together. Clearly the Yates kept ladies on the floor below if they could.

Gerald had complained that being on the northeastern corner, his bedroom was the coldest. So he must be at the far end, and the room facing the Gents bathroom must be Jonathan's. Next came another empty room in a very poor state, with water stained ceiling and peeling plaster. As Frank had said, there was still had plenty of work to do in the attic. Since it gave a view over the front driveway, however, Ambrose took another photograph from there.

Finally, opposite Gerald's room there was an old nursery, still boasting a wonderful rocking horse and a model railway on a vast table. The rails were shiny and a couple of sweet papers lay on the edge of the board. The set had been used regularly and recently. An image of Geraint, Jack and Gerald playing trains together made Ambrose smile. As the side window included part of the village and the main gates, Ambrose finished his film there.

Still without meeting anyone, he returned to his own room down the main stairs. It worried him that he'd been able enter Geraint's bedroom twice, without being challenged. If he could, so could others.

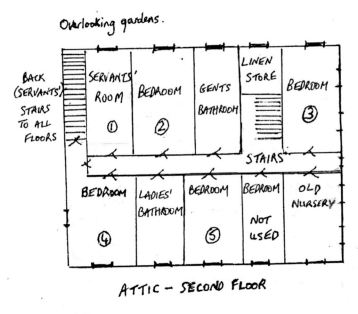

Overlooking gardens.

BACK (SERVANTS') STAIRS TO ALL FLOORS

SERVANTS' ROOM ①

BEDROOM ②

GENTS BATHROOM

LINEN STORE

BEDROOM ③

STAIRS

BEDROOM ④

LADIES' BATHROOM

BEDROOM ⑤

BEDROOM NOT USED

OLD NURSERY

ATTIC - SECOND FLOOR

BEDROOMS:
1. NOT USED   2. JACK   3. GERALD
4. D.I. AMBROSE, THEN GERAINT   5. JONATHAN

PC Sutton's hand-drawn map of the attic

Making a darkroom of bedclothes over his camera, Ambrose took out the film and put it safely into its canister. Then he found one of the envelopes left for guest use, placed the canister inside, signing his name across the seal. If anyone tampered with the envelope they wouldn't be able to replace the signature exactly. The chain of evidence secured, he put the envelope deep inside his dressing gown pocket.

As he changed his jacket, Ambrose considered what to do next. Rain was spattering on his window. He had no desire to walk to the village again. It would have to be the office phone this time, even if he had to evict Betty. With luck, Meadows would be back at the Station by now.

Ruth was chatting to a group in the lounge when Ambrose looked in, but Frank was in his study. That was too near the office. He might overhear.

"I'd like to know whether the Station have had any luck tracing Mr Coulson's family," Ambrose explained to him, "And I'll ask about the post mortem while I'm at it. Could you keep everyone in the lounge for ten minutes?"

"Glad to do so," Frank replied with a knowing sigh. "We don't want them getting all upset again. I'll tell them tomorrow's programme."

Meadows took longer coming to the phone this time. "She's looking after a lost kiddie till the Mum comes," PC Higgins apologized. "Poor little thing got left at the railway station. Meadows is playing noughts and crosses with her. I suggested Hangman, but she didn't think it was suitable. Anything I can do instead?"

"Thank you, but no," Ambrose replied. "I'll wait till she comes." He would have to explain later but at least Higgins wouldn't go spreading silly ideas until then. He was a sensible man.

"Have you found some Emerald Green?" Meadows asked as soon as Ambrose greeted her.

He smiled at her acuteness. "A large, well used tube, " he replied. "Looks old. Windsor and Newton, Artist Quality. How toxic will it be?"

"Depends how often your artist licks his brush. If he does it a lot, it'll be making him ill. Do you know how long he's been using it?" Meadows paused, hesitant at advising a superior. "I'd say he needs to go to hospital, and…" Her sentence trailed off uncertainly.

"And?"

"And if someone knowingly gave it to him, they didn't wish him any good."

Ambrose's expression hardened. "I want you to contact the pathologist at once," he ordered, "and if he hasn't already done the post mortem on Charles Coulson, ask him to check for traces of arsenic or indeed any other poison you can think of. Report our conversations to DS Winters as soon as he comes in, even if you have to stay after your shift. Say I'll tell him more when I see him at the Chalk Heath Arms tonight."

"Of course, sir," Meadows assured him.

"Charles Coulson," Ambrose repeated. "Got that? Ring the pathologist at once. Then go back to your noughts and crosses," he added more gently. "How old's the little one?"

"Six, but going on twelve. Her mother got off the train at the station for a quick fag and Sally followed her. Mum didn't see and got back on, leaving the little 'un on the platform. So Sally found a policeman and told him to take her home by car. We're having to wait until mum gets back to collect her."

"She'll cope with Hangman." Smiling, Ambrose put down the phone.

For several moments Ambrose sat in Frank's chair, staring at the busts on the bookcase. How could he prevent Geraint poisoning himself, without accusing Ruth? He had no evidence of deliberate intent. She'd tried to persuade Geraint to change to oil paints and had asked for her tube of Emerald Green back, in Ambrose's hearing. Whether she knew its effects was the issue. Ambrose suspected she did, though she might not have done so when she gave, or rather, lent Geraint the paint.

Ambrose decided his best course was to tell Geraint outright that the paint was dangerous. It was less certain he'd be able to persuade the young man to go to hospital. He'd steadfastly refused so far. But if he knew what might be wrong with him, maybe he would listen this time.

Then Ambrose frowned. If the pathologist found traces of arsenic in Coulson's body, the situation would change entirely. Ruth would be the prime suspect. But what would her motive be? If she'd deliberately poisoned Geraint, there must be something she could gain from his death. Or perhaps Ruth didn't need a motive?

No, Ambrose decided. Ruth Yates might appear fluffy and vague, but she was hard underneath. She must be, to keep a place like Chalk Heath Hall going. No matter what, Ambrose had to pass on the warning even if it jeopardised a future case. Not to do so would be inhumane.

Geraint was on his own in the library beside the window, paying little attention to the group in the lounge. He was staring out at the rain, his paintbrushes lying across the base of his easel, unwiped. Ambrose crossed to the window and sat beside him.

"How are you feeling?" he asked softly.

"Not brilliant," Geraint admitted. "I don't know what's up with me."

The others were chatting by the fire or had started returning to their rooms to get ready for dinner. It was a rare chance to speak to Geraint alone. "I don't want to frighten you," Ambrose began softly. "But you have symptoms of poisoning. Over the years, we've had quite a few cases of artists killing themselves accidentally."

His words frightened Geraint, as intended. "Poisoning?" he whispered hoarsely. "What the hell do you mean?"

"Stomach problems, general weakness, can't think straight." Ambrose still kept his voice down. "They can be symptoms of chronic arsenic poisoning. Not the acute sort you read about in books, but a killer all the same."

For a moment Geraint was silent. He seemed about to wave the subject away, for he moved his hand with a characteristic gesture. Then the smile faded. "Are you joking?" he looked concerned.

"Not in the least. You lick your brush when you're painting. I've seen you do it. If you have any old arsenic based paints, you could be ingesting them. Do you have any Emerald or Paris Green for instance?"

"I might have." Surprise and disbelief were becoming alarm, making Geraint's voice shake.

"I wouldn't use them any more," Ambrose advised. "And you ought to go to hospital and get yourself checked. Frank can call a taxi. You're not fit to drive."

"I'll see," Geraint replied, his voice unsteady. "If it *is* the paint, I should start to feel better soon. I won't be using it any more. Thank you for warning me."

Bewildered, Ambrose stared at Geraint. It would have been normal for Geraint to panic, either to ask for help or accuse others. Instead, he was trying to stay calm, even summoning some of his old charm. He wasn't in denial. His eyes showed he fully understood what Ambrose had said. But he didn't want others knowing it. And he was more frightened of going to hospital than of what might be happening to him.

"Don't ignore what I said," Ambrose insisted quietly.

"No. I won't."

There was nothing more Ambrose could say. He got up and left the room. He'd have to retire early after dinner, to get to the pub in time to meet Winters.

The Chalk Heath Arms was full when Ambrose entered that evening, though it was already near to closing time. As he opened the door a wall of the cigarette smoke and voices hit him. After the cold air of the street, the fug inside was almost tropical. A group of young men were propping up the bar, next to a sprinkling of girls. Their parents were there too, throwing darts or playing billiards. Even the old people of the village were huddled in corners, gossiping or bent over draughtboards and dominoes. There was more life in Old Chalk Heath than outsiders realised.

It took Ambrose ten minutes to get served. "Here you are, darling," the barmaid said cheerfully. "My, you're a tall one aren't you?"

Ambrose resisted the temptation to reply: "And aren't you a short one?" It would only earn him a funny look. Instead he said dryly

"So I've been told." He looked round for a seat. The only vacancy was over by the window. Trying not to spill his beer, he pushed his way between the tables and bodies to reach it.

As he sat down, a toothless old man in a cap looked up expectantly. "Ah!" he said, and began tipping dominoes out of a battered box. "How about a game? Penny a point?"

Ambrose was about to accept when one of the other old men called across to him. "You don't want to play with Bert," he advised. "He cheats."

"Thanks for the warning," Ambrose called back in amusement.

The babble around the bar suddenly went quiet. "Time gentlemen please," the landlord called loudly. "And ladies."

"What on earth…?" someone started but the bar maid put her fingers to her mouth, shushing him. She tilted her head slightly towards the door. Ambrose smiled to himself. DS Winters was at the bar, showing his warrant card.

For several seconds there was a stricken silence, then half the drinkers found pressing reasons to leave. Fortunately the door from the snug was open and there was a quick way out into the street. Even Bert swept his dominoes back into their box hurriedly and disappeared. There was no need for such a quick evacuation. There was still quarter of an hour before closing time.

"Just a courtesy call," Winters said to the landlord. "We're checking all the locals, to see they're keeping to licensing hours."

"Of course, officer," the landlord said. "Glad to see you're keeping an eye on things. We don't get many Bobbies on patrol this far out, and certainly not in plain clothes." He began ostentatiously gathering up glasses.

Ambrose got up and walked towards the bar. "DS Winters isn't it?" he asked. "Nice to see you. How are things going?"

"Fine. Didn't expect to see you here, sir. You on holiday?"

They walked out into the porch together, apparently chatting idly. "Any news?" Ambrose asked as soon as they were alone.

"Yes, sir. Meadows just caught the pathologist before he did the post mortem. There were no traces of arsenic in Mr Coulson's body, but Doctor Yates did find a drug. Something with a funny name. Hang on, I wrote it down. Dis-ulf-ir-am." Winters read slowly, squinting at his notes. "Yes that's it. Disulfiram. Apparently it's sold by the trade names Antabuse and Antabus. It's known to react badly with alcohol and Coulson's blood alcohol was well up. Yates confirmed that. He said the combination could have triggered a heart attack in someone with a weak heart and Coulson definitely had that."

"Disulfiram," Ambrose repeated thoughtfully. "Never heard of it. What's it used for?"

"Treating chronic alcoholism. Apparently it causes an acute sensitivity to alcohol. Makes you very sick I suppose and turns you off. Aversion therapy don't they call it? Anyway, it wouldn't have done Coulson any good having it in his system and then drinking so much."

"If he did," Ambrose said thoughtfully.

Winters nodded. "I'm beginning to see what you mean," he agreed. "It's all a bit too coincidental."

"We have to get Coulson's real name," Ambrose said quickly, "and speak to his GP. If Coulson wasn't prescribed the drug, then we need to know how it got into him. How's Meadows' search going?"

"That's the other news," Winters replied, more cheerfully. "She's traced the son. Lives only twenty miles away, believe it or not. The other side of Jenners Park. I'll leave word for Higgins to go out first thing to speak to him. I thought he might take Meadows, if that's all right with you, sir, being as she made the contact."

"At last!" Ambrose said in relief. "We're getting somewhere. Yes, Meadows can go too. She deserves a trip out after all her hard work."

"Goodnight, sir." Winters paused. "Sounds like we may have a murder case on our hands, sir."

"But not the one I expected," Ambrose replied as he walked away.

Book Two

Chapter Eighteen

Higgins drove. Meadows watched the raw estates of Chalk Heath through misted windows. After quarter of an hour the streets petered out and the road narrowed. Then they were in the countryside. For a few miles there was little to see but fields and fog until the new estates of Jenners Park began. Soon, rows of semi-detached houses stretched on either side, almost identical to those in Chalk Heath. Each boasted a newly planted privet hedge and square of lawn. Here though, the houses were packed tighter and the gardens narrower.

Meadows knew the town centre well and was able to direct. As they dropped down Corporation Avenue, she recalled catching the bus there with her mates from Chalk Heath Grammar. They would spend hours in Marshall and Heald's, trying on hats they couldn't possibly afford, until asked to leave by a very posh assistant. Now she was passing the store on her way to tell a family their father had died. It was hard to believe how much her life had changed.

"Sergeant John Taylor, you said?" PC Higgins interrupted her thoughts. "Can't say I've come across him."

Higgins was a quiet man, almost taciturn, and Meadows felt no reply was needed. She began thinking about names. Why did 'Charles Coulson' sound so much more interesting than 'George Taylor'? There was nothing wrong with the name Taylor. It was just too ordinary, not the name of a successful writer. And the man had once been very successful she gathered. The assistant at Chalk Heath Library said she used to have a waiting list for his books. Now both his titles were on the shelf and the gaps between the date stamps were getting longer.

Ordinarily, Meadows wouldn't have read police stories: it was too much like a busman's holiday. However Winters had asked her to find out everything she could about the dead man. Knowing what he wrote might help. The second book, *Adventures of a City Bobby*, was full of amusing stories that would attract an outsider but hardly a fellow officer. The first book, *The One that Got Away*, looked very different. It covered unsolved murder cases in the 30s and 40s, and was based on careful research. Though last night she'd intended just to glance at both books, Meadows had found herself engrossed. She was looking forward to reading another chapter after her shift ended.

Realising they were almost through Jenners Park, Meadows reached into the glove box. "We'll need the map now," she said. "I'm not so familiar with this side."

Last time she'd map read for them, Meadows had missed a turn and Higgins hadn't been impressed. She was determined to do better now and concentrated on every junction. Though they'd travelled less than twenty miles from Chalk Heath, they were now in another police division: 'Off our limits' as Higgins put it. DS Winters had obtained special permission for them to visit the Taylors, rather than a local officer. There wasn't a lot of co-operation between the two divisions. Canny thieves often sped up as they reached the boundary, knowing that a pursuing police car would be unlikely to follow. That boundary also explained why none of the officers at Chalk Heath had met Sergeant John Taylor.

Healds Hill, where he lived with his family, was rapidly being swallowed by its hungry neighbour. Soon it would be little more than an outer suburb of Jenners Park, but for now it retained a pleasant main street. Beyond the parish church and school was a line of very red semis, probably built after older cottages were cleared, either by Hitler or the local Council. The new ones were so out of keeping with the rest of the village, they seemed to have been dropped from above. At the far end of the row was the local police station with its adjoining house.

Mrs Taylor was waiting for them, standing at the window. As soon as the car pulled up she dropped the curtain back and hurried to meet them. "Do you mind parking down the alley?" she asked. "The neighbours don't like having police cars in the road. They lower the tone." Her smile conveyed more than a hint of irony. "I'll leave the kitchen door open."

"I'd hate to live round here," Meadows said as they drove back looking for the service road.

"You're quite safe," Higgins assured her. "You couldn't afford it."

They were almost at the church before they found the alley. It led round to an unmade track and a row of wooden garages. The backs of the new houses were far less impressive than the front.

"You begin the questioning first," Higgins said. "Just in conversation. You're better at that." He took his notebook out of his pocket and read it as he walked. "I'll come in with the ones about his drinking; questions 5 onwards. Understand?"

Meadows nodded. They each had the same list, drawn up at the station before they left. Winters had left them very clear notes on what he wanted. They walked down the back garden together, past rows of cabbage and broccoli. "Their winter greens are doing well," Higgins remarked. "Looks like good soil round here."

Mrs Taylor welcomed them into the kitchen. "Sorry about the mud," she apologised, seeing their shoes. "I should have warned you. The Council are supposed to be doing the alley. I'll believe it when I see it." She looked at the clock above the kitchen cabinet. "I wonder what's keeping John? He's usually back by now."

"We'll wait," Higgins assured her.

"Would you like a cuppa?" Mrs Taylor asked. "John'll want one."

"Thank you. That would be nice." Standing awkwardly by the kitchen table Meadows smiled.

"I'll have to go and fetch our little one soon," Mrs Taylor apologised. "My Mum has him while I'm at work. I'm a record clerk at South Cross police station, you see. Part-time. It's such a help being near my family again."

"You moved here recently?" Meadows asked.

"From London. When John got his promotion. He started with the Met, but he'd been trying to get back here for ages." She spoke too quickly, nervous at having such a visit. "Is there anything I can do until he arrives?"

Higgins shook his head. "I'm afraid we need to speak to him in person."

Her hand on the tap, Mrs Taylor paused. "Is it about his Dad?" she asked.

Higgins shuffled. "We'll wait until your husband comes," he repeated.

Mrs Taylor sighed, a deep painful sigh. Then she finished filling the kettle. "I guessed as much," she said. "When two of you visit together, it's never good news." She'd gone very pale.

Meadows went to her, quickly. "Here, let me make the tea," she offered. "You need to sit down."

"I knew something was wrong," Mrs Taylor repeated, her voice strangled in her throat. "Pops usually rings on a Wednesday. 'Reporting in', he calls it. What's happened? Is he in hospital?"

"I – um – I'm afraid it's worse," Higgins said.

"Oh!"

A key turned in the front door, and a voice called, "Hello darling. Sorry I'm late. The Super collared me as I was leaving."

Higgins went out to meet him.

For several moments there was the sound of the two men talking quietly in the hallway. Meadows made the tea and opened cupboards to find cups and saucers. When she turned back, Mrs Taylor was sitting at the table, crying quietly. That was the worst part of the job: breaking bad news to people. Sometimes you didn't need to say anything, like now. They were expecting it. But that didn't make the sadness any easier to watch.

The tea was poured and waiting by the time the men came into the kitchen. Sergeant Taylor crossed straight to his wife and put his arm around her shoulder. Neither of them spoke. Meadows had learnt not to interrupt such silences. Higgins waited too, helping himself to a cup of tea.

Finally Sergeant Taylor nodded. "Thanks for coming," he said. "Not just ringing."

"Poor Pops," Mrs Taylor said. "Was it his heart?" She fumbled in her apron pocket for a handkerchief.

"Yes, Love," her husband replied, holding her to him. They were both clearly fond of his father.

"Was it quick?" Mrs Taylor asked at length.

Higgins nodded towards Meadows. She was better with words than him, his expression said.

"Your father had a heart attack on Monday," Meadows began. She stuck carefully to the facts. "He was staying at Chalk Heath Hall. They run special weeks for artists and writers, and he was their guest speaker. We've had a job tracing you. He was known there by the name of Coulson."

Sgt Taylor sat at the table beside his wife. "Of course," he said flatly. "We nagged him to put our details in his diary. He had an attack five years ago, you see. But he was very independent. If you give me the address I'll contact this Hall place and make arrangements to bring his things here." A policeman himself, he was businesslike and practical, though his voice was unsteady with grief.

Mrs Taylor got up. "I'd better ring Mum and ask her to keep Jack a while," she said.

"I'll do it," Sgt Taylor said. "I'll tell her." He went out into the hall. Being a police house they had their own phone. Softly, he closed the door behind him.

Mrs Taylor warmed her hands on the teacup Meadows had passed her. "Poor Pops," she said, almost to herself. "I shall miss him. We all will. Little Jack thought the world of him." Remembering she was a policeman's wife, she tried to be hospitable. "Come into the lounge," she invited. "It's more comfortable there."

They moved into a neat little front room and sat stiffly on a plastic coated settee. They finished their tea as they waited for Sgt Taylor to join them.

168

"Your father-in-law was a writer I gather," Meadows said, not just making conversation. Her role was to obtain confirmation of the details they already had about the dead man. Quietly Higgins took out his notebook.

Mrs Taylor nodded. "His books sold ever so well," she replied, "We were so pleased for him. He was dreading retirement. He and my mum-in-law weren't all that close you see..."

"Why was that?"

"She was a civilian worker like me and, well, I think he looked down on her a bit. She hated having him under her feet all day. We thought there'd be sparks. Instead, he found a whole new life."

"I'm reading *The One that Got Away* at the moment," Meadows replied. "It's fascinating."

Pleased, Mrs Taylor managed to smile. "He wrote that while he was at South Cross," she explained. "Though it wasn't published until he'd moved to Nottingham. For a while he was quite famous. But fashions change, and to be honest, I think he'd used up his best stories." Mrs Taylor sighed. "He wanted so much to get another book published and now he never will." She lapsed into silence.

"But people still invited him to give talks?" Meadows prompted.

"He's a very good speaker." Unconsciously Mrs Taylor was slipping into the present tense. "Gets lots of invites from Town Women's Guild, churches, groups like that, but half of them don't pay a proper fee, just expenses, and a meal if he's lucky." She stopped. "Was lucky," she corrected herself. "I can't think of him as gone."

Sgt Taylor returned and stood beside the fireplace. The room was cold and he bent to turn on the electric fire. Artificial coals lit up below the bars. Everything was very modern and cheap, Meadows thought. The contrast with Chalk Heath Hall was striking.

She turned towards Sgt Taylor, trying to think of him as a member of the public who'd lost a relative, rather than a superior officer. "Sorry to trouble you at such a time, but there are a few questions

169

we'd like to ask you," she began. "Would you mind? Just to confirm things. It'll save us coming back later."

"Why?" Sgt Taylor asked sharply.

"Just routine," she assured him. "A sudden death away from home. You know how it is, sir. We need to make sure we've got everything correct. I've got your father's full name down as George Arthur Taylor, but that he wrote under the name of Charles Coulson. Is that right? "

Sgt Taylor nodded. "Yes. That's correct. You'll need to confirm the address too I suppose. He was living at Flat 1a, Cherry Tree House, Cherry Lane, Beeston, Nottingham. If you want his date of birth it was 12th August 1894 and he was born in Hackney. Is that sufficient?"

Higgins was writing quickly. "I gather he was moved to Nottingham when he was promoted to inspector," he prompted.

"Yes," Mrs Taylor confirmed.

"And he was happy living on his own? Not depressed at all?"

Mrs Taylor looked up with a puzzled expression. "I think he enjoyed it," she replied. "We wanted him to move nearer us, but he said travel was easier from Nottingham. He certainly wasn't depressed."

"And apart from his heart attack five years ago, he was in good health?" Meadows continued.

"Yes."

Higgins took a package out of his pocket and carefully unwrapped the silver hip flask Ambrose had found. "Do you recognise this?" he asked.

Mrs Taylor leant forward to look, and shook her head. "No. Should I?" she asked.

Sgt Taylor picked up the flask and examined it. Then he put it onto the coffee table. "Never seen it before," he said.

"You're sure it's not your father's?"

"Of course it isn't!" Sgt Taylor was getting annoyed. "Dad was teetotal," he replied.

Methodically Higgins noted the reply; then wrapped the flask up again. "You're sure of that?" he asked.

"Of course I am! Why are you asking all these questions?" Sgt Taylor demanded.

His wife took his hand, calming him. "I'm sure they have their reasons," she said.

Higgins persisted stubbornly. "We do," he said. "Bear with us please. The pathologist found a good deal of alcohol in your father's system. We need to be absolutely sure that your father wasn't drinking quietly, without you knowing."

"Dad never drank!" Sgt Taylor almost shouted. "If your pathologist said that, he was wrong."

"I've noted your reply," Higgins stated.

There was a long, awkward silence. "You say there was alcohol in his blood?" Sgt Taylor repeated. His expression was changing from anger to concern. A policeman himself, he'd started to understand what Higgins was implying. So too had his wife. "I can't guarantee Dad wasn't drinking still," he said in a stifled voice. "But I'm almost certain he wasn't."

"It sounds like he may have had a problem in the past," Meadows commented. "Is that correct?"

"Yes. Before he retired," Sgt Taylor conceded, calmer now. "You know how easy it is. You get into the habit of unwinding with a drink. One drink becomes two. But his heart attack gave him a fright. When his doctor said drinking too much might have been the cause, he vowed never to drink again."

Higgins glanced towards Meadows, slightly raising an eyebrow. It invited her to continue.

"And he stuck to his vow?" she asked.

"Oh yes." Mrs Taylor said softly. "For our boy Jack's sake. He said so only a couple of months back. We were celebrating John being made up to Sergeant and my brother brought some beers. Pops refused. He said he wanted to see his grandson grow up to be a good copper like his father."

Meadows had asked all her questions and couldn't think what else to say. Her own throat was going tight. Higgins was more matter-of-fact. He might be dealing with a superior in another division, but he was determined to obtain all the information DS Winters wanted. "One more question, please," he said. "We'd like to ask your father's GP whether he was treating him for anything other than heart trouble. It might have confused things. Do you have his doctor's name?"

Sgt Taylor sighed. "You've cause for suspicion, haven't you?" he remarked. "You wouldn't keep on like this otherwise. I'll ring his GP and see if I can get him to talk to you. You won't get past the receptionist otherwise."

He crossed to the bureau and took an address card out, then went into the hall to use the phone.

"What really happened?" Mrs Taylor asked. "Please tell me."

"Your father-in-law collapsed at dinner, apparently with a heart attack," Higgins replied. "The pathologist found a good deal of alcohol in his system. It might have contributed to his death. I can't tell you anything else."

"I don't understand," Mrs Taylor insisted. She shook her head in bewilderment

They could hear Sgt Taylor's voice in the hallway. "The GP will speak to you now," he called.

Higgins went to the phone.

For several moments Meadows sat in silence with Mrs Taylor, straining to hear the conversation outside. Finally Higgins returned. "Thank you, that was very helpful," he said.

"What did the doctor say?" Sgt Taylor asked.

"If you ring him, he'll talk to you about getting a death certificate. He confirmed your father wasn't drinking again. Not to his knowledge anyway."

"Then how...?"

Higgins cut in quickly. "You're in the business yourself, sir. You know we can't answer questions without getting the say-so. Our DS, Sam Winters, will get in touch with you as soon as possible. I'm not sure who'll be handling the enquiry while the DI's on holiday, but DS Winters will be able to tell you."

They got up to leave. "If someone caused my Dad's death, I want to know," Sgt Taylor said coldly.

"You will," Higgins assured him. "We're going straight back to Chalk Heath now. We should see DS Winters before we finish our shift. If we don't, we'll leave him a report."

"Sorry to be the bringer of bad news," Meadows said, offering her hand to Mrs Taylor. Then she followed Higgins out through the kitchen.

As soon as they were in the alleyway and out of hearing, she turned to Higgins, "Can you tell *me* what the doctor said?" she asked.

Higgins smiled grimly. "Dr Fletcher has never prescribed antabuse or anything similar," he replied. "Said he wouldn't ever do so, even if a patient was drinking heavily. He's one of the old school: believes in telling people to pull themselves together, not giving them drugs to make them sick."

"So how on earth could the pathologist find it? He couldn't be wrong could he?"

"Not Harry. I suppose he has been wrong once or twice, like marrying Gloria for instance. But I've never known him wrong on anything medical." Higgins turned his key in the car door, and paused reflectively. "Dr Fletcher mentioned something really interesting," he added. "Antabuse can be confused with another drug, coprine."

"What's that?"

"Apparently it's found in funghi, toadstools and mushrooms, things like that."

"You mean poisonous ones?" Meadows asked in surprise.

"They wouldn't be good for you, but coprine's not poisonous," Higgins replied. He got into the driver's seat and pushed the door open for her. "Not unless you've had a lot to drink," he added. "And have a heart condition too."

Chapter Nineteen

PC Greg Sutton sat on the old Anderson shelter, at the bottom of his garden, watching the sunrise. The stench of cat pee was unbearable, but sitting on the mound as dawn rose was still soothing. With all the tittle-tattle about him marrying so quickly, and to a divorcee, PC Sutton had been there a good deal over the last year. Chalk Heath got his goat. Half the town seemed to spend their whole lives gossiping.

He pulled his jacket round him. The mornings were getting colder. In a week or so the fogs would begin again. He hated November: walking the beat when he could hardly see two feet ahead. Goodness knew what could be going on, right next to him, undetected.

DS Winters would be arriving soon. For once the Woodbine Sutton was smoking did nothing to calm his nerves. He'd never helped run an incident room before. It was a compliment to be asked, but such a strange situation. It was hard to imagine a superior officer as a suspect in a murder case, especially DI Ambrose. He was one of the best: as straight as an arrow. Yet they had to treat him as a suspect.

"We've got to do everything by the book," DS Winters had stressed at the briefing the night before. "The DI helped cook the victim's last meal. If the press gets hold of that…" He left the sentence unfinished. Everyone could imagine the result. Never mind the *Chalk Heath Gazette*: the nationals would be down on them in hours. "However impossible it seems," Winters reminded them, "we have to question the DI like everyone else. He can't be given any inside information. While we wait for someone senior from South Cross to take over, I'm in charge of this case. Understand?"

Shaking his head at the thought, PC Sutton stared towards the church tower. The car would be calling for him soon. He wished he'd already set off on his own but Chalk Heath Hall would be a long way for him to cycle, particularly with his father's old attaché case strapped to the carrier. Kathy had packed him a clean uniform shirt and other essentials. What with his notebooks, torch and spare lantern, the case was heavy. So he'd accepted DS Winter's offer to pick him up, but it would be an awkward journey.

The man scared him. No. Scared was too strong a word, Sutton conceded, stubbing out his cigarette. Winters made him nervous, but then the DS didn't tolerate fools. Not that PC Sutton was a fool, but he felt like a rookie whenever he was with the DS. Which compared to what DS Winters had seen and done, Sutton was. According to the gossip at the Copper Kettle, Winters had been a Military Policeman during the war, had served in the Middle East and Italy. He'd even brought a fiery Italian wife back with him. Chalk Heath must seem like a dead hole in comparison. This was their biggest case for months. Greg Sutton was more used to dealing with the occasional brawl outside one of the pubs and they were easy enough to solve. Just a matter of who threw the first punch.

The sun was rising behind the chimney pots. Sutton glanced at his watch. He ought to go indoors.

"You off now, darling?" Kathy asked, still sleepy from the early start. "Here." She passed him a pack of sandwiches wrapped in greaseproof paper.

"Thanks, honey," PC Sutton kissed his wife.

"I thought you might not get anything else for hours," Kathy pointed out. "Posh folk don't throw their food about."

"Good job," Sutton replied dryly. "It'd be messy."

"You know what I mean!" Kathy laughed. "I'm not saying they're tight fisted, just broke," she explained. "Most of them are on their uppers now. You should see the state of the Hall. You might need those sandwiches."

Sutton gave his wife a hug. A horn sounded.

"Bye, darling." Grabbing his case, Sutton kissed his wife and hurried to the police car waiting outside. As he did so, net curtains dropped back across the neighbour's window. Nosey sods, even at this hour, he thought angrily.

DS Winters opened the passenger door for him. "Hop in," he instructed. "Before half the street injures themselves peering out. Higgins is joining us over there. He lives that way. Read the file?"

"Yes, sir," Sutton replied.

The police car pulled carefully around a cat sleeping in the road. Apart from the milkman, very little traffic came that way at this hour. "Any idea who might have done it?" Winters asked.

Not sure whether he was being set a trap, Sutton replied carefully. "I'm keeping an open mind, sir," he said.

"Quite right. But who do you reckon are the prime suspects? Who had the opportunity?"

Sutton considered the question. "It has to be the DI," he admitted uneasily, "and the girl who cooked with him. Then I suppose it's the host and hostess. She was in and out of the kitchen, and he could have gone into the dining room any time without people noticing."

"Yes. Mrs Yates is definitely worth watching," Winters replied guardedly. He'd decided to keep Ambrose's reason for being at the Hall to himself, for the time being at least. In fact, he'd decided to say as little as possible about their meetings over the past few days. He hadn't exactly been disobeying orders, but he was certainly going beyond them. Changing the subject, he asked, "What do you reckon for a motive?"

"I can't see that at all," Sutton admitted. "Certainly not for the DI. Not unless he'd met the victim way back. Even that's unlikely. South Cross division and ours rarely meet up." Watching a delivery boy wobbling on his bike up hill he paused, aware that his superior was assessing him.

To his relief, Winters smiled. "All very sensible," he said. "Any questions before we get there?"

Again, Sutton paused before he replied. He felt like he was back at school, with the Head standing over his desk, rapping his cane for an answer. "Well," he started slowly. "I thought we were meant to be waiting for South Cross to take over the investigation? What with the DI being unavailable, so to speak."

"That's right," Winters grimaced as he nodded. "The victim's son put the request in. He wanted someone from South Cross to take the lead. We'll get a Detective Super, or a DI at least."

Sutton wasn't sure if he should ask the next question. "So if we're meant to be waiting for someone, why are we starting the interviews today?"

Winters glanced over at him, annoyed. "Because none of us wants someone from another patch solving our cases," he explained.

Then Winters relaxed. He spoke more softly. "Look, this is how it goes. We have to report to the South Cross guy when he gets here, but we can be 'helpful' while we're waiting. Our Super asked me to set up the interview room. Now if we make a start on the interviews, today, we can hand our notes over to the new boss when he gets here. Besides, we can't keep the witnesses against their will so we have to get cracking before they leave."

Sutton was starting to understand. "Office politics!" he laughed. Then, "Is there anything particular you want me to do?" he asked. "Apart from fetching the witnesses?"

"Draw me some maps."

"Maps, sir?"

Winters nodded. "Yes. Do me some sketches showing the rooms on each floor, stairs, doors, French windows, that sort of thing. They'll help us work out who had access to the victim's food beside the cooks. That's why I asked you to bring a big writing pad. You did, didn't you?"

Sutton nodded.

"You might as well do one of the Hall and grounds too," Winters continued. "There's some funny business about a phone call from the village."

Though he couldn't consult DI Ambrose, Winters could follow his techniques. Ambrose often asked for a sketch to help him visualise things. With Meadows busy searching for a missing child, Sutton would have to do. He was a bright lad. Winters just hoped he was also good at drawing.

A coal lorry came out of a side road unannounced. The police car had to break hard to avoid hitting it. Winters could have stopped the driver and given him a severe lecture, but he probably hadn't been concentrating too well either. So instead he turned on the bell, giving the driver a nasty fright. The lorry pulled over urgently to let him pass.

Sutton managed not to smile.

They were heading out towards the Heath and the old village beyond. For a few moments both were silent. Then Sutton remembered another question. "What do we call the victim?" he asked. "Everyone at the Hall will know him as Coulson. If we call him Taylor, they'll get confused."

"Good point," Winters agreed. "We'll stick to Coulson. Any more thoughts?"

In the driver's mirror, Sutton could see his superior's expression: determined, thoughtful, a little uneasy perhaps. With his red hair and freckles he looked too young to be a Detective Sergeant. It must be hard for him too, Sutton thought. He and the DI often worked together. They got results. And now Winters was on the way to question his superior. That couldn't be easy.

"Well," Sutton began. "Just that the DI himself took samples of the meal, for testing, and he wouldn't do that if he was guilty."

"He might. It could be a clever double bluff. Like you said; it's wise to keep an open mind."

Suppressing a yawn, Winters forced himself to concentrate on the narrow road across the Heath. He'd had to change his shift to take over the case, which meant he'd only had a few hours sleep. His wife hadn't been impressed. "That Ambrose man! He make you work all the while again," she'd complained. "No better than last year, whatever he say. Your children do not know you."

That had hurt, and though he'd denied the accusation vehemently, Winters wondered if it was true. When he tried to explain that this time it was Ambrose he was investigating, Ginny had stared at him in disbelief. "Not possible!" she'd retorted.

"Not possible!" he kept repeating. He knew the DI wasn't guilty, but he had to go through all the motions. If he didn't, they'd never be able to convict the real culprit. No, he couldn't cut the DI any slack, even if the only evidence they had against him was circumstantial.

"What do you reckon to the note?" he asked Sutton. "The one the Williams woman found?"

Sutton was beginning to relax. The DS seemed genuinely to value his opinion. "It sounds like blackmail," he replied. "But it needn't be. It could just be telling someone to get cracking and do something. Or even part of someone's story. Though I don't think that's likely. I mean; you'd include a bit of description, wouldn't you? Not just a few words."

Winters nodded. Sutton would make a good detective: bright and thoughtful, able to look beyond the obvious, so long as he didn't let his personal life intrude. His sudden marriage last year, to a former suspect, had been a bit surprising. It suggested there was a good deal going on beneath the careful surface. Sutton would have to learn to balance his ambition with the other things that mattered to him.

That was something he'd never quite managed himself, Winters admitted. Perhaps if he'd chosen a different woman, he started. No, that wasn't worth thinking about. He might have had a quieter life but he wouldn't have loved her so much.

Tapping his hand on the driving wheel, Winters returned to the case in hand. The best way he could help the DI was to investigate the case properly. "And what about the cause of death?" he asked.

"More like a woman's method than a man's perhaps," Sutton replied. "Poison usually is a woman's crime isn't it? They'd have to be pretty clever and nasty too. I mean, knowing what adding alcohol would do and which mushrooms contain coprine. They'd also need to know that the victim had a weak heart. We may be looking for a very smart woman. Which definitely counts the DI out."

"Precisely," Winters agreed. He kept his mouth set in a hard line, resisting an urge to smile.

They sat in silence again until the main street of Old Chalk Heath appeared. Winters slowed down. The village was silent, two women waiting at a bus stop. Rooks cawed in the trees near the church. A dog slept on a doorstep. It was all so very English; as if the past three decades had never happened. The Hall gates had been left open. Carefully Winters drove between them and down a gravelled driveway.

"Blimey!" PC Sutton whispered. He'd seen the house from the road, but the gates were usually kept shut, and the trees along the drive blocked his view. Now he could see how gracious Chalk Heath Hall was. As they scrunched along the gravel, he almost felt excited at the prospect of spending a night in so imposing a house. Presumably he'd have to share one of the attic rooms with Higgins. He hoped the man didn't snore.

"It's all a bit run down inside," Winters warned. "Must have been beautiful once."

"It still is," Sutton insisted. "But look at that roof!" As the son of a builder, he knew the missing slates meant trouble, and an awfully large bill.

As arranged, Mrs Yates met them at the front door. "Ruth Yates," she said, trying to smile. "We've met I think," she added to Winters vaguely, "But you are…"

"PC Sutton," Winters replied, introducing his colleague.

"Pleased to meet you."

The perfect hostess even in times of trouble, Ruth shook their hands, but her voice was unsteady. Her eyes were swollen, as if she'd been crying. "I've put you in the games room," she said. "That'll be the best place. It's in the basement. You'll be private down there and there's a portable oil heater." She was talking too brightly. Despite her gracious manner, she was only just holding herself together. "Your colleague's already here," she added. "He's setting the room out. This way, please."

Winters had come to the front door before, but he'd been too preoccupied to notice the grand entrance hall. Impressed, he paused a moment, looking round. He saw the coat rack in the lobby. He recalled Ambrose's concern about the victim's coat; how it had suddenly appeared the day after his death. Yes, the coats were very accessible, so someone could easily have removed one and returned it later without being noticed. He was relieved that one of the DI's statements could be confirmed so easily.

They followed Ruth down a corridor. Doors lined the walls. Most were shut, but the first one on their left gave a glimpse of a cluttered office. Again recalling Ambrose's descriptions, Winters knew that one of the other doors must lead to a dining room, another to the guests' kitchen, but not which ones or how near they were to each other. And that might be important. "Yes, a map will be useful," he thought. "I'll never get my head round this place otherwise."

As they walked past, voices came from one of the rooms on the right. Then they stopped suddenly, as if the tread of heavy shoes had silenced everyone. "We've put all the guests in the lounge," Ruth explained. "My husband's with them."

"You've told them they can't leave until they've been questioned?" Winters asked.

"My husband has, but several are objecting. They don't see how Mr Coulson's death can have been anything but natural. I don't myself. It's all just too awful!" Ruth's self-control was nearly breaking and she blew her nose to hide her distress. "The stairs down to the basement are in our kitchen," she managed to add.

There was the sound of a door opening behind them and Ruth turned round sharply. "This is my husband," she said. "What is it, Frank?"

"Can I have a quick word?" Frank whispered, closing the door behind him.

"Of course." Winters assessed the man's appearance. He was concerned and nervous but there was nothing guilty in Frank's manner, and he was much less upset than his wife at having an official police presence.

"I've explained to the guests that you need to speak to all of us," Frank replied, "but it would be really helpful to know in what order. No one can settle to work if they think they might be called any minute. Besides, I'd like to arrange some activities. If we can't let our guests go home, we want to make their stay as enjoyable as possible."

Ruth nodded. "They have paid quite a lot of money," she explained. "And what's happened is so awful." Her voice trailed off.

It was a reasonable request. Winters tried to think what DI Ambrose would do. He'd want to inconvenience people as little as possible; keep things low key and informal, at least initially. "I'll draw up a list," he replied, "with rough times. Then people will know when they're wanted and can do other things till then."

"That's very good of you," Frank said and turned back to the lounge.

"Thank you for being so understanding," his wife added afterwards. Then she led them on, down the corridor. "The stairs to the basement are through here." She opened the door to their private kitchen.

Glancing back into the corridor, Winters saw the rack of keys hanging beneath the servants' bells. Unless the board was constantly checked, any of the guests could take keys to any door. Sutton had spotted the same possibility. "Why do they trust their guests so much?" he whispered.

"Because they're 'the right sort'. And they pay a lot," Winters whispered back.

They walked through the kitchen, to a flight of stairs at the far wall. "This way," Ruth led the way down. The steps were steep and awkward. Carrying trays of crockery or baskets of washing would not have been easy, especially in long skirts.

"Pity the poor skivvy!" Winters thought grimly. "Now that's a point," his mind added. "Ambrose didn't mention servants. That could complicate matters." Considering the state of the kitchen they'd just passed, he decided there probably weren't any.

They'd reached the foot of the steps. In front of them was a huge old kitchen area. Then a poorly lit corridor led them past more doors. The first two doors on their left were open. The next doors were tightly shut.

"Rum place isn't it?" PC Sutton whispered, looking around.

"How our ancestors lived," Winters replied softly. "Mine at least."

Finally, ahead of them, they could hear the sound of chairs being moved about and a kettle boiling. Light streamed from an open door. After the gloom of the corridor, it was hard to see for a few seconds. Then they made out the end of a ping-pong table and a dartboard on a wall.

"I hope this will be all right for you," Ruth said. "Let me know if you need anything." Turning abruptly, she went back the way they'd come and disappeared up the stairs.

"Well, I've worked in stranger places," Winters remarked. "Let's make ourselves at home."

Higgins looked up as they entered. "Morning," he said cheerfully. "Fancy a cuppa?"

"Now that's the most sensible thing I've heard all day," Winters replied with feeling.

Chapter Twenty

"But how long are we going to be here?" Christina demanded.

"It's like being in prison," Sheila agreed. "And for goodness sake, let's have some air!"

Ever since the announcement at breakfast, Betty and Phyllis had been virtually chain smoking. Now Jack had lit up too, the atmosphere in the lounge was becoming unpleasantly close. Frank opened the French windows but that made the room cold, so he had to settle for just leaving them slightly ajar. It was a lovely morning outside, the early mist rising from the woods and river beyond. The lawns near the terrace were a deep rich green, freshened by overnight rain.

"I want to be out!" Edith almost wailed. "We may not get another day like this."

"I have a sketch to finish," Phyllis insisted. "I started one yesterday near the old pond, such a lovely spot, not too far for me to walk and perfect for the fairy book I've been asked to illustrate. Have I mentioned that?"

"No, but I'm sure you will," Geraint remarked dryly. He was looking a little better, still pale and thin-faced, but his studied elegant manner was returning.

"I do believe you're jealous, darling!" Phyllis replied.

Breakfast had been difficult and edgy. Ruth looked near to tears and Sheila upset a teapot on the tablecloth. Even the normally patient Margaret had been irritable, almost losing her temper at Jack's constant banter. With an expression of distaste, she'd taken her poached eggs to eat alone at the far end of the table. Now they were cooped up together in the lounge, the tension was growing. DS Winters had insisted that no one be allowed to leave until their interview was over. Frank was going to have a difficult job keeping them from just walking out.

"This is such a bore!" Gerald complained.

Jonathan was more conciliatory. "The police have their job to do," he said. "I'm sure they'll be quick. They must have lots of real criminals to catch."

"All this fuss over a man dying of a heart attack!" Sheila agreed. "I'm very sorry. We all are. But these things happen. I can't understand why the police are involved."

Frank pushed his hand through his hair in a worried gesture. "Why are they?" he asked Ambrose. "Is it normal?"

Finding everyone looking at him, Ambrose considered his reply. "They must think something's suspicious," he said. "It could be quite trivial, but it would have to be investigated. Jonathan's right. They'll be as quick as possible."

"I'm frightened," Betty said. "What if I forget something or contradict myself? I always get things wrong."

"Don't be so silly!" Sheila almost snapped. Then she softened her tone. "There's nothing to worry about," she assured her. "We'll each be asked about Mr Coulson's death. Since we'll all say virtually the same we're not going to be much help. The police will take a few notes and go away. Won't they?" She turned to Ambrose.

"I imagine so," Ambrose agreed. "Just keep calm and tell the truth."

Inwardly though, he wasn't completely calm himself. He understood Betty's anxiety. Knowing that he was a suspect, however unlikely, was unpleasant. In future he would have more sympathy with the witnesses he questioned. It was also frustrating. Instead of being able to lead the investigation, he was cooped up in a lounge while his sergeant took charge.

He wondered how Winters would approach the situation. He'd do everything by the book, so he must be waiting for someone senior to lead the investigation, perhaps someone from a different division. That really would complicate things. Winters wouldn't want to admit he'd helped Ambrose investigate a case their Super had dropped. Nor would he want to cause trouble for a colleague, especially Ambrose. Ambrose would have to make sure he didn't say anything to implicate Winters. But he also couldn't lie…

Margaret interrupted his thoughts. "Let's not ruin our day worrying," she advised. "Frank, you said you had some activities for us."

With an expression of relief, Frank nodded. "I do indeed," he replied more cheerfully. "I have some ideas for the artists too. Everyone, come across to the windows with me."

They followed him dutifully. As they crowded at the windows Ambrose managed to whisper to Geraint, "How are you feeling today?"

"Better," Geraint whispered back.

"What have you done with the paint?"

"Given it back."

"Given it back?" Ambrose repeated in surprise.

"Ruth's asked for it often enough."

Shaking his head in disbelief, Ambrose wondered why Geraint would stay on at the Hall after what had happened to him. Why hadn't he accused Ruth in public or at least had a flaming row with her? There had been muttered voices in the Yates' kitchen late last night, but nothing other guests would have noticed. Geraint seemed determined to play down what was possibly an attempt on his life.

"I want you all to look at the gardens," Frank was saying, "and remember somewhere you've liked. Don't think about it. Just let the picture come."

PC Sutton was walking across the lawn. He was carrying a big notepad and staring intently at the back of the house.

"What's he doing?" Christina whispered.

"Looks like he's sketching," Jack suggested.

Ambrose smiled to himself. "Sam's got him drawing maps," he thought. "Very sensible. With a place like this it'll help to know who was where and when." He would have done the same himself.

"Ignore the police," Frank insisted. "Picture somewhere in the gardens. Where are you, Jack?"

"Umm…" Put on the spot, Jack hesitated.

"I said don't think," Frank reminded him. "Let your subconscious do the work."

"In the market garden," Jack blurted out. He was as surprised as the others.

"And where are you, Sheila?"

"In the woods," Sheila replied, laughing. "I see what you're up to. It's like automatic writing."

"You what?" Edith asked.

"Madame somebody-or-other used to do it before the war. It was all the rage. Now you do it. Where are you?"

"Goodness. I don't know. Near the old cabin perhaps." Edith frowned. "Talking of which, I'm sure someone's been in there recently. When I looked yesterday, there was a faint footprint on the boards."

"Really?" Frank asked in surprise. "It's supposed to be locked."

For a moment there was an awkward silence. Then Christina spoke. "That was me," she said. "I hope you don't mind. You said we could go where we wanted, Frank, and I can concentrate better in the quiet. I saw the key hanging on the rack. You're not cross, are you?"

"No, of course not. Just make sure the door's locked after you, please. We've had tramps in there."

"But the key doesn't fit," Ambrose nearly said, and stopped himself. He watched Christina's expression. Why would she lie about such a trivial thing?

"And you, Jonathan?" Frank asked.

As Frank spoke, Ambrose saw Sheila touch Christina's hand. It was the slightest of gestures but it conveyed a great deal. "Of course!" Ambrose thought. Sheila and Gerald were using the cabin as a meeting place. They must have taken the key and put a substitute on the rack. They came to the Hall regularly so they could be together. Presumably they would put the real key back before they left. And Christina had just covered for them. No wonder Sheila was grateful to her.

He glanced at Gerald and wondered what a woman like Sheila saw in him. "Maybe he's like Jack," he thought. "Different on his own." He had certainly been quieter at the beginning of the week, even hesitant. Perhaps that was what Sheila liked about him. She could mother him as she'd mothered Ambrose when they first met. The fact that Gerald was married probably gave the sense of danger she missed in peacetime. It also meant she didn't have to make any commitment to him.

"And you, Paul? Where did you picture yourself?"

With a start, Ambrose realised he hadn't heard the last answers. He'd just have to hope he wasn't repeating what someone else had just said.

"In the formal gardens," he replied. "Sitting in one of the arbours."

"Excellent!" Frank clapped his hands, as he often did at the end of a successful exercise. "Now I want you to describe your place, in words or paint. Geraint you can take the artists to Ruth's studio. There's a box of photographs there that might be useful. You don't need to draw accurately. A memory of a colour or a mood will do fine. The writers stay with me. We have another game to get your juices flowing."

The reference to photos jogged Ambrose's memory. He ought to give DS Winters the film he'd taken yesterday. "Do you mind if I go upstairs to get a pullover?" he asked.

"Don't be long. The police might want you."

"Won't be a minute."

Frank's reference to 'the police' rather than 'your colleagues' troubled Ambrose. The man had spoken to him as a friend, someone he trusted. And yet Ambrose had been gathering evidence against Frank's wife, observing them all in fact. It felt like a betrayal.

Running upstairs to his room he took the film from his dressing gown and stuffed it into his pocket. Grabbing a pullover, he struggled into it as he ran back downstairs. Even so when he returned to the lounge, the writers were already at work. "What have I missed?" he asked.

"My instructions," Frank said, getting up to meet him. "Take a book off the shelves in the library, any book, and open it at the fifth page. Count down to line five and along to the fifth word. Your challenge is to write a story or a poem beginning with that word, set in the place you imagined earlier."

Sutton's figure passed the French windows, closer this time. "Ignore him," Frank advised. "I don't know what he's up to, but it looks like he's enjoying himself. Help yourself to a book."

Frank had opened the sliding doors between the lounge and the library. The combined room felt light and airy. For a few moments Ambrose stood in the library section, wondering where to begin. Near him was a shelf labelled 'Nature'. "The fifth word", Frank had said. He might as well take the fifth book too.

Counting from the left, Ambrose took out a guide to English wildflowers. As he did so, he noticed a book on toadstools and mushrooms on the shelf above. It was misplaced in a section headed 'Hobbies'. Automatically he removed it, to put it back in the Nature section. Then he paused. Ruth had been looking for a mushroom book on the first day, to identify the toadstools she'd painted. She and Frank had searched thoroughly. It was odd that they hadn't found it then. Very odd.

Ambrose flipped through the pictures, stopping abruptly at a clump of toadstools. His mouth tightened. Ruth's watercolour was hanging on the far wall, together with other paintings completed during the week. The funghi in the book were definitely the same as the ones she'd painted.

Sitting down at one of the reading tables, Ambrose pretended to be counting lines and letters. Urgently he read the caption below the drawing:

"Coprinus atramentarius. Common Ink Cap. A medium sized species. The cap is grey-white but turns black. On liquefaction, it makes an inky substance that was once used for writing, hence the popular name. It grows along woodland paths and in lawns, appearing July to November. Although edible it contains a chemical similar to the drug 'Antabuse' and causes sickness when eaten in conjunction with alcohol."

Ambrose quietly copied the caption into his notepad, and replaced the book exactly where he'd found it. Then he tried to start writing but he couldn't concentrate, his mind was whirring. Whoever had used the book before him must have realised how they could kill Charles Coulson. They must have gone back into the woods and picked the ink caps Ruth had painted. Then they'd dropped them into the basket of wild mushrooms in the kitchen. But where had they got the alcohol at such short notice? And how had they added it to Coulson's drink without being seen? Ambrose paused in concern. These were the missing pieces of the jigsaw...

PC Sutton stuck his head round the door to the lounge, surprised to see the much larger combined room. "Could DI Ambrose come, please?" he asked. "Do you mind, sir?"

"Not at all," Ambrose replied, getting up. "It'll get it over with." As if mechanically, he picked up his writing pad and took it with him.

Sutton was embarrassed, not knowing whether to adopt a formal tone, as he would with any normal witness or to be more relaxed, colleague to colleague. As he was very much the junior officer, even that would feel odd. He decided silence was safest. Walking ahead of Ambrose, he led the way to the basement. Together they went through the old kitchen, to the Games room.

191

Hearing steps coming along the corridor towards him, DS Winters took a deep breath and looked at his notes. Even before he set out for the Hall, he'd planned to speak to his superior first. Knowing what more the DI had discovered could be invaluable. Given the irregular situation, however, it would be wise not to tell Sutton and Higgins about the DI's true reason for being at the Hall.

There was an awkward pause as Ambrose entered the room.

Chapter Twenty One

Ambrose eased the atmosphere. "Is this under caution or an informal interview?" he grinned. "I can give you my name and details if you want them."

"I think Higgins knows them already," Winters said with a wry smile. Then he started more formally. "We're investigating the death of Charles Coulson, and as you were here at the time, we need to ask you a few questions. Do you mind if Higgins and Sutton both take notes? In the circumstances, it'll be wise to do everything extra carefully."

"Indeed," Ambrose agreed. "You need to cover everyone's backs. Are you heading the investigation?" he tried not to sound surprised.

"Technically, no," Winters replied. "We're waiting for someone from South Cross to take over."

"Ah, and you're starting the interviews now, just to get the ball rolling," Ambrose nodded. He'd have hated reporting to someone from another district, so he understood completely.

He crossed to the tiny windows and looked out. Sunlight was beginning to filter through. As he turned back, he picked up some playing cards scattered on the table. Automatically he gathered them together. "This is awkward for all of us," he said. "So how about I recount what I saw and heard? Afterwards you can ask me anything that's not clear."

With relief, Winters nodded. He would have found it difficult to question Ambrose as if he were a normal suspect. "That sounds sensible," he said. "Tell us anything you think might help."

"I'm afraid that's not a lot," Ambrose admitted. He settled into a chair near the card table, thinking how to word his statement.

"I came here on holiday," he began. "The owners, Ruth and Frank Yates, host house-parties; what you might call retreats. They're aimed at people who want a quiet week to write or paint. Mary bought me a week for my birthday. I write short stories occasionally you see." He said nothing about working on a novel. He wasn't ready to share that.

"All the guests have to take it in turns to cook an evening meal," Ambrose continued. "The first one was cooked by our hostess. I signed up for the second evening, with a Miss Edith Greenwood. Earlier that day our guest speaker arrived, the victim Charles Coulson, and he was giving a talk during the dinner. He was a replacement for another speaker who had cried off, probably because of the fog."

Ambrose paused, choosing his words carefully. "I formed the impression Coulson was nervous, possibly frightened of someone. His behaviour was strange. As if he didn't want to be left alone..."

"Did you see anyone threaten him?" Winters asked.

"No. He might just have been nervous about giving a talk. Everyone expected someone more famous." Trying to visualise the scene at the ruined chapel, Ambrose paused. No, he still couldn't see who or what Coulson was avoiding; just that he was afraid to be on his own.

"And you cooked the meal with Miss Greenwood?" Winters prompted.

"Cooked is being kind," Ambrose replied and smiled. "Mary's always seen to our meals. I had no idea how to prepare dinner for fourteen people. The menu was pretty elaborate too. Edith Greenwood had been before and at least she knew where things were, but I wouldn't have said she was a cook either. We muddled through, with help from our hostess." Once again Ambrose frowned, recalling the hectic few hours he and Edith had spent in the kitchen.

Noticing that Higgins was having trouble keeping up, Winters let his superior lapse into silence.

"I didn't see either Edith or our hostess add anything to the victim's meal," Ambrose continued, "and I certainly didn't. I do have an idea how it was done, though. I copied this out of a book in the library just before you called me, a book that went missing by the way. It's turned up again as if it was merely misplaced, but I'm sure someone's hidden it for several days." He tore the page out of his notebook and passed it to DS Winters. "We had beef and wild mushroom casserole that night," he added.

"Goodness!" Winters said as he finished the extract. "Are there any toadstools like these about?"

"In the woods near the river. Ruth Yates did a painting of them. She showed it to all of us. Someone could easily have gone back later and picked them. It would have been equally easy to add a few extras to the basket of funghi in the kitchen. Edith and I wouldn't have known the difference. They were all shapes and sizes, not your greengrocer's mushrooms."

"Did you see anyone go into the kitchen?"

Ambrose paused, considering his answer. "Lots of people," he said. "We're allowed to make drinks and help ourselves to biscuits."

"What about the alcohol?" Winters asked. "Presumably the killer brought that with them?"

"Only if they're a secret drinker. The booking form specifically asks guests not to bring any alcohol with them, and there's none in the house."

"There's a pub in the village," Winters pointed out.

"I doubt if anyone had time to walk up there, get served and smuggle a drink out before dinner. It's worth checking if they have an off-licence, though. The barman might remember selling a bottle of spirits."

Winters made a note to do so. "Who prepared the drinks for the evening meal?" he asked.

"Margaret – Mrs Astin. We were way behind, so she helped by putting the lemonade on the table. She might have tipped some vodka into the victim's drink, if she had any to hand...." Ambrose paused again. He didn't want to think of Margaret as a suspect, but clearly she'd had the opportunity.

"I have found one thing out," he added. "There's a short cut from the back of this place into the village. One of the guests could have made a call from the phone box there, and stopped us phoning for an ambulance."

The oil heater was making a sputtering sound and Winters got up to check the wick. "How?" he asked, as if it was a new idea.

"By leaving the phone off the hook. One of the guests, Sheila Butterworth, ran up to the box and said the receiver was off when she arrived."

"I remember that happening once at the station," Winters remarked thoughtfully. "The desk sergeant didn't put the phone back properly and we got all hell afterwards. He'd been talking to his opposite number in South Cross."

Higgins had gone very red. "That was me, sir," he muttered. "I didn't half get it in the neck. South Cross weren't able to ring out for half an hour. Fortunately I heard our phone making a funny noise and replaced the receiver."

"Now that *is* interesting," Ambrose said. "If someone cut through the woods they'd have to know the route. It was our first full day. So that suggests someone who's been here before."

"That narrows it down," Winters agreed.

Without intending, Ambrose and Winters were slipping back into their usual practice, bouncing ideas off each other. Sutton looked up curiously, just as Higgins glanced his way. "Do you know what's going on?" Higgins' expression asked. Very slightly, Sutton shook his head. They both looked down at their notes again, quickly.

"That's what gets me!" Ambrose said. "It's all so darn clever, yet it has to have been a crime of opportunity. No one knew Charles Coulson was coming until the evening before. Not even the Yates or Coulson himself. You'd think it had taken weeks of planning. Someone very clever is living amongst us, joining in the activities, or arranging them, and I still don't know who it is. That's getting worrying."

"You need to watch your own back, sir," Winters advised.

Ambrose nodded. He remembered the roll of film in his pocket. There was no way he could avoid referring to the Marshall case, even with the other officers in the room. "You'd better take this and get it developed," he said bluntly.

Winters took the canister. "What's on it, sir?" he asked.

"Some shots of an old tube of Emerald Green paint. It was in Geraint Templeton's bedroom. If he's been licking his brushes while using this, he'll have been making himself sick. Ask Meadows what old style Emerald Green can do. She has facts and figures."

Once again Higgins and Sutton glanced at each other. Being the oldest and with less to lose, Higgins could risk a question. "Is this a separate case, sir, or to do with Coulson's death?" he asked. "I'm not sure what to record."

Ambrose smiled. "Just take notes. Let DS Winters decide what goes on record afterwards," he suggested. "Off the record, I've been following an allegation that a previous guest was poisoned while staying here. I have been on holiday, but I've also been…" He sought the right word. "Watching, shall we say? My being here when Mr Coulson died may have been a coincidence or the two cases may be related. DS Winters knows the background. Is that sufficient?"

"Of course, sir."

"Do you know how he got the paint?" Winters asked.

"Ruth Yates gave it to him."

"Then surely we have grounds to arrest Mrs Yates?" Winters brightened up. "We can charge her with attempted murder. That may well mean she also poisoned Charles Coulson."

Getting up, Ambrose crossed to the table tennis. For a full minute he bounced a ping-pong ball against a bat, without answering. Winters knew not to prompt him. Whenever Ambrose went silent like this, he was considering all the facts, trying to come to a conclusion.

"I don't think she did," Ambrose said at last.

Winters frowned. "With respect, sir, why?" he asked. "You said she came into the kitchen, and that the toadstools grow in her grounds. Besides, if a woman poisons once, she's more likely to do it again. Everything points to her."

Once again, Ambrose bounced the ball in silent thought. "There's no way she'd poison the speaker," he decided.

"Why not?" Winters asked. He wondered whether the DI was allowing his judgement to be clouded. Clearly he liked the woman and didn't want to think she might be a murderer. That was understandable. But it was also the reason why even a DI must be treated like any other witness.

"Making someone poison themselves while they paint is pretty cold and calculating," Winters persisted.

"True," Ambrose admitted. "If she did it deliberately."

"So you think it was an accident?"

"I don't know." Thoughtfully Ambrose put the bat down. "Even if she did poison Geraint deliberately," he added, "I don't think he'll give evidence against her."

"Why on earth not?" Winters asked.

"I don't know. Perhaps she has some hold over him."

Both of them lapsed into an edgy silence.

"I'll bet my bottom dollar that's what she did to James Marshall," Winters said suddenly. "Gave him another tube of the stuff so he fell ill after he left here."

"It is possible," Ambrose had to agree.

"I'd say it's very likely. He was probably painting all the time he was in India, killing himself as he did it. That has to be one of the most heartless crimes I've heard of. It's time we started questioning her."

Ambrose still wasn't convinced. "We can't prove she knew the paint was harmful," he pointed out. "Nor, if she did, that she intended to kill Geraint. She asked for the paint back in my hearing. We don't even know James Marshall had any paints, from her or anyone else. All his effects were stolen or destroyed after his death, and the Indian authorities didn't keep records."

"But what about the letter to his fiancée? Isn't that enough evidence for you?"

Realising they were beginning to argue in front of Higgins and Sutton, Ambrose stopped. The old oil heater was smoking now. This time Sutton went to trim the wick. He took a guarded look at his superiors as he did so. Neither of them was showing irritation outwardly but he could sense the abrasive atmosphere between them.

"Just hand all the information over to whoever heads the case," Ambrose instructed. "It's his case."

Winters nodded. "It is indeed," he agreed. "But we'll speak to Mrs Yates next. Who knows, we might have her confessing before the new chap even gets here."

"Only if she's guilty I hope," Ambrose warned. "Do yourself a favour and speak to Margaret Astin first. She poured the drinks. Ruth Yates didn't."

"Maybe they were acting together."

Ambrose came back from the table and stood at the window again. "Now that is an idea," he agreed. "It's worth following up. I gather they've known each other for years. Do you need me for anything else?"

"Thank you, no, sir. You've been very helpful." Winters adopted a formal tone again. "PC Sutton will escort you back upstairs and fetch Mrs Astin."

Hearing his cue, Sutton got up quickly.

He accompanied DI Ambrose back through the kitchen and up the stairs, towards the lounge. As they walked, Sutton didn't dare ask questions about the case. A sense of unreality was beginning to trouble him. He'd never been inside such a grand house before, or been involved in so complicated a murder case. Two cases it now seemed. Even if he was little more than a messenger boy, he felt almost sick with nervousness. He must get everything right.

He was relieved to get the DI safely back in the lounge, without having to open his mouth and risk putting his foot in it.

Mrs Astin was charming though, putting him at ease immediately. "This place would have been full of steam when it was in use," she remarked as they passed the old laundry. "The boilers would have made everyone hot and sticky. Hardly the 'good old days'!"

"My Mum worked in a laundry," Sutton admitted. "Langlands Supreme." He stopped. Why was he telling a woman he'd only just met such a private detail? Mrs Astin seemed to draw confidences, just by smiling and being pleasant.

"I remember Langlands," Margaret replied. "It had a splendid chimney. An easy target for the Luftwaffe. Have you seen the monstrosity they're putting up in its place?"

They walked towards the games room, chatting as they entered. Still on edge from the interview with Ambrose, Winters found such familiarity annoying. Mrs Astin's easy confidence irritated him too. "Go and do some more of your maps," he instructed Sutton curtly. "You're not needed here."

"Good morning," Margaret greeted Winters politely. "Your young Constable has been very pleasant. It helped relieve the tension."

Winters saw the exotic shawl casually draped over Margaret Astin's shoulders, her elegant green dress, and thought, "Wealthy Old Colonial. Used to throwing her money about." She clearly had style though, and what his mother used to call 'breeding'. That annoyed him even more.

As soon as the preliminaries were over, he began questioning her brusquely. "I believe you prepared the drinks on the night Mr Coulson died?" he asked.

Margaret raised an eyebrow slightly. "Not exactly," she replied. "Ruth, that is Mrs Yates, had already prepared bottles of home-made lemonade. Paul and Edith were struggling to get the dinner ready on time, so I offered to help. They asked me to fill the carafes and set them out on the dining table."

"Carafes?" Winters asked. "Can you explain please?"

"Ruth enjoys doing things elaborately. I think it reminds her of her youth. Her parents' house parties were famous. This week each of us has our own personal little carafe, with our name on it, beautifully written of course."

"Go on."

Margaret was not going to be hurried by brusque little sergeants. She smoothed her skirt elegantly. "Might I have a glass of water please?" she asked. "It's very hot in here."

Higgins looked round for a glass and finding only cups, filled one from the kettle for her. "I'm afraid it's been boiled, Ma'am," he said.

"That will be fine." Margaret smiled at him before taking a sip. "On the night Mr Coulson died," she continued, "Paul and Edith were so far behind, the carafes were still in the sideboard. I filled one for each of us, put a label on it, then set it on the table to mark each person's seat. I found a jug for the lemonade that was left, and placed it on the sideboard, in case anyone needed more."

"Did you add anything?" Winters asked.

"Of course not. Ruth makes an excellent lemonade."

"Did anyone else come into the room?"

"Ahh!" Margaret said. "You think someone added something to Mr Coulson's drink, to make him ill. That is possible. There were lots of comings and goings, but I didn't see anyone. I went upstairs to change soon afterwards." She paused. "In retrospect, one thing does strike me as a bit odd, though. There were two labels for the speaker, so I did two carafes for him. I suppose Ruth has found speakers get thirsty and need a second. Certainly Mr Coulson drank both, and then helped himself to more from the jug."

Winters was beginning to regret his hasty assessment of Margaret Astin. She was a good, careful witness. Or a very good liar. "Tell me about Mr Coulson's death," he asked. "Did you see him collapse?"

"We all did. He was obviously unwell, looking very hot and drinking a lot. For a while he managed to go on with his talk. It was very amusing and we were all watching him, not each other. Then Jack asked a typical Jack question, rambling on for ages. I looked away in embarrassment. Most of us did. The dessert plates were being passed around too. There was a lot going on. Suddenly Mr Coulson collapsed. I'm sorry I can't give you exact details of how he did so. It was all a blur."

"You definitely saw no one add anything to his food or drink?" Winters checked.

"I've already answered that question. No."

Glancing to see if Higgins was keeping up, Winters paused. Higgins looked up in gratitude and sharpened another pencil.

"I believe you and Mrs Yates have known each other a long time," Winters commented afterwards.

"Of course. Our families met regularly. I grew up at Winterburn Hall, only six miles away. I knew Ruth's older brother better than Ruth. He was more my age. We used to play tennis together. Then he left for France. He fell at Passchendaele, like a lot of that group." There was a catch in Margaret's throat as she spoke. "If he'd lived he would have inherited this place," she added, "and saved Ruth a lot of worry and expense."

Despite his earlier dislike of the woman, Winters was warming to her. "Winterburn Hall," he said thoughtfully. "That's a teacher training college isn't it?"

"Yes. A very good one" Sighing slightly, Margaret looked into the past. "It's more use to the Education Department than it would ever have been to me or my sister. When our parents died I was in India and she was in Scotland. Benedict should have inherited, but he was dead. None of us needed a draughty old pile we couldn't afford to heat."

Winters nodded. Then he decided to see if he could startle her. "Do you think Mrs Yates is capable of murder?" he asked.

"My goodness!" Margaret replied. "What a question!" She thought about her answer. "No. But she might consider it. She's a strong lady. Has to be to do all she does, with a husband who's, well, not exactly handy. No, she loves this place too much to risk losing it by doing something stupid. And why should she kill a guest speaker? She needs them more than they need her. Can I go now, or is there anything else you want to ask me?"

"That will be all for now," Winters replied, and got up. "PC Higgins will see you safely upstairs." Then to Higgins, "bring Mrs Yates next, please."

The words were hardly out of Winters' mouth when the door flung open. A large, red-faced man stood in the corridor. He looked out of breath.

"Damn! There are a lot of stairs," the newcomer complained. "Sorry Ma'am, didn't think there'd be a lady in here." He bowed slightly as Margaret left the room.

"DCS Dudley's the name, from South Cross," he continued, turning to Winters. "So you've started the interviews have you? No problem. Just fill me in while your chap gets the next witness, there's a good man."

Chapter Twenty Two

DS Winters knew the signs of guilt: the slight gestures of the hand, an inability to meet a questioner's gaze.

He saw guilt in Ruth Yates from the moment she entered. Her eyes were red and she looked round the room as if barely seeing it. Her voice was shaking as she gave her details. She was twisting her wedding ring round and round. Winters picked up the film Ambrose had given him. "Do you know what's in here?" he asked and gave the canister a little shake.

Ruth looked at him. "No," she replied. "Should I?"

"In here are photographs of a tube of paint – paint you've been using to poison one of your guests."

"Poison?" Ruth repeated. Her voice sounded faint but surprised. "No!"

"You gave Mr Geraint Templeton this tube of *poisonous* paint, knowing that it would make him sick."

Winters had expected another hot denial. Instead, Ruth looked at him with wide, frightened eyes.

"I believe it's called Emerald Green," he continued. "You knew it was harmful if swallowed, and that Mr Templeton often licked his brushes. That's why he's been so ill recently."

"That's also how you killed James Marshall," DCS Dudley added.

"James?" Ruth had gone very pale.

"Yes. James Marshall. You murdered him while he was in India."

"No!"

"I say yes."

"No!!!" The colour was rushing back into Ruth's face. "That's not true!"

"Oh but it is, Mrs Yates," Dudley said coldly. "You're a very clever lady. You killed a man in another country. He must have died a horrible death. Sick and alone amongst foreigners, in all that heat…"

Ruth's eyes were filling with tears. She fumbled in her cardigan pocket, trying to find a handkerchief. "I never meant to harm him," she protested.

Winters could barely believe their luck. Within minutes they had the beginnings of a confession. Dudley clearly didn't hang around.

"What do you mean?" Winters demanded.

Once again Ruth was silent. She looked wildly up at the window, as if longing to escape through it.

"You gave Mr Marshall a tube of paint to take with him, knowing it would make him ill," Dudley repeated. "In India, with the heat and disease over there, he wouldn't survive long. His resistance was weakened. Very clever and utterly callous."

"It wasn't like that!" Ruth insisted.

"Then how was it? Tell me why James Marshall believed he was being poisoned here, and died soon afterwards. And why Mr Templeton has that tube of paint. You gave it to him. You must have known it was dangerous."

Though she caught her breath, Ruth didn't reply.

"It's a bit of a coincidence," Winters remarked.

Still Ruth said nothing.

"Let me make it clearer for you," Winters said in a quiet voice. "A guest staying with you believed he had been poisoned while he was here. He died soon afterwards. This film shows another of your guests has a tube of paint that is dangerous if swallowed. You gave it to him. He's now sick. You killed the first guest and are at the moment trying to kill the second."

Ruth shook her head vehemently but said nothing.

"Answer us!" Dudley shouted, making both Ruth and Winters jump.

Her breath coming in sudden jerks, Ruth rose from the chair. Higgins got up too, standing between her and the door. "I need some air," she gasped. She seemed to be having some sort of attack, but Dudley ignored it.

"Sit down!" he ordered.

"I didn't kill James!" Tears engulfed her. Sobbing uncontrollably, Ruth put her hands to her face and flopped back into her chair. "I only meant..." The rest was lost behind her hands.

"What was that?" Dudley barked. "You only meant what?"

"I just wanted to teach him a lesson..."

"Oh yes," Dudley mocked. "And what lesson might that be?"

It took Ruth several minutes to reply. All the time, Winters watched her, hoping she wasn't going to collapse on them. He nodded to Higgins to get her a cup of water. Ruth's hand shook as she took it from him. She drank the whole cupful and asked for another. Then, steadier, she was able to talk.

"He was such a good artist," she said. "But he was arrogant, full of his own talent, and..."

"So you thought he needed bringing down a peg?" Winters suggested.

"It wasn't like that. I meant him no harm. But he needed to learn to listen. He patronised everyone, like he was a god, and we were mortals...." Ruth drank more water, then paused, trying to explain. "He couldn't go on treating people like dirt," she added, "or he'd make enemies. I wanted to teach him that he didn't know it all, that he shouldn't keep licking his brushes. Not when I'd told him not to..."

"So you did it for his own good? Pull the other one," Dudley laughed loudly.

Dudley got up and began walking around the room. He knew the movement would disorientate Ruth.

"I didn't mean him any harm," Ruth repeated. "I knew he wouldn't be able to take his paints with him. He'd just feel sick before he went and I'd warned him about licking his brushes. Only I don't know whether he was listening. I'm certain it isn't my fault he died. It can't be..."

Winters could feel Ruth's guilt swelling like a boil. A little more pressure and it would burst. Clearly that was Dudley's view too.

"You must have known Emerald Green was dangerous," Dudley persisted, walking up and down the room. "You teach art. You know such things. They're your trade."

"I'd heard it might make people sick but I never dreamt it could kill. Not until I read an article, and even that said it wasn't certain. I tried to get my tube back immediately, but James had already set off for India." Ruth was talking quickly now, so quickly Higgins was struggling get it all down. "I knew he would be all right, though. He wouldn't be able to carry big tubes like mine with him; only his travelling box. He said he was leaving most of his things with his sister."

"What if he did take the paint with him?" Dudley asked mercilessly.

Fear and grief thickened Ruth's voice. "He wouldn't have done," she repeated.

"Can you prove that?"

Ruth shook her head and lapsed into silence. They let her sit there for several moments, stewing.

PC Sutton passed along the terrace above them, his upper body hidden from view. With annoyance Winters watched the legs go one way and then the other. "What on earth is the lad doing?" he asked himself. Then he remembered he'd ordered drawings of the house. Presumably Sutton was sketching the rear aspect. "Well, it's keeping him occupied," Winters thought. He wondered if they'd need the maps. Maybe they had the murderer there with them, slumped in the chair, her head in her hands. She didn't look like a cold-blooded murderer he had to admit, but few murderers did.

"Well?" Dudley prompted, deciding it was time to break the silence.

Suddenly Ruth sat up straighter, as if realising something. "I can't be sure either way," she said more calmly. "After I heard James had died, I went to his sister, to say how sorry I was. I asked about his paints and brushes, and could I buy them for my pupils? His sister said she'd already sold them, to help pay for his funeral. Everything he had with him on the train had disappeared. His passport, money, everything."

She didn't add, "So you can't prove whether he took the Emerald Green with him or not," but Winters understood. In annoyance he watched as Sutton moved past the window again. Either Ruth Yates was very lucky, or much cleverer than she appeared. He began to understand DI Ambrose's warning. It might indeed be difficult to prove anything against her. Even Winters wasn't convinced she was guilty of murder, so how could he expect to persuade a jury? They'd think her merely foolish or vindictive, but not worthy of hanging.

"And I suppose you only meant to teach Mr Templeton a lesson, too?" Dudley demanded.

He'd surprised her, as he'd hoped, but she didn't reply.

"What did he do wrong?" Dudley asked scornfully. "You can't deny you gave him the tube of paint. There are photos of it here." He pointed to the canister now sitting in Winters' lap. "We'll have these developed and used in evidence against you. We'll charge you with causing bodily harm by poisoning, at least, if not attempted murder."

"I didn't try to harm Geraint," Ruth insisted. She seemed to be finding some inner strength now and had stopped crying. "Why should I? He's my best student, he's getting known. But he paints too quickly. I keep telling him his work will lose its value if he goes on churning it out. I just wanted to slow him down, make him take time off for a bit. As soon as I realised it might make him really ill I asked him to give me the tube back. I've asked him again and again…"

"So it's his fault really?" Dudley mocked.

"He wouldn't give the paint back," Ruth insisted. "I wouldn't harm him for the world."

"So it was nothing personal? He wasn't arrogant and condescending?"

"Geraint's always teasing me," Ruth conceded. "I can take it when there's just him. I'll admit it was harder that week, when there was the two of them, egging each other on. But I honestly didn't mean either of them any harm. When Geraint wouldn't give me the tube back I made him change to oils, so he wouldn't lick his brush. I've done everything I can to undo any harm I've done. I'm very fond of him."

"I hope you never get fond of me," Dudley retorted.

He seemed frustrated. Winters felt the same. A few moments ago, he was sure they'd have a full confession and a formal charge. Now it seemed to be slipping away from them. Ruth Yates was guilty of attempted murder at least. She had virtually said as much but was that enough?

"So what about Mr Coulson?" Dudley asked suddenly. "What lesson did you need to teach *him*?"

In surprise, Ruth stared at him. "Mr Coulson?" she repeated.

"Yes. Your visiting speaker. Why did you kill him?"

"I didn't!" Ruth answered hotly.

"Really?" Dudley said firmly. "You have a pattern of trying to poison people. Are you asking me to believe that when your speaker collapsed at the dinner table, you didn't have anything to do with it?"

"But I didn't!" Ruth insisted. "I've told you the truth about James and Geraint. Why should I lie about Mr Coulson? What possible reason could I have? I'd never even met the man until that day."

"I doubt if you need a motive. You kill for the fun of it!" Dudley said, but he felt less confident than his voice suggested.

"That's not true!" Ruth said, her voice shaking with shock and anger. "I want Frank. He'll tell you I didn't kill Mr Coulson. You can't accuse me like this. It's bullying!"

Uneasily Winters looked at his watch. If they carried on much longer they might indeed be harassing her. They weren't getting anywhere. He had a feeling they could go round and round like this for an hour or more. Despite her partial confession, there wasn't enough evidence for an official charge.

Winters glanced over at Dudley. The man looked even redder than before, as if he was taking Ruth's failure to confess personally. Suddenly Dudley stood up. "Ruth Yates, we are taking you to the Police Station where you will be questioned formally about the murder of Charles Coulson," he announced, "and the attempted murder of Geraint Templeton."

Appalled, Ruth stared at him, utterly speechless. She rose from her seat and appeared to be about to run from the room. Higgins barred the way.

Dudley nodded to Higgins, who took Ruth gently but firmly by the arm. Winters watched as they left the room. He hoped they were doing the right thing.

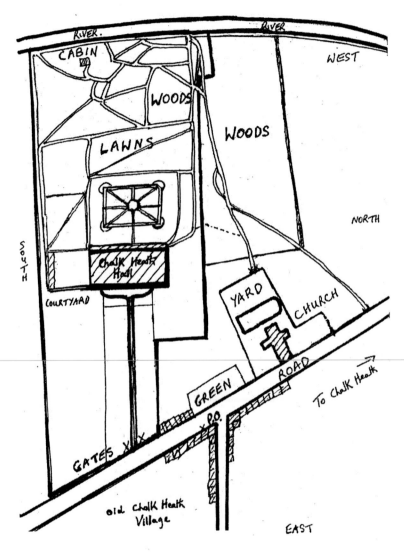

PC Sutton's map of Chalk Heath Hall grounds, showing the village & church

Chapter Twenty Three

They sat in silence. Five minutes passed, every second marked by the tick of the grandfather clock in the corner. Finally Jonathan stood up. "We might as well go home," he said huskily. "What an awful day!"

"I still can't believe it," Sheila agreed. She was standing behind Frank's chair with her hand on his shoulder, comforting him.

"Don't go!" Geraint said suddenly.

In surprise everyone turned towards him.

"Help me prove Ruth didn't do it."

Geraint's appeal reinforced Ambrose's unease. "You think she's innocent?" he asked.

"Of course. Ruth wouldn't deliberately hurt anyone. Certainly not a speaker at one of her retreats. It'd be stupid."

"She was making you ill," Ambrose pointed out.

Now everyone looked at Ambrose in bewilderment. "How?" Edith asked.

"You'd better ask Geraint."

Staring into the empty fireplace, Geraint didn't reply.

Edith crossed the room and stood in front of him, arms folded. "All right, I'm asking," she said. "How has Ruth been making you ill?"

Looking up at her earnest expression, Geraint smiled. "I love it when you're cross with me," he said.

"I could hit you!" Edith retorted. "You haven't answered my question."

"The police think Ruth was trying to poison me."

"Why?" Sheila demanded.

"She gave me a tube of Emerald Green paint. It has arsenic in it. I don't know whether Ruth knew it was dangerous. I hope not.

When she realised it might be making me ill, she asked for it back, but I kept it. She warned me against licking my brushes. I didn't listen then either." Geraint shrugged his shoulders. "If it's anyone's fault, it's mine. Besides, I really do have a liver problem. It's why I flunked out of medical school."

"Why didn't you tell me?" Edith asked. She sounded near to tears. "You're a silly chump!"

"So I've been told." Geraint gently touched her arm.

Shaking her head, Edith turned towards the French windows. Despite the sunshine outside, the room was cold and miserable. "Can't we have a fire?" she asked.

"Of course." Rousing himself, Frank became very busy with the box of kindling and the coalscuttle. "I was thinking," he said. "Yes, please stay till Sunday. There'd be no charge, of course. There's plenty of food left. I'd be grateful for the company, and if you can prove Ruth didn't do it…" He began laying twists of newspaper and firewood in the grate but his hands were shaking.

"Here. Let me," Jack said and took over. "Are we staying?" he called over his shoulder.

"Please," Geraint said simply.

Ambrose wondered why Geraint didn't hate Ruth, or why he'd want to defend her. "I'm willing to stay if others will," Ambrose agreed. "I don't think she poisoned Mr Coulson either. But I won't be allowed to investigate the case. Someone from another division has been brought in. I don't want that or for there to be a miscarriage of justice."

"That would be awful!" Christina agreed. "I'll stay."

"So will I," Margaret nodded. "Ruth and I have known each other for years. I can't believe she could kill someone."

Others nodded in agreement. The fire flared up suddenly, nearly catching the sheet of newspaper Jack was holding to draw the flames. Hurriedly he pulled the paper away.

"I can't see much chance of the police changing their minds," Jonathan said, "present company excepted. But if we can help..."

"How can we?" Gerald asked. "Like Jonathan said, once the police have made up their minds..." Flushing, he glanced at Ambrose. "No offence meant," he apologised, "But it often seems that way." He turned to Geraint. "What do you suggest?"

"I don't know. Try to prove Mr Coulson died from natural causes. Or that someone from outside killed him."

"How could they? We'd have seen..." Edith began. Then she stopped suddenly. "It must have been an outsider," she corrected herself.

"Of course!" Phyllis agreed.

Ambrose wished he shared their confidence. Glancing round at people's expressions he knew, whatever they might say, others had begun to think the unthinkable. A sense of shared horror had held them together since the police took Ruth away. Now it was being replaced by uneasiness and suspicion. No one felt safe, but equally no one was willing to admit it.

"Why don't you question us, Paul?" Jack asked. "See if we noticed something. You're a detective, after all."

"That's my day job," Ambrose agreed. "What do the rest think? Would you mind? People often don't realise they've spotted something until they're asked."

"Of course we wouldn't mind," Margaret replied firmly. "I'm sure you'll be able to solve it."

Ambrose was flattered but wasn't sure he agreed. Looking up, he saw relief in Betty's eyes. There was something she wanted to tell him, and Jack had provided the opportunity. He recalled her behaviour on the landing the second day.

"Of course!" he nearly said out loud. He'd been so immersed in the Marshall case and Charles Coulson's death, that he'd almost forgotten the beginning of the week. He hoped no one else had seen Betty's expression.

Quickly Ambrose considered what to do next. A fortunate coincidence occurred to him. "Tell you what," he suggested. "I'll take over Frank's study and you can come to me in alphabetical order. You can get on with some writing or painting until it's your turn."

At the mention of painting, there was an awkward silence. "I'll cover for Ruth," Geraint offered. "Frank will take the writers."

Frank nodded, still too stunned to object. Geraint was taking over organising everyone and proving rather good at it.

"Christian names or surnames?" Christina asked.

"We know each other by Christian names, so let's go by them," Ambrose replied. "It won't take long. There's no point in telling me about Mr Coulson's death, unless you saw something others couldn't have." He turned to Betty. "I think you're first," he invited casually. "We might as well walk down together."

Betty got up and followed him to the door.

As soon as they were in the study, Ambrose said, "You've been trying to talk to me for a couple of days. I'm sorry. I should have noticed."

"I need to tell you something," Betty replied.

Clearing a pile of papers Ambrose perched on the edge of the desk, while Betty sat in the armchair opposite. He had a sudden memory, of listening to Frank's comments on his work. It seemed months, not days ago.

"It was your flask wasn't it?" Ambrose asked.

"Yes."

"How did it end up in Mr Coulson's pocket?"

"I don't know." Betty shuffled awkwardly in the chair. "I couldn't tell you in front of the others," she said. "I was too ashamed." Her voice shook, but she spoke quickly, relieved to share her secret at last.

"You have a bit of a drink problem," Ambrose remarked gently. "Tell me about it. I won't be shocked. You wouldn't be the first or the last."

He wanted to tell her to hurry up. She must tell him everything, quickly, or the murderer sitting calmly in the lounge would fear she was saying too much.

Her face going a deep red, Betty tried to find the right words. "Mum could be very trying," she began, "and watching her die was awful. It was too much, after we'd already lost the baby and my brother. It helped to have a little drink occasionally. But it got out of hand until I couldn't do without. That's why Henry paid for me to come here. He knew it was Teetotal, and that writing helped me. It was kind of him, but the idea terrified me. So many strangers! And all of them cleverer than me! I hid two bottles of vodka in my case, to have a little sip if I needed it."

Ambrose nodded. "I was nervous about coming, too," he said.

"Why?" Betty asked. "You're clever."

"Not when it comes to which knife to use."

"It is so tricky, isn't it?" Betty agreed, smiling slightly. "I looked at the table before dinner on the first day and panicked. So I had a few sips while changing, to give me courage; only I drank more than I'd intended and made a fool of myself. I was so ashamed I hid the bottles and my flask at the back of a drawer. I thought if I couldn't see them I wouldn't be tempted again. But when I got ready the next morning I felt awful." She looked at Ambrose in appeal, willing him to understand.

"And you found the flask had vanished?" he prompted.

"With one of the bottles. Someone had taken them while I was in the bath." Betty shuddered, visibly frightened. "They'd been through my things, and found them. I couldn't tell anyone. I shouldn't have brought the bottles in the first place."

In concern Ambrose tried to picture the other rooms near hers, and the position of the staircase. It would have been easy for a thief to come from almost anywhere in the house. They would hear the bath running and know they had time to search her room. "Why didn't you say something later?" he asked. "When Ruth and I found the flask?"

"I was petrified. One of our group must have used my vodka to make Mr Coulson ill. Then they'd put my flask in his pocket, so we'd think he was a secret drinker. I wanted to tell you but there was no chance, not without the others overhearing..."

She'd gone very pale. Her fear was well grounded, Ambrose thought grimly. Whoever had taken that flask had killed Charles Coulson.

"Don't tell anyone what you've just told me," Ambrose warned. "When you go back to the others, say we talked about a tramp you saw in the grounds. Then stick close to Frank. You'll be safe with him. He wouldn't let Ruth be arrested for something he'd done."

"But what about when he's talking to you?" Betty pointed out.

"I'll see him at lunch. He's leading the writing group now. As soon as we can contact your husband, we'll take you home. We'll say you're sick."

"Please don't."

In surprise, Ambrose paused. "Why not?" he asked.

Betty stared up at the shelves of books, seeking inspiration. "Because I've started to feel like *me* again," she said, "the real *me* before the children were born and Mum was ill. I finished what was left in the second bottle, and after that, I had to go without. I've managed it. If I stick this week out I'll be able to say to myself: 'You coped in a strange place, with strange people, and with all the horrible things that happened. If you can do that, you can cope at home.' Do you understand?"

"I think so," Ambrose said. He smiled. "You're a brave young woman."

"No one's ever said that to me before," Betty admitted. She smiled with pleasure. For a moment she looked almost pretty, all the cares and unhappiness leaving her face.

"Be careful, though," Ambrose warned. "Someone in that lounge is capable of hastening a man's death, perhaps of murder."

He got up, ready to escort Betty back to the lounge. As he did so, he recalled another detail. "Were you ill the night Mr Coulson died?" he asked.

"Very. Margaret had to stay with me."

"Did you have something to drink before the meal?"

Flushing deeply, Betty nodded. "That's when I finished the second bottle."

Ambrose was relieved. Everything was becoming clearer. "We'd better get back," he warned. "You mustn't talk to me too long."

As he opened the door, Betty asked, "One last thing, has anything come of the note I found?"

"Not yet," Ambrose said. "Perhaps it was just from someone's story after all."

The writers were gathered around the lounge fire as he and Betty re-entered. Heads were bowed in concentration. Even Frank looked a little happier, doing something he understood. "Christina?" Ambrose called quietly.

Putting her pad and pencils onto the chair, Christina followed him down to the study.

"Ask me anything you want," she invited. "If it will help."

As Ambrose had expected, she added little that did actually assist, apart from saying again that Charles Coulson no longer drank. Edith wasn't much help either. He talked to them both for about the same length of time Betty had been with him, trying to decide whether they were genuinely innocent or very good liars. It was hard to tell. Edith explained about the scholarship she'd won to come on the retreat, but mainly she spoke about Ruth and what might happen to her. "I can't believe they'd hang a woman!" she protested.

After she'd gone, Ambrose felt quite distressed. He'd grown to like Ruth. It was awful to think of her being condemned for

218

murder. "Don't let personal feelings come into it!" he warned himself sharply.

Talking to Geraint made that even harder.

"I have a duty to help Ruth," Geraint insisted. "I owe an awful lot to her." There was a seriousness in his voice Ambrose hadn't heard before.

"How?" Ambrose asked.

"My parents wanted me to be a doctor. So I went to medical school and messed about, painting instead of studying. Catching glandular fever was a mercy, saving me from being sent down." Getting up, Geraint wandered around the bookcases, taking out the occasional book as he talked. "While I was convalescing I had some lessons with Ruth. She was brilliant: gave me every encouragement. But as soon as I was better, my parents wanted me to go back to Edinburgh. I refused. We had a humdinger of a row and I ended up here at midnight, asking for a bed." Shrugging his shoulders, Geraint smiled ruefully. "Can you see *me* as a doctor?" he asked. "I'd pass out at the sight of blood."

Ambrose doubted that Geraint was as weak as he pretended, but he smiled. "You're quite a successful artist now," he commented. "Getting known. Have your parents changed their minds?"

"My father died before I could tell him," Geraint replied quietly. "The mater's coming round. My paintings sell well nowadays. She understands money."

"Do you live with her?"

"Lord, no! That would be an easy murder to solve. I have my own bijou place and cadge weeks here, in return for teaching Ruthie's students. Like I say, she's very good to me."

Becoming uncomfortable, Ambrose stood up. As he did so, he knocked the bookcase near him. The whole thing wobbled alarmingly, the bust of Milton falling flat, half on, half off the top shelf. In concern Ambrose lifted it down to check it was unharmed. It was too light to be marble. Turning it over he found a ridge at the base where the plaster of Paris had been detached from the mould. He felt cheated. Even Milton was a disappointment, like the author whose study they sat in, like the whole week in fact. Ambrose had looked forward to being able to write, and here he was working as usual.

Putting the bust back, he forced himself to think clearly. He took a notebook from the clutter on Frank's desk and wrote out the words of the blackmail note. "Do you know anything about this?" he asked, passing the sheet to Geraint.

"No. Should I?" Geraint asked, shrugging his shoulders. He turned the paper about, as if it might reveal something upside down or back to front.

"You don't recognise the words?" Ambrose persisted. "They're signed 'GT'."

"Not by me. It sounds like blackmail. Presumably you'll be asking Gerald. He's GT too. It could be from one of his horrible stories. That man has an unpleasant obsession with gore. He's probably hen pecked at home and fantasises about getting his revenge!"

Ambrose had to hide his smile. "How did the business with the paint come about?" he asked, putting the note back on the desk.

Geraint became very interested in the book he was holding. "It was my fault," he said quietly, "always teasing Ruth and being a pain. Owing her so much embarrassed me." Again there was that studied, elegant shrug of the shoulders. "When James Marshall was here we were like a couple of schoolboys, egging each other on. He was a good artist but a conceited ass, and I was getting big for my boots too. Ruth probably did think we needed bringing down a peg. But she wouldn't have meant to harm us. Even if she did, I won't bring charges against her." Geraint's stare challenged Ambrose to disagree.

"You could be summoned to give evidence," Ambrose warned.

"Only if you have a case, and you don't. Everything's circumstantial. And you have even less proof that she killed Mr Coulson."

"So who do you think *did* kill him?" Ambrose asked.

"If I knew that, I'd be legging it out of here. Before they realised I knew."

Putting the book back on the shelf, Geraint lounged against the bookcase. "Is that it?" he asked. "Can I go now?"

"Send Gerald along," Ambrose replied, sighing. He found Geraint very difficult to handle.

Gerald was equally puzzled by the words on the paper. "I've no idea what it means," he said hotly.

"It's signed GT," Ambrose pointed out.

"Well I didn't write it," Gerald retorted. "Have you asked Geraint? It's the sort of daft joke he might play." He nibbled the skin on one of his fingers. "Do you mind if I have a fag?"

"I don't think Frank would like it," Ambrose replied. The man was clearly nervous. He decided to unsettle him further. "I wondered if that note was about you and Sheila," he remarked.

In alarm Gerald stared at him. "Me and Sheila?" he repeated.

"Yes. Does your wife know you come here to meet your 'bit on the side'?"

Aghast, Gerald stared at him. He tried to reply but no words came out.

"I don't suppose Miss Butterworth's employers know she's having an affair with a married man either," Ambrose continued.

"Please don't say anything," Gerald pleaded. He seemed to have crumpled into his chair.

"Why shouldn't I?"

"Because Sheila isn't my bit on the side, not to me. And I don't want to ruin her career."

The gentleness of his tone surprised Ambrose. "Do you love her?" he asked.

Mutely Gerald nodded.

"Why don't you leave your wife?"

"Sheila doesn't want me to. She likes things as they are. No commitment."

A bike sounded on the drive, its tyres crunching the gravel all the way down from the gates. Listening to its approach, Ambrose considered the man before him. He could see why Gerald would find Sheila attractive, but not what would attract her to him. Perhaps he was a surprisingly good lover. They seemed to spend a lot of time vanishing to the cabin together. "The fact that your wife has the money is nothing to do with it?" he asked.

Gerald looked at him angrily. "What would you do?" he demanded. "If Sheila would have me, I'd cut and run. But she won't. So there's no point in being out on my ear. Besides, Hazel would make sure I never saw the children again. So Sheila and I come here, and a few other places. When we can."

The bicycle had reached the front of the house. "The postman," Ambrose decided. Such trivial everyday events made their conversation seem unreal.

"Do you reckon the others know?" Gerald asked afterwards.

"Christina does. She covered for you. And Margaret's guessed. I don't think either of them will gossip. But I wouldn't go to the cabin again. Don't push your luck."

"No," Gerald agreed emphatically. "Thank you." He let out his breath in relief. Automatically he felt for the cigarette packet in his pocket, then remembering, stopped. "Why did you think that note was about me and Sheila?" he asked.

"I wondered if someone was blackmailing you."

"It wouldn't be signed 'GT' if it was," Gerald pointed out. Taking up the note again, he read it slowly, his mouth moving with the words. "You know what to do…" he repeated aloud. "It does sound like blackmail," he admitted. "If I was writing a story I'd put quotation marks, 'he said', 'she said' that sort of thing. Stage directions. But this is – well, a threat, isn't it? Where did you find it?"

222

"Somewhere in the house," Ambrose replied vaguely. "Send Jack to me," he asked, bringing the meeting to a close. "And please don't say anything about the note. It could be important."

"And you won't say anything about me and Sheila?"

"Not unless it becomes evidence."

Pausing at the door Gerald nodded his thanks. He'd gone very pale. "What a horrible week," he said. "Murder's different in real life. No fun at all."

Chapter Twenty Four

WPC Meadows sat in the 'Copper Kettle' café, staring at her cup. Doreen had left the pot stewing on the stove again. Without at least two spoonfuls of sugar the tea would be undrinkable. Thoughtfully Meadows reached for the sugar shaker. "Would Ruth Yates kill Charles Coulson?" she asked herself. "In a room full of people?"

Killing your guest speaker would be very bad for business, she thought wryly; and those fancy retreats were all about money, to maintain a rambling old house. Even an accidental death might lead to cancelled bookings. No. It didn't seem plausible.

Her meal should be coming soon. Anxiously Meadows looked at her watch. If she was going to call at the library on her way back to the Station, she'd have to leave earlier than usual. There might be a queue at the desk.

She returned to her problem. Who was she to question a senior officer? DCS Dudley was sure he had the right suspect. Or at least he'd seemed certain when he'd first arrived at the Station. Meadows suspected he wasn't now. He looked thoroughly frustrated as he left the interview room, a deep frown creasing his forehead. "Not going well," Higgins had whispered as Dudley walked past.

Meadows sighed. At the next table, a couple of market traders were making their way down a mound of Spam fritters. The smell made her feel even hungrier.

"'Am egg an' chips," Doreen's voice called from the counter. In relief, Meadows waved her hand.

For several moments she concentrated on Les' excellent chips. Once the first pangs of hunger had subsided however, the questions were niggling again. She'd finished the last chapter of *The One That Got Away* curled up next to the gas fire last night and looked through the footnotes and appendix in bed. After that, she'd fallen asleep, only to wake up suddenly, sure something wasn't right. But what was it?

Reaching for the bag near her feet, Meadows took out the library book. The plastic tablecloth was greasy so she wiped it with her handkerchief. Then she placed *The One That Got Away* in front of her. Eating with one hand, she checked the contents list and flipped through the chapters. Previous readers had written comments in the margins on some of the pages, and a whole paragraph was underlined in pencil. "Sounds like the Miller case," one note suggested. Another replied furiously, "NO!! Where did he get that from?" Fascinated, Meadows almost forgot to eat.

PC Sutton was entering the café, looking round for a table. It would be churlish not to indicate one of the empty chairs near her. "I'm leaving early," Meadows said, closing the book as he joined her, "But I've time for another cuppa. The last barely touched the sides."

Smiling, Sutton hung his coat over the chair and went to order at the counter. He came back with two cups of tea. "We're in luck," he said. "A fresh brew!"

"You don't get many of them to the pound," Meadows agreed. "Aren't you going home for your meal?"

"Kathy's got a couple of days teaching. I might as well eat here as sit at home on my own."

"Do you mind her working?"

"Why should I? We need the money." Shrugging his shoulders, Sutton sat opposite her. "Hope I'm not disturbing you," he apologized. "You looked deep in thought."

"I was thinking about the Coulson case," Meadows admitted. "None of my business, but I've been reading the man's books. I feel I know him."

"That DCS from South Cross thinks he's got it sewn up." Pausing, Sutton considered Meadow's expression. "But you don't?" he asked.

"It's not my place to say."

Doreen waved a plate in their direction. "Over here!" Sutton called. "That was quick," he whispered afterwards.

"Probably meant for someone else," Meadows suggested. "Tuck in before she realises."

"Why don't you think the Yates woman did it?" Sutton asked, through a mouthful of shepherd's pie.

"I can't see why a woman in Mrs Yates' position would risk killing so important a person. And why would she confess to one charge but deny the second? The methods are different, too. Someone who knows about paints doesn't necessarily know about toadstools."

"Fair point," Sutton agreed.

"She doesn't seem the sort either."

"Why? Because she's the arty type? Staying in that freezing old Hall would make me bad tempered."

"Never!" Meadows teased. They got on well. They'd joined the same year, and both were still treated as raw recruits by some of the older coppers.

Then she was more serious. "When Mrs Yates arrived at the station," Meadows continued, "her dignity impressed me. 'I deserve punishing,' she said, 'But not for this.' Or it could have just been a good act."

"It could," Sutton warned. "I know what you mean, though. When we were in the car, she seemed to be praying. Usually the religious sort get up my nose, but Mrs Yates seemed to mean it."

"I keep wondering if we've got the wrong person. It's hard to explain. Just a niggle: what Ambrose calls 'a gut feeling' I suppose."

"If that's all you've got, you'd better keep quiet," Sutton warned.

"But what if she's innocent and still condemned?"

Sutton shrugged his shoulders. "I imagine it happens," he said. "The sooner they repeal the death penalty the better."

For several moments they sat in silence. Meadows began to feel depressed.

Pushing her empty plate to one side, she took out a cigarette. She ought to give up smoking, she thought ruefully. She would never afford that Butlins holiday if she didn't, and her kid sister had set her heart on it. But a quiet smoke helped her think. "Do you mind?" she asked as she lit up.

"Not if you don't blow it over my dinner."

Savouring her cigarette, Meadows sent the smoke away from the table. She pictured herself sitting reading by the gas fire. Concentrating hard, she visualised herself in bed afterwards, half asleep as she read the appendix and credits at the end of the book. One page in particular had puzzled her. Again she tried to picture the page: chapter headings to the left in slightly larger print, notes below them and a greasy thumb mark to the right...

"That's it!" she said suddenly.

Sutton started, nearly spilling his tea. "What is?" he asked.

Urgently Meadows stubbed out her cigarette. Picking up the book she turned to the appendix. "A chapter's been cut out at the last minute. Some of the notes are still here, but not the chapter. Look!" Stabbing her finger at the reference, she carried on. "Here's the bit. 'Barrage Balloons helped defend the big cities from bombing raids. Sally Burton served with Number 32 group in Gloucestershire, and at its HQ at Claverton Manor near Bath, before she was transferred to South Cross.'"

Sutton stared at her, mystified. "So?" he asked.

"There's nothing anywhere in the text about a Sally Burton or barrage balloons. Last night I kept wondering if it was significant. I mean, no one's suggested a motive, have they? What if the killing was connected to a case in Coulson's book? Perhaps to this missing one? It mentions South Cross."

PC Higgins had come into the café and was standing at the counter ordering. Sutton glanced in his direction. "He might know," he suggested. "He's got a mind like a filing cabinet."

Getting up, Meadows went across to the counter and greeted Higgins. "Come and join us," she invited.

Higgins glanced at her suspiciously. "I know that tone," he said. "You're after something."

Meadows smiled her best smile. "Just some advice," she replied. "I think I may have spotted something in the Yates case, but I don't know whether it's worth troubling that new Super."

"Ah," Higgins said. "Glad you've finally learnt some caution." He followed her to the table by the window, nodding to Sutton as he sat down. "So, what have you spotted?"

Once again, Meadows picked up the library book. "This is Charles Coulson's first book," she explained. "It's a good read, but I think a chapter's been cut at the last minute. Two references were left in the chapter before but they don't fit." She passed the book across to Higgins, indicating the reference she'd already read to Sutton. "The next one seems to be about the same case too,"she continued, pointing to the sentences: "The bit where it says 'Burton was promoted to Corporal two years later. Her accuser was transferred to other duties, down south.' There's nothing about that case anywhere else in the book."

Higgins read both references carefully and then checked the Chapter headings, "Sloppy writing," he suggested.

"Maybe," Meadows agreed. "But what if Coulson knew something he couldn't prove? He was accusing people of getting away with murder, literally. Presumably he changed the names, but whoever Sally Burton was, she could have found out he was writing about her. Maybe she threatened him until he took the chapter out."

"Or the publisher was afraid of a libel case?" Sutton suggested.

"Either's possible," Meadows agreed. "But what if Sally was at the Hall? She might have decided to shut him up, forever."

Sutton let out his breath slowly. "A couple of the women looked like WAAF types," he said.

Higgins sat quietly, his expression thoughtful. They waited for him to speak. The door to the café jingled several times.

"His family said Coulson wrote the book while he was in South Cross," he recalled. "But he didn't get it published until after he left. There was a case involving a WAAF while I was there. I don't remember her name." He drank his tea reflectively. "Tell you what, an old mate of mine used to work over there: Bert Blake. He's retired now, but we keep in touch. Bert might know about it." He turned to Meadows. "I'll ask the boss if we can call on him. He lives above one of the shops. We can walk there."

"Do you think we'd be allowed?" Meadows asked cautiously. "That new chap might not like us investigating his case when he's got a suspect."

"I wasn't planning to ask DCS Dudley," Higgins replied. "I know DS Winters doesn't like having someone from another district breathing down our necks…" He left the sentence unfinished. "If we can solve the case without help from South Cross, that'd be a feather in our cap." He turned towards Sutton. "You can help too," he added. "Examine the records we've pulled on everyone at the Hall. See if any of them have ever been accused of murder or changed their names."

"I've made other notes about them too. I'll pass them over," Meadows volunteered. She saw their surprised expressions. "You haven't heard me say this," she continued, "but DI Ambrose was investigating another case at the Hall, undercover. He asked me to find out what I could about the guests, before the Coulson case was made official. DS Winters knows. He was helping."

Higgins nodded: he knew about the Marshall case already but he was surprised Meadows did too. He looked at his watch. "I'll fix us that visit," he said. "Bert'll enjoy it. A fresh young face'll do him a power of good, and he might remember something. Now you'd better be getting back to the Station before you're missed."

For the next hour Meadows kept glancing at the clock, willing Higgins to appear. It was very quiet: just a report of a dog loose on the main road and some clothes missing off a washing line. She spent most of the time catching up on paper work. When PC

Higgins stuck his head round the door, she was mid yawn. "Sorry. I didn't sleep well," she apologised.

"A walk'll wake you up," Higgins said cheerfully. "Bert's expecting us."

Snatching up her coat, Meadows signed out, and followed him into the street. "Does he mind us coming?" she asked.

"Pleased as punch."

Higgins walked quickly, his long legs covering the pavement faster than Meadow's. She had to run a couple of times to keep up with him. They reached the old market square and crossed the road, hurried past the theatre, then on towards the less fashionable edge of Chalk Heath centre. In less than ten minutes Higgins was pausing outside a shop called Solomon's Outfitters. It seemed to specialize in ladies' lingerie. In the window a couple of headless mannequins were encased in fearsome looking corsets, and a dozen cami-knickers were draped across a display. It was all very tasteful and very pink.

Meadows was puzzled. It didn't seem the sort of place to find a retired police officer. Seeing her expression, Higgins nodded. "When you're allocated a police house, it goes with the job," he pointed out. "If you don't find something for your retirement early enough, this is all you get." He gave a door beside the shop a push. "The 'force was Bert's whole life." The door opened. "Come through."

They went up a flight of steep stairs to a flat above the shop. Before they even had time to knock, an elderly man was welcoming them and inviting them in for tea. His voice was still strong and mellow and his appearance smart. He looked about seventy, tall and straight and fit, but the arthritis in his fingers suggested he was nearer eighty. He was every bit Meadows' image of a retired Police Inspector.

"A WPC, eh?" he commented, shaking her hand. "They let you go out on cases? They wouldn't have done in my time! Our loss of course."

Resisting the temptation to reply defensively, Meadows smiled. "We're getting around a bit more," she said.

"Good to meet one of the new breed. Always good to see you, Mick."

Meadows glanced around her discreetly. An African mask challenged her from above the gas fire. Crossed spears decorated the other wall and carved antelopes stood on the window ledge. It was as though she'd stepped out of an English shopping parade into colonial Africa. She'd expected police memorabilia, and there was plenty of that scattered around: books and photographs, even an old fashioned truncheon on the sideboard. But this retired copper had visited much more interesting places than Chalk Heath.

"Watched you coming from my window," Bert explained. "I can see right across town." Pulling the net curtain aside, he demonstrated the view.

Higgins didn't rush things. They chatted for half an hour, filling Bert in on the latest news and gossip, while he repaid them with slices of buttered malt loaf. Most of the time Meadows sat and listened, feeling very young and inexperienced. Finally, though, Higgins explained why he'd brought her.

Taking out Charles Coulson's book, she showed it to Bert.

At first he looked puzzled. Minutes ticked away on the clock on the mantelpiece. Higgins helped himself to another piece of malt loaf while Meadows looked out of the window. A delivery van was unloading at one of the shops nearby, making a lot of noise, but it didn't disturb the elderly man reading intently. Finally he looked up and smiled broadly. "Well I'm blowed!" he said. "Charles Coulson, eh?"

"You knew Mr Coulson then?" Meadows asked, glancing towards Higgins. He merely raised an eyebrow in encouragement.

"DS Taylor you mean. I suppose the fancy name was his publisher's idea. Yes, he was at South Cross. We kept in touch after he transferred. I knew he'd got a book published but had no idea it would be so popular." Curiously Bert flicked back to the frontispiece. "Third imprint eh? I never thought it'd look this good, let alone sell three prints. He didn't either. Went on about how they'd cut some of his best bits at the last minute. No pleasing some people."

Once again Meadows glanced towards Higgins. "Some bits were cut out?" she repeated.

"Two or three chapters he said. Apparently publishers do that sort of thing."

"Any idea what they were?" Higgins asked.

"One was a case we investigated together in South Cross. Ironic, as that started the book off. Don't know about the others." Putting the book down, Bert looked at them shrewdly. "So what's happened to him?" he asked.

"He was murdered this week," Higgins replied bluntly.

Bert grimaced. "I warned him accusing people of murder wasn't healthy," he remarked. "Most of the people were dead he said, and those that weren't wouldn't dare draw attention to themselves. Sounds like he got that wrong."

"We've no idea of motive, yet," Higgins replied carefully. "But young Meadows thinks there may be something in his book that'll help. Tell us about the South Cross case. She's found a couple of notes about a Sally Burton. Would that be the case you worked on?"

"She wasn't called Burton," Bert replied. "What was her name?" He frowned with the effort of memory. "Norton, that was it. One of the WAAFs based nearby. The Super was convinced she'd killed her lover, but nothing stuck. There was a war on. People had other things to think about. Clever woman."

"And you say that started the book off?" Higgins prompted.

"George had developed a special interest in poisons, pretty knowledgeable he was too. If he'd been brought in on the Norton case earlier he might have cracked it, but the woman disappeared after she was demobbed. He collected a couple more local cases, and realized there were quite a few nationally. Tell you what, I'll sit down after you've gone and write down everything I can remember. I'm not so good on names straightaway. I can drop a note at the Nick for you. I have to pop out to the chemists'."

"Would you?" Meadows asked in delight. "Please?"

"Anything for a pretty face," Bert replied, smiling.

As soon as they were out in the street, PC Higgins was striding back towards the Station. "Good work!" he said gruffly. "We might be getting somewhere. We need to know about the other cases though. If only we had the original manuscript."

"Perhaps his publishers have a copy," Meadows replied breathlessly.

"Or maybe it's still in his house. They'll have to break the door down if that neighbour doesn't come back soon."

PC Sutton greeted them as they came back into the Station, his face flushed with pleasure. "You look pleased with yourself," Higgins said testily.

"Yes sir. Sorry sir," Sutton replied, flustered. "I've had a bit of luck though. I've traced the telephone operator who took the call to the Hall. She remembers someone asking her to put them through on the evening Mr Coulson died, and that it was a very long call. I've given her details to the DS."

They looked at him in surprise. "I'd forgotten about that," Meadows admitted. "Well that's easy. Was it a man's voice or a woman's? That'll narrow it down a bit."

Sutton grimaced. "She said she couldn't be sure. It was either a woman with a low voice or a man 'squeaking', like he was in a rush."

"That's hardly helpful," Higgins groaned. "And?" he asked. "You look like you've something else to crow about."

"There's been a call from Nottingham. Mr Coulson's neighbour's back: Brigadier Barrington. Been on holiday. He's opened up the house and wants to know if we need anything sending up."

"See if he can find the original manuscript!" Higgins replied at once.

"Manuscript?"

"The manuscript of the first book," Higgins snapped, grabbing the library book from Meadows' bag and holding it up. "If he does, we'll need it driving up straight away. We can't wait days for it. I'll see the DS right now to authorise the expense."

Chapter Twenty Five

"I love bubble-and-squeak," Edith said, spooning leftover cabbage and potatoes into a frying pan. Frank hadn't exaggerated. There was plenty of food left. Even without Ruth's guidance they would eat well.

"We'll have to draw up an extra cooking rota," Christina said.

"Would it be better if we all cooked for ourselves?" Betty asked. Her voice tailed off, but they all knew what she meant. There may well be a poisoner still amongst them.

"I vote we start tonight," Sheila said. "Frank can't do it all on his own."

"It would be rather a lot," Frank agreed, "without Ruth here…" He stopped short.

"I'm game to have another bash at cooking," Jonathan offered.

"Why don't we all do our own cooking?" Edith suggested. "But we can certainly do the washing up together." She flicked a tea towel at Geraint. "That includes you!"

Lunch was long and leisurely but the strain was difficult to hide. "We could all do with a walk!" Frank announced afterwards. "This might be the last fine day we have." He looked uncertainly at Ambrose. "Would that be all right?"

For a minute Ambrose paused, wondering if it was too big a risk. "So long as we all stick together," he said. "I'll need to get my jacket first. It's in your room."

As he passed the library Ambrose had an idea. Everyone was still in the kitchen or dining room. Quickly he found the book on funghi, still misplaced amongst 'Hobbies'. Hiding it amongst some papers in Frank's office, he snatched up his jacket and joined the others on the terrace.

Together, they followed Frank through the gardens to the woods beyond. A gap in the fence led them to the river. October sun slanted through the trees and glistened on water. Small currents lapped at the muddy banks in a gentle breeze. Geraint found a stone and skimmed it across the water.

"What is it about men?" Sheila asked. "As soon as they're near water they turn into boys."

Edith picked up a twig. "I don't see why they should have all the fun!" she called. "Let's play Pooh sticks!"

Within minutes they were all playing, watching as twigs floated down river or became caught in the bank. For a few moments, the guests could forget Charles Coulson, Ruth, the whole awful week. But it was cold near the water, and Phyllis and Betty started to shiver. "We'd better go," Frank said. "Paul hasn't had chance to talk to everyone."

His reminder was like a splash of icy water. As the group walked back through the grounds in twos and threes, voices were more subdued. The atmosphere of suspicion returned. However pleasant other guests might appear, one of them could be a murderer.

As soon as he was back in Frank's office, Ambrose rang Mary. "I'm afraid I won't be home until Sunday afternoon," he apologised. He heard her sigh, but she was too used to his work to comment. "Sorry. This case is dragging on. How's Joe?"

"Fine." There was an awkward pause. "Perhaps it's a good job you're away tomorrow. Joe's band is coming."

"Good grief! Will you stand it?"

Mary laughed. "I imagine so. They've got their first booking. I've told them they can use the attic, so long as they keep the windows shut. Joe's getting quite good you know. You should listen to him sometime."

"What about his homework?" Ambrose asked in concern.

"We did a deal: rehearsal space for two hours' study each night."

"Bribery and corruption," Ambrose teased. There was a knock on the door. "Must go, Love." Smiling, he put the phone down.

Jack had arrived. He looked smaller, scruffier. Reluctant to sit down, he wandered the room nervously. Since the man clearly wanted to say something, Ambrose kept quiet, waiting patiently. Finally Jack asked, "Do you think one of us is a murderer?"

Ambrose turned the question back on him. "Do you?"

"It looks like it. Unless Betty really did see a tramp?" Shrugging his shoulders, Jack looked at Ambrose for reassurance.

Ambrose refused to be drawn. "I'm interested in what you saw, not Betty," he said. "Did you notice anything the others might have missed?"

"No. Unless you count Geraint ogling Edith. Funny really. He acts as camp as a field full of tents. Christina was falling for Charles Coulson too. They'd have got something going if he hadn't died."

Ambrose was surprised by the man's perception. "You watch people pretty closely," he remarked.

"In my job you have to. 'If you want to sell a man something, you need to know the man.' That's what I think anyway."

"Did you watch Mr Coulson?"

"We all did. He was acting strange." Narrowing his eyes, Jack recalled the scene. "He seemed afraid of something. I wondered if a ghost from his past had turned up." He rubbed one shoe against the other to clean it. "Didn't have time to do them this morning," he apologised. "Overslept. I'm usually on the road by six. It's a treat to lie in."

"You hate your job, don't you?" Ambrose remarked. "You're probably not very good at it either. Is that why you put on an act? To convince yourself you're big and brash, like your colleagues?"

Jack flushed, a deep uncomfortable red. It was several moments before he replied. "Nonsense" he said. Though he tried to laugh Ambrose's question away, it had clearly stung.

"Talking of acts," he added suddenly. "Phyllis isn't as lame as she pretends. She's my prime candidate. She could have ditched her crutches and run to the dining room, slipped something in Mr Coulson's drink, then scarpered upstairs without any of us suspecting."

"Why do you say that?"

"Catch her when she's on her own," Jack advised, "and her crutches'll be propped on the wall. By the way, has Sheila told you about the phone being off the hook?"

Ambrose shook his head.

"She will," Jack predicted. "It's on her conscience. Like Betty's drinking must be on hers. Pissed as a newt the first night! Have you asked her where she got the grog? I could do with a dram myself."

Though he spoke lightly, Ambrose could hear fear behind Jack's words.

They talked for another five minutes, chiefly about Jack's book, until Ambrose had kept him roughly as long as he'd kept Betty. When they parted, it was on friendly terms.

"You're not at all like I imagined a detective," Jack said as they shook hands.

Unlike Jack, Jonathan showed little outward nervousness, though Ambrose noticed the way he repeatedly pushed the hair off his forehead. "Dreadful business!" he began. "I feel bad about my own part."

"Why?" Ambrose asked in surprise.

"I assumed Charles was back on the booze."

"You knew he was an alcoholic?"

"He told me so himself." Jonathan pushed his hair back again. "He promised me he'd dried out. His work's been getting erratic though, missed deadlines, sloppy writing. Fame's a fickle mistress, and can suddenly turn her back on you. A little drink cheers you up. Lots of writers go down that route. But perhaps I did Charles an injustice. I liked the man. He was one of my first clients. If I could apologise to him, I would."

"As his agent, you must have known him well," Ambrose remarked. "Did he have any enemies?"

"The felons he sent down weren't happy."

238

"And the ones who got away," Ambrose asked, "the people in his book? Could any of them still be around?"

"I never knew the actual cases," Jonathan explained. "He'd changed all the names. Even if they did recognize themselves, surely they wouldn't have tracked him here? We didn't know he was coming ourselves until the night before. He must have died of natural causes. Nothing else makes sense."

After Jonathan had gone, Ambrose sat for several moments on his own, thinking. No, it didn't make sense, he agreed. Few cases had puzzled him so much in recent years. Usually by now he had a short list of suspects, and some idea of motive.

Suddenly the telephone rang, startling him. "Person-to-person call for Detective Inspector Paul Ambrose," the operator's voice said.

"That's me," Ambrose said in surprise.

"I have a Brigadier Barrington for you. Will you accept the call?"

Ambrose was about to refuse, assuming a member of the public had discovered he was at the Hall. They probably wanted to make a complaint. But he could think of no Brigadier Barrington living nearby. "Yes," he agreed. "Put him on."

"Harold Barrington here," a voice boomed. "Your Sergeant suggested I call. Apparently he can't speak to you himself. Some procedural matter. I'm George Taylor's neighbour or was, I should say, poor fellow."

"Sorry, who's neighbour?" Ambrose was confused.

"My apologies," the Brigadier replied. "Presumably you know him as Charles Coulson. Your Sergeant asked me to check if there was a manuscript in the house. Had to hunt. George wasn't the neatest of men. Found it in his desk. I'd already read the book, of course. George gave me a signed copy when he moved here."

Immediately, Ambrose was interested. "Have you found any cases in the original manuscript that weren't in the book?" he asked.

"Three poisonings. George was a bit of an expert. Would it help if I gave you a summary?"

If he could have shaken the man's hand down the phone line, Ambrose would have done so. "Please," he said, grabbing a pad and pencil.

"First one: a WAAF called Sally Burton. A pilot at her base hit the deck on a training jump. Burton was accused of putting arsenic in his dinner, so he was too sick to open his chute. They were lovers and had a flaming row the day before. Nothing proved. There wasn't a lot left of the poor bloke so no one examined the corpse."

Ambrose was writing furiously. "Case two?" he asked.

"Chap in London during the last war," he replied. "Probably murdered his wife for her money. She died while he was away, so it was difficult to pin anything on him. Silly woman ate rhubarb leaves. Any countryman'd tell you they're deadly, but one of the government booklets said you could add leaves if there wasn't enough stalk. Daft buggers! The book was there in the kitchen. George reckoned it was all a bit too convenient."

The Brigadier paused for breath. "Case three's a well-to-do young girl accused of feeding rat poison to her fiancé. Both families were pushing her to marry him, but she couldn't stand him. Happened in 1916 and hushed up, so she got away with it. Charles called her Helen De Burgh, from Keslington Hall, but I've never heard of such a place.

"One of our local Bobbies is about to call by. He's driving the manuscript up your way. You should get it by dinner. Must be important."

"It is," Ambrose said. "Thank you very much, Brigadier. You've been most helpful."

"Always glad to assist Her Majesty's Constabulary."

For a long time after he put the phone down, Ambrose sat thinking. The solution to the present case lay in one of those missing chapters, he was sure of it. And suddenly the blackmail note made a bit more sense too.

He wasn't sure how to proceed: whether to question people again to see if they had links to any of the cases or to continue as before.

He decided changing his approach might alert the murderer. If they felt threatened they'd go home and probably disappear forever.

Going to the library, Ambrose called for Margaret.

As soon as they went into Frank's office, she closed the door. "Never keep a lady waiting," she said gently, but with a slight edge. "Not when she wants to talk to you."

Ambrose smiled, intrigued. "What about?" he prompted.

Crossing the room, Margaret stood beside the bookcases. Mechanically she cleaned dead leaves from a spider plant near her. It needed watering. "Frank's been getting us to visualise places," she said. "So I visualised the dining room the night Mr Coulson died. It made me remember something."

The plant was almost tidy now.

"When I set the table, the labels for the carafes were on the sideboard," she continued. "I noticed them, because I was amused that Ruth had gone to so much trouble. Then I went to the basement with you. You kindly carried the lemonade into the dining room, and left me. I picked up the labels and filled a carafe for each one…"

Still standing beside the bookcase, Margaret stared ahead, picturing her movements. Ambrose didn't hurry her, though inwardly he felt a growing sense of urgency. "There were two labels marked, 'Speaker'," she recalled, "so I filled two carafes. But I'm sure now that when I first saw the labels, those two weren't there. Someone put them on the sideboard while I was out of the room. At the time I was too busy to notice."

"How can you be sure?" Ambrose asked.

"I have what I believe is called a photographic memory. Ruth's handwriting is immaculate. When I picture them now, one label isn't as neat as the other. I think someone took the proper label and copied it. Presumably you can check."

"We will," Ambrose promised. "Everything went to the laboratory for analysis. Did you see anyone near the dining room?"

"No, but I heard the door close opposite."

Ambrose recalled hearing a door himself, but didn't say so. "You realise you're high on the suspect list?" he asked instead. "You had means and opportunity. Perhaps you wanted to ruin Ruth's business for some reason? You never intended her speaker to die but…"

Margaret cut him short, her voice even lower than normal. "Perhaps," she agreed. "But I didn't."

After Margaret had gone, Ambrose noted what she'd said. He could see why the murderer might add a second label, to ensure Coulson drank more.

His interview with Phyllis was little help. "No, I didn't tamper with anything," she said firmly. "How could I? I was in my room writing or getting ready for dinner."

"You're not as lame as you pretend," Ambrose pointed out. "You could have gone down by the back stairs, unseen."

"I could have done," Phyllis admitted, flushing, "but it would have been difficult." Avoiding Ambrose's eyes, she looked at her crutches propped against the desk.

"You don't need those, do you?" Ambrose asked.

There was a long pause. "I do…to prop me up," Phyllis replied. "In every way. When I first hurt my leg, people were sympathetic. After I got better people were impatient if I limped. They were more understanding if I used my crutches. I still need them when I'm tired, but nowadays I use them mainly to make me, well, different I suppose."

"So you really do have an injury?" Ambrose asked.

"A jeep turned over on me and broke my leg in several places. There was a raid on our base and a bomb exploded near us. The officer I was driving was killed. I survived."

"I see," Ambrose said softly.

"No you don't. I was engaged to the man who died, and I might have saved him if I'd reacted quicker."

242

For an instant Ambrose saw the pain behind the woman's bright red lipstick and manicured nails. "I doubt if you had time to do anything," he replied, more gently. "Blaming yourself achieves nothing. Believe me, I know." For a few seconds he stared into the past. Then he smiled. "Coming here to find a husband wasn't a good idea either," he added.

Startled, Phyllis looked at him.

"That is why you came, isn't it?" Ambrose persisted, passing her the crutches.

"Partly," Phyllis admitted, sighing deeply. "At least it's made me feel better about being on my own. Imagine living with Jack or Gerald! Even Geraint would drive me mad in a couple of months."

"I'd give him three days," Ambrose replied, smiling again as he helped her up.

He was about to fetch Sheila when there was a knock on the door. He got up to open it.

"Paul," Frank said softly. "Your daughter's here."

"My daughter...?" Ambrose began and stopped himself. "I thought she was on duty," he added.

"She says it's urgent. Shall I show her in?"

Chapter Twenty Six

"Is she in uniform?" Ambrose asked.

"Yes. She's cycled straight from work," Frank replied. "Said it was a family matter. Hope it's not bad news. Shall I show her in here?"

Ambrose thought quickly. WPC Meadows would surely not have come again unless it was important. "Can you take her round to the tradesman's entrance?" he asked. "If one of the guests sees the uniform they might get worried."

"I'll take her down to the old kitchen," Frank suggested. "You can talk in peace there. I'll give you a call when she's ready. She'll have to park her bike."

Puzzled, Ambrose waited. As he did so, he remembered the book he'd taken from the library. Finding it under Frank's papers, he read the full title: "A Handbook to British Funghi, with original photographs by L.E. Stillson." Once again he turned to the page on Ink Caps and read the description.

He turned to the credits at the front. "Nature Handbooks and Co. Dorking," had published the book six years ago. According to the biographical information L.E. Stillson was a prize-winning nature photographer who lived in Norfolk.

"I wonder," he said to himself thoughtfully.

Frank knocked again. "She's waiting," he whispered.

Ambrose followed Frank into the Yates' kitchen and down the servants' steps to the basement. WPC Meadows was standing beside the table in the old kitchen. She smiled as if to a relative. "Sorry to interrupt your holiday," she began.

As soon as Frank had left them the smile had gone, and Meadows was apologising nervously. "I'm sorry sir. I know you said..."

"And I meant it," Ambrose cut in. "You're also risking your job. I'm one of the suspects. You shouldn't be even wishing me the time of day."

Meadows was breathless with cycling so far so fast, and with nervousness. Winters had warned her she would have to hold her own. She put her hand on the table to steady herself. "There have been a lot of developments in the Coulson case, sir," she said, "DS Winters felt you should be briefed, for your own safety."

"He knows you're here?" Ambrose asked in surprise.

"Not officially. But…"

Raising his hand, Ambrose stopped her. "I don't want to know," he said sharply.

The kitchen was gloomy, the late afternoon light slanting through the high windows. There was a damp musty smell Ambrose hadn't noticed earlier in the week. He wished he'd asked Frank to bring the young policewoman to the office. The chance of her being seen by the guests wasn't great, and being taken to the basement must have been intimidating. He indicated one of the chairs beside the table. "Sit down," he invited, softening his tone. "You look exhausted."

Meadows sat down gratefully, though on the edge of the seat. She was indeed shattered. The day had exploded since she visited Higgins' old mate. Though she was officially off duty now, it looked as though it would be a long time before she could go home. She was probably also getting herself into terrible trouble. DS Winters had assured her he would support her if anyone did find out, and she believed him. Sam Winters was straight as an arrow. But he would probably be in trouble too.

"Does the chap from South Cross know?" Ambrose asked.

Catching her breath, Meadows shook her head. "DCS Dudley has left, until Monday," she explained. "South Cross have a double murder on their hands. Winters is in charge until he comes back."

"So what's happening about Ruth Yates?"

"We've been ordered to detain her. The odd thing is, she hasn't even asked for a solicitor. The DCS says the case is as good as closed. She'll crack when he questions her again, he says."

"But Sam doesn't agree?" Ambrose asked, smiling inwardly.

"No sir. He now thinks the killer is one of the guests. He says they'll be thinking Mrs Yates is taking the rap and may be off guard. We might nail them if we act quickly. If we wait until the DCS comes back, the guests will go home. It'd also be a feather in Chalk Heath's cap if we can tie up the case ourselves."

"It would indeed," Ambrose replied. He'd met DCS Dudley a couple of times and hadn't particularly liked him. He had a bullying manner Ambrose would never dream of using himself. "Fortunately we've got one more day," he added. "The retreat's been extended 'til Sunday."

Taking a sealed envelope from her pocket, Meadows passed it across the table to him. "DS Winters asked me to bring you this update," she said. "Three cases were cut from Coulson's book. We think the murder may be connected with one of them. We've also found a good bit more on your suspects. And Coulson's real name was George Taylor."

Ambrose nodded. "Brigadier Barrington rang me this afternoon," he said. "I know about the cases. So, what else have you found?" He began to skim-read Meadows' hand written notes. "You've been busy," he remarked, smiling. "Well done, all of you."

"There are lots of gaps," Meadows admitted. "It's Friday afternoon and people have gone home early. Greg Sutton's been chasing records, though, and PC Higgins' called in favours. I got quite a bit of help from Doreen at the Copper Kettle. She knows most of the gossip round here."

Nodding, Ambrose continued reading. "No wonder Sheila finds the library boring," he remarked dryly at one point, and "Jack's wife left him last year? Hardly surprising," at another.

Curiously Meadows looked around her, at the old range and the shelves on the walls, some still laden with copper pots and pans. The room was huge. Her own little bed-sit would probably fit into the pantry. She tried to imagine a fire burning in the range and servants coming and going. Her grandmother had been in service as a cook before she married. She must have spent most of her time in such a basement kitchen, preparing meals for the gentry above. Involuntarily Meadows shuddered. She would have hated having so little light or fresh air. However demanding her job was: rushing about the place and working long hours, she had a far better life. "The good old days weren't that good, even for the gentry," she reflected. "Though it would be nice to have someone to cook your meals…"

For several moments Meadows waited with a sense of growing anticipation. When DI Ambrose went quiet like this it was usually followed by rapid instructions, or the answer everyone else had missed. Finally he looked up, smiling grimly.

"So what do we do now?" he asked. "How do you catch a killer who'll let someone else hang for their crime?"

Meadows wasn't sure whether he was asking her opinion or thinking aloud. "Set a trap, perhaps," she suggested.

"My thought entirely," Ambrose agreed. "But how?"

He paused. "I gather one of the telephonists remembers the call here?" he asked. He looked through the pages again, trying to find the right note.

"This area doesn't have direct dialling yet, so there's still an old fashioned switchboard," Meadows explained. "Greg Sutton rang them. A Miss Mavis Ridgeway recalled someone asking for this number the night the victim died. They said it was likely to be a long conversation, so to make sure they weren't cut off. 'And don't disturb us' they added, which really offended her. She had no idea how long the call took or what it was about, but thought it lasted at least an hour."

"Would she recognise the voice again?" Ambrose asked.

"She told Sutton she might. She was so annoyed, the call stuck in her mind. But she couldn't tell us whether the caller was male or female. Are there any women here with really low voices?" Meadows asked.

"Yes, there are." Ambrose seemed miles away. Suddenly he came to a decision.

"Hmm, it might work …" Ambrose said softly. Getting up, he walked around the kitchen. Twice he glanced at Meadows, wondering whether it would be fair to ask so much of her. She was bright and keen, but still inexperienced. He could be putting her at risk. But he could see no better way of baiting his trap.

"Is Coulson's original manuscript coming tonight?" Ambrose asked suddenly.

"It should be at the Station by nine o'clock."

Ambrose walked to the old range, examining the pots and pans.

"Right," he said finally. "Here's what we'll do, that is, if you're willing. You go back to the Station on your way home, and ask DS Winters to send the manuscript here. I'll get Frank Yates to announce at dinner that Charles Coulson's publisher is bringing out an unabridged edition of *The One That Got Away*, in his memory. We're being lent the original manuscript, which will be arriving about eleven o'clock and put in the library, ready for guests to look at in the morning, as a sort of recompense for having their week spoilt."

Urgently Meadows took out her notebook and scribbled Ambrose's instructions down.

"Ask Sam to persuade Miss Ridgeway to come here tonight with you. We'll put her in the lounge where she can hear anything said in the library but not be seen herself. Not if we close the sliding doors between the two rooms. Then we'll see whether our suspect bites. If I'm right, they won't wait till morning but will have a go over night. By the time everyone else reads the manuscript, one case will be missing. Would you be willing? I'll be in the lounge too, watching your back."

Mystified, Meadows stared at him. "Of course," she said, "but I'm not sure what you want me to do."

Ambrose smiled. The girl was right. His ideas had come too quickly. "You'll be in the library guarding the manuscript," he explained. "If our killer comes in, you'll try to keep them talking long enough for Miss Ridgeway to recognise the voice. I'll give you a ring later to confirm you can get hold of her and to finalise details. Are you willing? Have a think about it."

It took less than half a minute for Meadows to come to a decision. With DI Ambrose in the other room, she would be safe enough, and it would be good to catch a killer; far more interesting than minding lost children. "Yes, sir," she agreed. "But wouldn't you rather have Sutton or one of the other PCs?"

Ambrose laughed. "You'll be far more effective," he assured her.

Later that evening the police car crunched down the gravel drive, its headlights picking out the front door and the steps up to it. A little behind, Meadows and Miss Ridgeway walked softly on the grass verge, hidden by the shadow of the trees. Both were wearing plimsolls and dark clothing. If any of the guests woke and glanced in their direction, the car's headlights would distract them. Miss Ridgeway was agile for a woman in her fifties. "I go rambling every weekend," she'd confided before they set off. She was also surprisingly game. "I haven't done anything so interesting since I served at the War Office," she'd added.

The trickiest bit was getting into the library unobserved. Their steps hidden by the noise of the car turning round, the two women darted quickly from the trees, into the shadow of the house, and then along the terrace to the French doors. Fortunately there was a light still on in one of the attic bedrooms, so they could see the door handle. Ambrose let them in.

The library was in darkness but Ambrose had a small torch. Shading it with his hand, he guided them into the room, nodding his thanks to Miss Ridgeway as he did so. As soon as the curtains were safely closed, he showed her through the sliding doors to the lounge, and indicated an armchair. The telephonist had brought a thick shawl with her and settled into the chair at once. She would be able to hear any conversation in the library but not be seen.

"Frank Yates and Higgins will come in here," Ambrose whispered to Meadows, "They'll pretend not to see you."

Meadows took up position in the far corner, between two stacks of books. She could hear Frank Yates showing Higgins to the library. He put on the light. If either of them saw her crouching there, they made no sign. "Put the manuscript on the table, please," Frank said, with the door still open. He spoke softly, as if trying not to disturb the house, but anyone listening on the landing would have heard him. "Thank you so much for bringing it over tonight. We'll be able to let people see it straight after breakfast. We have to get it back to the publisher's tomorrow afternoon, and quite a lot of people will want to read it."

"You're welcome," Higgins' voice replied. Then he switched the light off.

For a few moments the two men stood in the corridor near the open doorway, talking softly. "Beginning to feel a bit Autumnal," Higgins said. "The car windows were covered in condensation when I left."

"It won't be long before the first frost," Frank agreed. He shut the library door firmly.

Under cover of their conversation Ambrose checked the sliding doors between the lounge and the library were firmly closed. Meadows listened intently. He hadn't locked them so he could give assistance quickly. The door from the corridor into the lounge was secured with a chair under the handle. That way no one could get into the lounge where they might sense Miss Ridgeway and Ambrose waiting in the darkness.

Meadows made herself more comfortable. She heard Frank and Higgins walk back to the front door. Their feet echoed on the tiled floor. Soon afterwards the tyres of the police car scrunched on the gravel outside, and then drove towards the gates.

Two hours went by. She had to fight drowsiness. For a few moments she almost gave way, only to jerk herself awake, shivering with cold and tension. Miss Ridgeway probably was asleep. They'd agreed she could rest, so long as she didn't snore. "I never snore!" the woman had replied hotly. Meadows hoped she was right. Ambrose would be awake of course, watching and waiting too.

Suddenly a board creaked. At once Meadows was alert. Faint steps came down the main stairs.

They turned towards the kitchen. She relaxed again. One of the guests had come down to make themselves a drink. That was all.

After few moments the muffled steps came out of the kitchen. But instead of going back to the stairs, they crossed the corridor, towards the library door. The door handle turned. Meadow's nerves tightened. Melting back into the darkness, she watched as the door opened. A shadowy figure came in, holding a small torch, pointed downwards to mask the light. She could just make out a pair of brown house shoes and a long dressing gown.

The intruder faced the door and a key turned in the lock. Then the shadow moved softly past her hiding place. The dressing gown became clearer: a silk jacket with an oriental design running down the front. It seemed to be a gold dragon rearing upwards. To Meadows' alarm the figure then moved towards the sliding doors to the lounge and locked them too. When she and Ambrose had discussed the plan earlier, they'd anticipated an intruder taking the key from the hanger, to lock themselves securely in the library while they read the manuscript. They hadn't expected the sliding doors to be locked, too. "We should have thought of that," Meadows admitted. "If we're worried about someone coming in through the lounge, they must be too." Hopefully it wouldn't matter.

Satisfied, the intruder turned to the table and pulled up a chair, as coolly as if it was the middle of the day. Placing the torch on the desk to give sufficient light, the figure sat down to read. For an instant, Meadows saw a handsome profile and hair greying at the temples. She recognised the description Ambrose had given her. "Jonathan Prentice!" she thought with satisfaction. So, Ambrose was right.

Jonathan opened the manuscript and turned the pages. Suddenly he looked up, and around the room. Meadows flattened herself back into her corner.

The pages of the manuscript were held in place by a large bulldog clip. Softly page after page turned. Then Meadows heard the clip being opened. There was the rustle of pages being removed. In the faint light she could see Jonathan pushing them into the pocket of his jacket. Closing the clip back up, he replaced the manuscript on the desk and rose from his seat, his back still towards her.

At once, Meadows flicked on the light switch. Jonathan spun round, his face distorted by surprise and anger. "Who's there?" he snarled.

Meadows didn't answer. Instead she walked across the room towards him.

Jonathan recovered himself surprisingly quickly. "Good Lord!" he said. "You gave me a fright young lady. What the hell were you doing, lurking in the darkness?"

"What were you doing?" Meadows retorted.

"Reading my writer's manuscript."

"At night?"

"I couldn't sleep, so I thought I'd have first look." Almost invisibly Jonathan pushed the pages further into his pocket. "He really did write well. Such a pity!" He sounded almost affable again.

"Why couldn't you wait until morning?" Meadows persisted, standing close to him.

"I was cross," Jonathan admitted disarmingly. "As Charles' agent I should have been consulted about any new edition. We had a contract."

"You were removing pages," Meadows said firmly.

"Nonsense my dear. Why would I do that?" Jonathan looked at her with approval. "What a pretty little thing to be crouching in a corner!" he remarked. "Who put you up to this?"

The conversation wasn't going how Meadows had intended. "I was asked to guard the manuscript," she replied, beginning to feel foolish. The man was taking the initiative, and she shouldn't be allowing it.

"How quaint! Why on earth would it need guarding? Technically it's my property, even if our host thinks he owns everything. Be a darling and let me borrow it for an hour or two. I won't tell him."

"Why do you want it?" Meadows asked.

"To see whether it's worth me kicking up a fuss and taking over the deal. I'll bring it back before morning. Cross my heart and hope to die."

He was very persuasive, but Meadows wasn't in the mood to be persuaded, particularly with Ambrose listening beyond the sliding doors. "I've been told to make sure it stays here until morning," she replied. "And that's what I intend to do."

"Very noble of you, I'm sure," Jonathan said. "Such a fuss over nothing, though! Is this Paul's doing? Once a policeman always a policeman! He's taking a liberty, making you lose your beauty sleep."He smiled, a condescending, knowing smile that thoroughly annoyed Meadows. "You're looking quite dark under the eyes, sweetheart. You should look after yourself better." Still smiling, he turned towards the door.

Urgently Meadows thought how to detain him. She must make him use some of the words from the list Sutton had given her, to help Miss Ridgeway remember the voice. "Did you phone the Hall the night Mr Coulson died?" she demanded.

"How could I? I was here."

"You went up to the telephone box in the village," Meadows insisted.

"Why would I make a call from a telephone box?" Jonathan shook his head as if to a puzzled child.

"So no one could ring for an ambulance."

"How on earth would that work?" He sounded genuinely curious.

Meadows took a deep breath. She wasn't going to be beaten. "You deliberately left the village phone off the hook, to jam this line," she replied. "We have an operator who remembers you. You asked to be connected here and told her it would be a long call."

"A long call? I don't think you have any idea what you're saying," Jonathan smiled again.

"And that you wanted to make sure you weren't, what's the word…."

"Disturbed, perhaps? I rather think you're the one who's disturbed," Jonathan laughed.

There was a faint movement beyond the sliding doors. "That's the voice!" Miss Ridgeway whispered. "It's the way he said 'disturbed'. I'm sure it's him."

She'd spoken very softly but Meadows had heard her, and so had Jonathan. Before Meadows had chance to move, he grabbed her shoulder, pulling her back against him. "Whoever you are in there," he called. "I've got your pretty policewoman. I'm going out the house now and she's coming with me." He held her so tight he was squeezing the breath out of her chest.

"Don't be so stupid!" Ambrose called back urgently.

"If that's you Paul, listen to me," Jonathan shouted. "I want the keys to my car, my wallet, and no one to prevent me leaving. Otherwise…" With his free hand he clutched Meadows' throat, making her gasp in pain. "Hear that?" he demanded. "Any attempt to follow me, and I'll strangle the silly girl."

Chapter Twenty Seven

As soon as he heard Jonathan shout, Ambrose leapt up in alarm. He had another key to the sliding doors but in the darkness it was difficult to find. Urgently he flashed his torch, looking for the keyhole. "Put the light on!" he shouted to Miss Ridgeway.

"I'm so sorry!" she said. "Did he hear me?" It seemed like ages before she found the light switch.

Then the key wouldn't go into the lock. Jonathan had left his own key in it, so the lock was effectively jammed. Ambrose cursed his own stupidity. He should have guessed the man would take every possible precaution.

He heard Meadows cry out. At once he thrust his shoulder against the sliding doors. Stubbornly they held, though they bowed inwards.

Miss Ridgeway had tugged the chair from under the door handle. "This way!" she called to him.

There was the sound of a heavy thump in the library.

"Fetch Mr Yates!" Ambrose shouted. "He's in the far room on the right."

They almost fell out of the door into the corridor together. Miss Ridgeway ran towards Frank's kitchen calling, "Mr Yates! Mr Yates!"

Ambrose thrust the spare key into the library door. Luckily Jonathan hadn't left his key in this door. Urgently Ambrose rushed in. He could see two figures on the library floor, one lying flat, the other crouching on top. To his surprise the smaller figure was uppermost.

Meadows looked up in relief. "Help me hold him down," she called. "Stay still, you stupid git!" she shouted furiously, pushing the man on the floor back down.

"I presume you mean him, not me," Ambrose said. He couldn't help laughing as he strode across the room.

Jonathan was getting up, almost crawling towards the French windows. Snarling and cursing, he was very different from the urbane man they'd known all week.

"Do as the lady says!" Ambrose instructed, and shoved him back down.

"Well done!" he added to Meadows. "Pity I don't have any handcuffs with me."

Frank ran into the room. "Good grief!" he said. "What the hell's going on?"

"Call 999," Ambrose instructed. "Then come back and help me." Powerful as he was, and used to holding criminals who resisted arrest, he found it difficult to restrain Jonathan. The man had the strength of fear and desperation.

Suddenly Geraint was in the room too, holding a large frying pan above Jonathan's head. "Stay still or I'll brain you with this pan!" he shouted. He clearly meant it.

Jonathan stopped struggling. Together Ambrose and Geraint hauled him into a nearby armchair and pushed him down into it, hard.

"You skunk! You absolute skunk!" Geraint said still holding the pan, ready to hit Jonathan if he moved. "I've a mind to brain you all the same. You'd let an innocent woman swing…!"

Others were appearing, running down the stairs. "What's going on?" Edith demanded. "I heard a noise," another voice agreed, "What's all the shouting about?"

Frank returned. He had to push his way through the guests who were already entering the library, or gathering in the corridor. Standing by the French windows he blocked that exit. Miss Ridgeway waited uncertainly in the doorway. "Is there anything I can do?" she asked.

"See if the girl's all right," Geraint suggested.

As soon as he spoke, Meadows realised she felt a little faint.

"Sit down," Miss Ridgeway instructed. "My goodness, you're going to have a nasty bruise. Shall I get you a cold compress? Where's the nearest bathroom?"

"I'm all right," Meadows assured her. "Just a bit shaky."

Ambrose looked up in concern. "Open the sliding doors, please," he asked Sheila. "Then take everyone through. It's getting a bit crowded in here." He turned back to Jonathan, now sitting quietly watching them all. His poise was returning, as if he thought he could still get away, or argue his way out of the situation. The man's arrogance annoyed Ambrose intensely.

"Jonathan Prentice," he began. "I am arresting you for the murder of George Taylor, otherwise known as Charles Coulson; and also on suspicion of murdering your wife, Geraldine, some time during 1944. I must warn you that anything you say will be taken down and used in evidence against you."

There was an awestruck silence. Jonathan sat straighter in the chair. "Prove it!" his manner said, but he didn't speak.

"His wife too?" Margaret asked softly.

"I suspect that's what it's all been about," Ambrose replied. "But we'll have to let a court decide." He couldn't tell them any more, for fear of prejudicing the case.

"Of course! I get it!" Geraint said, putting the frying pan down with an apologetic smile. "G.T. – George Taylor. Let me guess. Our illustrious guest knew Jonathan had murdered his wife and tried to blackmail him. Jonathan shut him up. That's why you asked me about the note, Paul."

"And me," Gerald called from the doorway. "As if I would blackmail someone!"

A police bell could be heard coming down the driveway. Clearly Higgins hadn't gone far when he'd left the Hall. Ambrose guessed Frank hadn't had to telephone: he'd simply gestured from the front door to the waiting police car. Ambrose watched Jonathan warily, prepared for him to make a sudden bid for freedom. With so many people appearing it was becoming more and more difficult for him to get away.

"Paul can't answer you," Frank pointed out. "He's got to do everything properly. But if you want, I can tell you what I think happened."

The rest of the guests were crowding into the two rooms, excited and shocked. Even Phyllis and Betty had made it downstairs in their dressing gowns, drawn by the noise. "Yes, do tell us!" Sheila said. "Put us out of our agony."

The bell was nearly at the front door. Frank glanced in its direction. He was back in professional mode, keeping his guests interested while they waited for something to happen.

"This is only my opinion," he insisted. "When Charles wrote his book, he didn't realise one of his unsolved murders was committed by his own agent. Jonathan must have recognised it, but decided the book was going to sell very well and no one would make the connection. At the last minute he panicked and cut the case out of the manuscript. As a distraction he removed another couple of chapters and told Charles it was the publishers' fault."

Pausing, Frank looked towards Jonathan, seeking confirmation, but the man's expression gave no answer. Everyone else was listening with rapt attention. They could hear the front door opening.

"By the time of Charles' third book," Frank continued quickly, "Jonathan had lost interest in him. He'd moved on to the latest big thing. Agents do that sometimes." There was a note of bitterness in his voice. "Charles returned to the three unused cases, hoping to get another best seller out of them. Somehow he realised the man who poisoned his wife in the war might be his own agent. Jonathan knew about natural poisons, he specialised in Natural History books, and had been left a lot of money when his wife died. Then Charles tried to use what he knew to put pressure on Jonathan to find a publisher for his third book."

Frank sighed. "Poor silly man!" he said reflectively. "We all want to be published, especially if we're become a bit of a has-been," he admitted ruefully, "But it's not a good idea to threaten someone who's capable of killing. Am I right?" Frank ended, turning towards Jonathan, and then Ambrose.

"You do make up some splendid stories," Jonathan replied coldly.

"I couldn't possibly say," Ambrose replied, but he nodded very slightly.

"What evil luck," Margaret remarked, "those two being here together. I bet Charles had no idea what was waiting for him when he came to the Hall!" She shivered and pulled her wrap closer about her. "I felt that evil."

Christina sighed. "Charles warned me about wanting anything too much," she began. "He should have listened to his own advice." She turned suddenly on Jonathan. "He was just a silly man, but you! You're evil, as Margaret says. All this week you've been with us, smiling and joking. And yet you knew you'd killed your wife. And then you set about killing poor Charles as if it was just a…" Words failed her. "Game," she added lamely. She couldn't express her contempt.

"Are you finished?" Jonathan asked her coldly.

"No, but you are!" she retorted.

Epilogue

There was already a queue. Half the town had come it seemed, plus everyone in Chalk Heath village. Notoriety was good for sales.

"Welcome to Chalk Heath Hall!" a woman sitting at a table said, smiling broadly. "It's our first open day." She counted three bright red tickets from the reel in her hand. "We only acquired the Hall a month ago."

Mary smiled, taking the tickets. She passed one to Joe. "You'll want to do your own thing. See you here in an hour?"

Joe almost nodded. Ambrose had been surprised when his son agreed to come. Apparently seeing a room where a real murder had been committed was more attractive than moping in a bedroom. They were beginning to get somewhere.

A woman in a tweed skirt and jacket clapped her hands. "I'm taking the first tour round now," she announced. "The rooms are quite small, so no more than thirty at a time I'm afraid."

With Mary beside him Ambrose joined the party. To his amazement, Joe was still with them.

"We're restoring the rooms to their original layout," the woman explained, taking them up the front steps and into the entrance lobby. "Have a glance at the ceiling while you're here. Isn't it beautiful? And just look at those stairs! They're coming up beautifully. The whole place is 'a work in progress'. Fortunately Mr and Mrs Yates have kept a lot of the old fitments, and they have the original plans. We intend to take the house back to its eighteenth century layout. Of course, most of the grounds have gone, but we'll be restoring the lily pond and the formal gardens."

"Where was the murder?" Joe asked her, getting straight to the point.

For a second the guide looked cross, then she smiled. "In what used to be the guests' dining room," she replied. "We'll start there now and work our way back along the corridor."

Joe pushed himself towards the front.

"Here we are!" The guide opened the door and the party surged forward curiously. A red velvet cord hung from two stands, preventing access, so people had to take it in turns to move to the front and look.

The table and chairs were still there. Ruth's entire dining service and silver had been laid out, as if for a formal dinner. The infamous carafes were in place and there was even a candelabra in the centre of the table. "We'll be moving everything to the original dining room," the guide explained, "as soon as we've stripped that out. The Yates used it as their private kitchen. Of course, in the old days, all the cooking was done 'below stairs', so ultimately we won't have a kitchen on this floor at all. You'll be able to go down the servants' stairs in a minute. The old kitchen and laundry are hardly changed..."

"Where was the victim sitting?" Joe whispered.

Ambrose smiled. At least his son was talking to him. "On the far side," he whispered back. "He was standing, actually, giving a talk. I tried to bring him round there." He pointed to the floor. Seeing the room again made it all vividly real. "Poor man," he said softly. "But it doesn't pay to make threats."

They moved on, to peer into the lounge. "This was the original library," the guide continued, "All we'll have to do here is remove the sliding doors and open the whole room up again. Such a lovely view, don't you think? We don't know yet whether to keep the terrace or demolish it. I mean, it's part of history isn't it? Some of you may remember when the Hall was a convalescent hospital. There was a whole line of camp beds out there with wounded soldiers recovering in them."

Joe went to peer at the terrace and imagine the line of wounded men.

Thoughtfully Ambrose turned back to the corridor. As he did so, he was surprised to find Frank Yates standing beside him. "I hoped you'd come," he said, shaking Ambrose's hand vigorously. "Thank you so much. Ruth sends her very best wishes. She couldn't face seeing people tromping all over the place. Not that she minds really. She's delighted in fact. We both are. How else can we save the house?" He was talking too quickly, nervous and uncertain.

Ambrose nodded. "It's the right decision," he said reassuringly. "Will you stay?"

"Yes. We'll have the attic. It'll make a nice flat when it's refurbished, and we'll be able to use the rooms below when the house is closed to the public. In fact we'll be having a party here in a few weeks' time. Edith and Geraint are getting engaged. "

"Engaged?" Ambrose repeated, and burst out laughing.

Frank grinned. "Yes," he insisted. "A bit of a surprise, eh? You'll be invited of course."

"Mmm," Ambrose began reflectively. "I hope they can make a go of it. They might. They'll fight of course, but don't we all?"

With a rueful smile, Frank nodded. "You can imagine the last few months," he said. "At first Ruth wouldn't have anything to do with the idea, but giving the house to the National Trust really was the only solution. This whole sorry business nearly finished us off." His voice shook with anger. "I ought to feel sympathy I suppose," he admitted. "Being found guilty must be terrible but at least Jonathan didn't get the death penalty. I still can't find it in my heart to forgive him. Ruth does though. That surprised me."

"She has some idea how it feels," Ambrose said quietly. He could have added Ruth was lucky not to be charged herself.

The party was surging out of the lounge. "Ah! Mr Yates!" the guide said in delight. She turned to the people around her. "We are most privileged," she enthused. "Allow me to introduce Mr Frank Yates, the owner of this beautiful house, and a famous novelist too!" She saw Frank's expression. "Oh dear," she added, laughing. "I'm embarrassing him."

Frank smiled at Ambrose, then beat a hasty retreat along the corridor. He watched as the tour went up the stairs to the first floor. He suddenly became aware of a figure in the darkness

262

behind him. Whirling round, Frank was surprised to see DS Winters.

Shaking his hand, Winters smiled. "I always knew your wife was innocent," he insisted. Frank didn't reply.

"But there is just one thing I have to ask," Winters continued. "I must know," Winters looked anxious. 'Is DI Ambrose writing his memoirs? I mean, what does he say about me?"

Frank laughed for the first time in months, if not years. "Don't worry," he reassured Winters. "Paul is writing romance. He has done for ages. Maybe you've read some of his stories, without realising? His pen-name is Maggie St James."

FOUL PLAY

If you enjoyed Poison Pen you will enjoy reading *Foul Play*, DI Ambrose' first mystery by PJ Quinn:

It is 1958. Britain is emerging from post-War rationing and bomb damage. Teenagers are falling for James Dean or teddy boys. Soon it will be the Swinging '60's.

The sleepy town of Chalk Heath is shocked by a vicious crime at the theatre. The local Players are rehearsing when the leading lady is attacked on stage. Was it an outside job or was one of the Players trying for instant promotion?

Detective Inspector Paul Ambrose is sent to investigate with his colleagues: the ambitious DS Sam Winters and smart WPC Pauline Meadows. Ambrose is a gentle giant, coping with a wayward son and his own memories of wartime Britain.

Ambrose solves the mystery. Can you?

And a few reviews of *Foul Play*:

A great murder mystery

I was lucky enough to have been received this book as a gift. Otherwise, really being averse to crime, detective and murder mystery, I would not have chosen it. However it didn't take long to be captivated by the descriptive nature of the book and that is one of the key reasons why I couldn't put it down. The characters are well chosen and there is much humour throughout bringing light heartedness to what could otherwise be another typical crime novel. A great twist at the end too.

Michelle (UK), 12 July 2012

Read This

Anyone who was brought up on the "Whodunits" of Margery Allingham, Ngaio Marsh and Dorothy Sayers will welcome this beautifully written return to a much missed genre. Cleverly set in the fifties - that unsettling era of post-war change - and capturing perfectly the feeling of the times, PJ Quinn (alias mother and daughter duo Pauline Kirk and Jo Summers) has produced a highly enjoyable crime mystery with a splendid cast of characters. Two more novels from the same pen are already promised. Look out for them!

Mary SN, 12 Dec 2011

A Great Detective Story

It kept me guessing until the very end. I managed to solve some parts but the end was still a mystery.

An unputdownable book and one which I would recommend to anyone who enjoys a well written and well thought out detective novel.

Next one please!

Philippa H, 20 Sep 2011

An Excellent Book

It gripped me from the start and kept me guessing (incorrectly!) all the way through. I look forward to the writers' next novel.

Kerry, 16 Sep 2011

First of a series, I hope

The clues are set cunningly throughout but I hadn't solved it by the end. The bright WPC is set to be a star in future episodes, I hope. DC Winter's domestic bliss was brilliantly done. Worth following this writing duo.

John, 3 Sep 2011

Excellent reading

This is a book that once you pick it up, you won't put it down until you have reached the last page.

Sandy, 31 Aug 2011

A Good Read

I don't normally choose to read detective novels but was very pleased to be given PJ Quinn's *Foul Play* to read as I really enjoyed it! Informed by a sound knowledge of English Law and Police work I found *Foul Play* a most gripping and entertaining detective novel which kept me guessing and speculating to the end. I look forward to reading more of DI Ambrose's and his team's sleuthing.

Margaret, 30 Aug 2011

Other publications available from Stairwell Books

First Tuesday in Wilton	Ed. Rose Drew and Alan Gillott
The Exhibitionists	Ed. Rose Drew and Alan Gillott
The Green Man Awakes	Ed. Rose Drew
Carol's Christmas	N.E. David
Fosdyke and Me and Other Poems (with Fighting Cock Press)	John Gilham
frisson	Ed. Alan Gillott
Feria	N.E. David
Along the Iron Veins	Ed. Alan Gillott and Rose Drew
A Day At the Races	N.E. David
Gringo On the Chickenbus	Tim Ellis
Running With Butterflies	John Walford
Foul Play	P. J. Quinn
Late Flowering	Michael Hildred
Scenes from the Seedy Underbelly of Suburbia	Jackie Simmons
Pressed By Unseen Feet	Ed. Rose Drew and Alan Gillott
York in Poetry Artwork and Photographs	Ed. John Coopey and Sally Guthrie

For further information please contact rose@stairwellbooks.com

www.stairwellbooks.co.uk